WHISPER OF BONES

A CASSIE QUINN MYSTERY

L.T. RYAN

with
K.M. ROUGHT

LIQUID MIND MEDIA

Whisper of Bones

Cassie Quinn Mystery Book Two

L.T. Ryan with K.M. Rought

The authors wish to thank the following for their contributions...

Bill, Carol, Dianne, Elizabeth, Gene, George, Karen, Katherine, Kevin, Linae, Lynn, Marcia, Marty, Melissa, Rita, Steve, and Walt

THE CASSIE QUINN SERIES

Path of Bones

Whisper of Bones

Symphony of Bones

Etched in Shadow

Concealed in Shadow

Betrayed in Shadow

Born from Ashes

Love Cassie? Hatch? Noble? Maddie? Get your very own Cassie Quinn merchandise today! Click the link below to find coffee mugs, t-shirts, and even signed copies of your favorite L.T. Ryan thrillers! https://ltryan.ink/EvG_

1

DETECTIVE DAVID KLEIN TOOK A MOMENT TO ENJOY THE AC BEFORE exiting his sedan and making his way to the crime scene in the warm Savannah sun. It was early November, but temperatures were still in the seventies and eighties, and he wasn't looking forward to spending more time in the heat than necessary.

Not for the first time, David wondered what it would be like to move somewhere cooler, somewhere quieter. Lisa would laugh at him for even entertaining the idea. "You love this city too much," she'd say. "You'll be here until the day you die."

She was right. Usually was, in his experience. Lisa knew him better than anyone else on this planet. She knew him better than he knew himself. If she said he'd never leave, he had no choice but to believe her.

But damn if he didn't want to get away every once in a while.

The last few months had been rough. Savannah had just gotten over a brutal serial killer, one that had killed by ripping the hearts out of young women and draining them of their blood. However, the killer hadn't been working alone. William Baker had been the true mastermind of the operation and he was now six feet under.

Good riddance.

As usual after a heavy investigation, life had slowed down. The world had gotten quieter. Decades on the force taught him cases came in waves. There'd be a horrific, vomit-inducing murder, and then a quiet crime of passion. Neither was ideal, of course, but if you asked anyone on the force, they'd tell you in no uncertain terms which one they preferred.

But they didn't get to pick and choose. And there was no telling what was normal anymore. Was it normal for life to be calm and peaceful? Or was it normal for life to be bat-shit insane?

He didn't care to think about those questions anymore. For the past few years, what mattered was getting from one case to the next. One day to the next. It was easier if he didn't think too far into the future. He could handle today. Tomorrow might be another story.

David switched off the ignition and stepped out of the car. The humid air clung to him like a wet sweater. The hot coffee mug burned the inside of his hand, but when he took a long sip, that same heat refreshed his throat. It was worth the physical discomfort to have a few drops of energy in his bank.

As he usually did these days, David took stock of his body. His knees and hips were stiff. In his shoulder, a pinched nerve. A slight headache forming over his left eye. His feet hurt like something else, but nothing out of the ordinary. He'd be more worried if he woke up pain free.

With a deep sigh and the resignation that only came after years of working as a homicide detective, David walked toward the underside of Harry S. Truman Parkway. The officer who'd called him this morning about a dead body there had mentioned he might find it of interest. Other than that, he was in the dark about the subject.

A few officers stood at the edge of the underpass, keeping a group of the homeless away from the crime scene. The Chatham-Savannah Homeless Authority did its best to make sure the camps never got too out of hand, but the Truman Parkway was a hotbed for individuals trying to stay cool and dry.

A female detective stood closer to the body, waiting for David to nod his way past the officers, one of whom lifted the crime scene tape for him. He ducked underneath it, stifling a groan as his shoulder twinged in defiance of the movement.

When he straightened, the female detective lifted a hand in acknowledgement, and David returned the gesture. He saw Detective Adelaide Harris around the precinct nearly every day, but they never had much time to say anything more than a simple hello.

He'd always liked Harris' work ethic and dedication to the job, but he was more grateful to her for keeping Cassie Quinn safe when the two came face to face with William Baker. Cassie had a tendency to throw herself into situations without considering an exit plan. Harris had gotten her out alive.

Harris offered a small smile. "Good morning."

"Is it?"

"Could be worse." She looked over her shoulder at the body. "Could be better."

"What've we got?"

Harris walked David over to the body. "Male. Mid-60s. Strangled, legs crushed. Been here a day or so. We can't tell whether someone killed him here or dumped him. There's been too much traffic in and out from the homeless. We've got one guy, Randall Gibson, who says they didn't know he was dead right away. Just figured he was sleeping. Not sure how true that is considering the state of the body, but when they finally figured out the man was dead, most of them got spooked and took off for another area. Mr. Gibson reached out to the Homeless Authority. They called us."

David was listening, but Harris sounded further and further away the more she talked. "Strangled *and* crushed legs?"

"Yeah." Harris drew the word out in anticipation of getting to this point sooner than later. "That's why I called you."

"How'd you know—?"

She laughed. "I've done my research, okay? The name David Klein would be one of myth and legend if you weren't still on the force, proving to people that you're real. I was interested in what type of cases you'd tackled over the years, what type of cases you'd solved. What type of cases you hadn't solved. This one stuck out."

"That was over twenty years ago." David shook his head. "Are you sure it's the same?"

"No. Not at all. But I figured you'd be the one to ask." Harris waited for David to say something, but when he remained silent, she took a step toward the body. "Want to walk me through what you remember?"

David followed her to the man's still form. His hair was gray, as was his skin. He'd been dead long enough for the blood to drain from his face. He looked peaceful, but a deep bruise around his neck meant he'd suffered as he died. His crushed legs showed he couldn't have gotten away as someone had slowly stolen his life.

"In the early '90s," David began, "we had figured out someone was killing addicts around Savannah. Within a few weeks of being released from prison, they'd show up dead. Our perp dumped the first three in the ocean. They washed up on shore soon after, and it was easy to tell they'd been killed in the same way—someone had crushed their legs, then strangled them. And pumped them full of heroin."

"The first three?" Harris asked.

David figured she knew the answer to her own questions, but he played along. Explaining the details to her out loud would force him to remember working the case when he was still a rookie cop. Maybe he'd remember something critical that could help them now.

"We discovered the next four bodies while searching the woods for a missing girl. It'd been about two years since the three bodies had washed up onto shore. The perp didn't bury one deep enough, and one of our dogs had sniffed it out. We couldn't tell if the perp strangled him, but he'd crushed his legs, just like the others. When we kept looking, we found three more. Seven bodies total."

"And then nothing?"

"And then nothing." David gestured to the body at his feet. "Until now, I guess. Do we know anything about this guy?"

"Not yet. I'm gonna have the boys do their thing, but I wanted you to have the first look at the body and the crime scene."

David bent down to get a closer look, this time allowing himself to grunt as his knees resisted the movement. Harris said nothing, and he was grateful. Staring into the face of a dead man not much older than himself was enough to make him feel like he was on death's door.

He took in what he could of the body without moving it. The man had on casual clothes—jeans and a polo—and had no distinguishing features. He looked average, bordering on handsome, with a clean-shaven face. He wore a wedding ring on his left hand.

"It's been a while." He looked up at Harris. "But he doesn't look much like what I remember of the other victims."

"How so?"

"The three we found on the shore were malnourished. They were addicts and looked like it. This guy looks healthy, all things considered. And he's wearing a wedding ring."

"Were the others not married?"

"Not that I can remember, but we'd have to go back to the old case files to find out for sure."

"What do you make of the wounds?"

David turned back to the body. "Strangulation. Hard to tell without a closer look, but it doesn't look like the perp used a rope. Back then, we thought maybe he was killing people with a tourniquet."

"And the legs?"

David's gaze shifted to the man's lower body. Blood had seeped through his jeans, but even without that sign, it would've been obvious something was wrong. The knee on his right leg was out of place, and his left leg bent at a strange angle. Broken.

"Done to incapacitate the victim. Make sure they couldn't run away. Then the killer could take their time strangling them."

"So, it's personal?"

"Can't know for sure." David placed his hands on his knees and stood up with another grunt. "But seems likely. The killer was trying to send a message, we just never figured out what it was."

"Think this is the same guy?"

"I don't know. Feels similar, but that was over twenty years ago. It's been a damn long time since we had a body. We always figured there were more victims, but we never found them. So, why now? Why him?"

"That's the million-dollar question." Harris waited until David caught her eye before she spoke again. "You gonna call her?"

David didn't have to ask to know she was talking about Cassie Quinn.

"No," he said. "Not yet. She deserves as much of a break as we can give her."

2

CASSIE DIDN'T BLINK AS SHE STUDIED THE GHOST OF THE YOUNG BOY standing in the corner of her therapist's office. She'd only been there a few minutes before he'd materialized, translucent and stoic. He brought a slight chill to the air. She'd been seeing him outside of her own bedroom walls more often as of late, but she still had no clue why. He had only spoken to her once, uttering the name Sarah Lennox, before returning to his silent watch of her everyday life.

His presence had become more comforting than not. After the ghost of Elizabeth Montgomery had replaced him, he had come and gone as he pleased, and she couldn't help but look for him when he wasn't there.

Where did he go when he wasn't watching her? Did he haunt other people? Did he have other objectives to fulfill? She would ask him these questions every once in a while, but he never responded. He'd just stare at her until she went back about her day.

"Cassie?"

The voice of Cassie's therapist, Dr. Rebecca Greene, brought her back into the present. The woman was in her fifties, with brown hair streaked with gray. She always dressed professionally in a monochrome pantsuit. She had at least three for every color of the rainbow. Her closet must've been so satisfying to look at.

Today, she wore a periwinkle blue pantsuit with a white tank top underneath. Cassie had seen at least three other blue pantsuits over the years, but this one was the palest. It made Cassie feel warm and light. It was the exact color of the Savannah sky on a cloudless summer day.

"Sorry," Cassie said. "What were you saying?"

Dr. Greene's smile was calm and serene. Her eyes sparkled behind her black-rimmed glasses. "I asked you how you were doing."

"Oh." Cassie laughed. "I'm sorry. I haven't been getting much sleep lately."

"What's been going on?"

"Um." Even after years of being with Dr. Greene, she sometimes felt strange about opening up. It was her fatal flaw. "I've been having this recurring nightmare."

"Want to tell me about it?"

Cassie shifted in her seat, glancing back over at the ghost of the little boy. Was it for reassurance? She wasn't sure. "It starts off with me driving a car. It's not mine."

Dr. Greene nodded her head.

"It's nighttime, and I'm on the highway. I can't steer the car. I keep drifting back and forth across the line, but no matter what I do, I can't control it. Then I see people in the distance, just standing in the middle of the highway."

"Do you recognize these people?"

Cassie nodded. "When I get closer, I see it's my parents and my sister. My parents look like they do now, but my sister is about five or six years old. She's pretty young."

"Is your sister often young in your dreams?"

"I'm not sure." How many times had she actually dreamed about her sister? "I don't think so."

"What happens next?"

"I get closer. It feels like the car is speeding up. I keep trying to step on the brakes, but nothing happens. I get so close that I can see the terror on their faces. My sister is crying and screaming. I try to swerve, but there's no stopping the car. Right before I hit them, I wake up."

"And how do you feel once you wake up?"

And how do you feel when... Dr. Greene had asked Cassie that kind of question thousands of times over the years, and yet it was always strange to analyze her own thoughts and feelings. She'd much rather keep her head down and carry on with life, but that didn't fix any of her problems.

"Scared." Cassie's laugh sounded nervous, even to her own ears. "Terrified, really. Sad. I'm usually crying or sweating or both."

"Anything else?"

"Regret."

"Hmm." Dr. Greene wasn't the type of therapist who kept a notepad in front of her to make notes on, but every once in a while, she'd make an affirming noise and pause, as if she were filing the information away in her mind. "Do you know why you feel regret?"

"Not really. I understand the fear and sadness, but not the regret. I tried everything I could to stop the car. It wasn't my fault."

Dr. Greene pushed her glasses further up her face. "So, as long as you do everything in your power to stop something bad from happening, you won't feel any regret?"

Cassie smirked. Dr. Greene was good at asking questions to flip Cassie's perspective on a situation. "No, of course not."

"Regret is a good indicator that a situation may not feel resolved to you, even if you've done everything in your power to fix it. Sometimes these things are out of our control. It's what you do with that feeling of regret that matters most." She paused here for a moment and rested her chin in her hand. "When did you first have this dream?"

Cassie looked up at the ceiling while she thought. "Maybe a couple weeks ago."

"About the time you decided to see your sister again?"

Cassie's gaze snapped back to her therapist's face. "Yeah, about that time."

"Is it possible that these dreams relate to your anxieties about seeing your sister? It has been a few years, after all."

"It's more than possible." Cassie blew out a long breath. "Seeing her again has been weighing on me."

Dr. Greene leaned forward slightly. "How come? What are you worried about?"

Cassie decided to let it all out. "Oh, everything." She laughed. "We were close as kids, but it's been so long and so much has changed. Will we still get along? Will she still feel like my little sister? Will she treat me like I'm made of glass, like most people do once they find out what happened to me?"

"Have you asked her any of these questions? Raised any of these concerns?"

Cassie looked away. "No."

"Hmm. I'd bet Laura is nervous, too. You're her big sister, after all. She looked up to you when you were kids. What do you think she's afraid of?"

Cassie bit the inside of her lip as she tried to put herself in her sister's shoes. "Probably the same things? Whether we'll get along. Whether it'll be awkward. Whether we'll still feel like family."

Dr. Greene leaned back. "So, you seem to share the same fears. That means you have a middle ground, a common issue. And, as always, the best way to solve a situation like this is with—"

"—communication."

"Exactly." Dr. Greene's eyes sparkled again. "I knew you'd been paying attention."

Cassie tried smiling, but it came out more like a grimace.

Her therapist didn't miss a beat. "What else are you worried about?"

"I'm not the same person I used to be. She isn't either. My life is so different now. There's so much I want to tell her. So much I want her to know." Cassie's eyes once again drifted to the ghost boy. "But she'll need time and energy and a willingness to listen."

"Is there anything that has told you Laura isn't willing to listen?"

"No, but that doesn't mean she will be."

"True." Dr. Greene shrugged her shoulder. "But as much as we'd love to, we can't control other people's reactions. Or their emotions. Or their actions."

"That's stupid." Cassie elicited a laugh from her therapist.

"I don't disagree with you there. Life would be much easier if we could predict how people will interact with us." Dr. Greene checked her watch. "We're almost out of time for today. Did you ask Laura if she'll be joining us next time?"

Cassie dropped her head. "No, not yet."

"Okay, well, no pressure. It's there if you want it. If not, I'm sure we'll have plenty to talk about."

"Don't we always?" Cassie shook her head. Even after a decade of therapy, there was always something to talk about. But her weekly routine with Dr. Greene was reassuring. She might not tell her therapist everything—like the fact that she could see ghosts and sometimes got psychic visions—but it was nice to talk to someone who wouldn't judge her, no matter how anxious her thoughts were. She owed her therapist a great deal of gratitude.

Dr. Greene stood and walked to the door. "When will you be picking up your sister?"

Cassie checked the time on her phone. "Four hours and counting."

She tried not to the let the dread that had built up in the pit of her stomach show on her face.

3

Cassie's heart drummed against her chest as she stood in the Savannah Airport baggage claim area, wondering if she would spot her sister before Laura spotted her. Her palms were sweating, and she felt dizzy as mobs of people shuffled back and forth, grabbing their bags and hugging their loved ones. Their collective body heat made the air heavy and oppressive. The noise was almost enough to drown out her thoughts.

How long had it been since she'd last seen her sister? Three or four years? Longer? She had returned to Savannah for a few days in the spring to visit her old friends. She hadn't even stayed with Cassie. But they'd met up for an awkward dinner. It was nice, but superficial.

This time felt different.

Laura was visiting *her*. She was returning to Savannah to be with *her*. The plan was to spend a long weekend catching up, getting reacquainted, and visiting some of their favorite spots in town. Then, they'd pack their bags and head to Charlotte to talk to their parents as a unit. It was time to change the relationship among all four of them, and it would start tonight with her sister.

Cassie caught a flash of red amidst a sea of blondes and brunettes.

Laura's hair had always been brighter than Cassie's auburn locks, which made it easier to spot her in a crowd. When Cassie turned, she caught sight of her sister, who was making a beeline for the conveyor belt. It gave Cassie a moment to catch her breath.

For all her fears, Laura hadn't changed much in the last few years, not physically. She was a little shorter than Cassie, but more athletic. Tonight, she wore leggings and a long shirt with a pair of flats. A backpack hung off one shoulder, and as she leaned forward to grab her bag, her soft curls fell in front of her face.

Once Laura snatched her suitcase and set it on the ground, pulling up the handle so she could lug it behind her, she scanned the crowd and found Cassie's gaze. For a moment, the two stared at each other in shock, and then broke out in twin smiles.

Cassie waited until Laura pushed her way through the crowd, still nervous about what the next few days would entail. Once Laura was in front of her, she felt her arms reach out and pull Laura into a hug so tight her sister squeaked in surprise.

"Watch the ribs," Laura said. "I kinda need those."

"Oops." Cassie pulled back and tucked a piece of hair behind her ear. "How was your flight?"

"Not too bad." Laura shrugged and started making her way toward the door. "It's not that bad of a flight. I just hate sitting next to gross dudes who don't know how to refrain from manspreading."

Cassie cringed. "Ew. Have you eaten?"

"Yeah, they fed us on the plane. Surprisingly, not terrible."

Cassie drooped a little. She'd hoped to take her sister out tonight. The sooner they got back to her house, the sooner they'd have one-on-one sister time, and Cassie wasn't sure she was ready for that yet. What would they talk about? What if they got into a fight? What if they got along great and she ended up regretting not reaching out sooner?

Maybe her therapist was right about the true meaning of her dream.

Cassie spent the entire walk to long-term parking thinking about what she should say to her own sister, and by the time they'd reached her car, she hadn't said a single word. She popped the trunk and helped Laura lift her bag into the back.

"Damn, did you pack a bunch of bricks?"

Laura's laugh was a welcome sound. "Fifty pounds exactly. I was so scared it would go over. But I needed to make sure I had enough clothes, just in case."

"Just in case what? The apocalypse?"

Laura's smile faded. "Just in case I needed to stay longer than a week."

Cassie slammed the trunk and looked at her sister across the top of her car. A streetlight was out nearby and the darkness engulfed them, but she could still make out the sheepish look on her sister's face.

"Why would you need to stay longer?"

"In case Mom or Dad need me." Laura waited for Cassie to unlock the car doors and opened the passenger door, but stopped short of getting in. "Or in case you need me?"

Cassie slid behind the wheel and waited for Laura to shut the door before giving an incredulous look. "Why would I need you?"

"You know, just in case. I don't know Cass, I'm just trying to be helpful."

"I've been doing fine for years, Laura." Cassie barely contained the anger in her voice. She hated when people treated her like she had FRAGILE stamped on her forehead. "And maybe Mom and Dad will want my help. I live closer."

"It's not a competition." Laura rolled her eyes and snapped her seatbelt into place. "I'm just trying to be helpful."

Cassie took a moment before she responded. She knew she was being defensive. Unreasonable. "I know. And I know I have a long way to go to make everything up to them—"

"You're their daughter." Laura put a hand on Cassie's shoulder. "You don't have to make anything up to them. Besides, they'll kick us out before we can volunteer to help. God knows Mom doesn't want anyone to baby her, even with a brain tumor."

Laura's words didn't make Cassie feel better. She still hadn't talked to either of them. Cassie had pitched her and her sister's visit as a surprise, but the truth was she didn't want to give her parents a head's up in case they didn't want to see her. Or just in case she decided at the last minute that she didn't want to go.

Realistic? Maybe.

Cowardly? Absolutely.

Cassie stuck the key in the ignition and twisted. Her car roared to life, and the headlights illuminated the surrounding darkness. The gasp that left her mouth was automatic, and she didn't have time to cover her reaction before Laura jumped and followed her gaze.

"What? What's wrong?"

"Nothing," Cassie said. She searched for a plausible lie. "I thought I saw a cat run off. Scared me."

"Jesus, don't do that." Laura clutched a hand to her chest. "I thought we were being kidnapped."

Laura seemed to realize what she said as soon as it left her mouth.

"Cassie, I'm so sorry. I wasn't thinking. I—"

"It's fine." Cassie forced out a laugh. "You don't have to walk on eggshells around me. Let's just get home, okay?"

Laura nodded and turned back to the front of the car. Cassie followed suit, and once again locked eyes with the ghost of the little boy who had been haunting her for months. He seemed to show up more frequently outside of her bedroom as her sister's visit had drawn closer.

Was it a plausible connection or simply coincidence?

Cassie couldn't say for sure, and she wasn't looking forward to solving that mystery. She'd already lied to her sister, and they weren't even home yet. How would she nonchalantly ask Laura if she had any connection to a little boy who had died twenty or thirty years ago?

Cassie twisted in her seat and carefully pulled out of the parking spot, knowing there was no simple answer to her question.

4

CASSIE GRIPPED THE STEERING WHEEL UNTIL HER KNUCKLES TURNED WHITE *and her hands ached. Her headlights illuminated the road right in front of her, and the rest was so dark she felt like she was driving through a void in space. She could sense, rather than see, the trees whipping by as she sped down an empty highway.*

Her foot slid off the gas pedal, but the car didn't slow down. She slammed her foot on the brake, and the pedal went right to the floor with no resistance. The car didn't shudder or stop, no matter how many times she stomped her foot. There was no slowing down.

Cassie looked around, wondering if she could use something—anything —to help her slow down and stop. There were no guardrails, and the inky blackness scared her more than the road ahead. If only she could find an exit and maybe an empty field to help her slow down.

The car drifted to the left, but no matter how hard she yanked the steering wheel to the right, she couldn't correct her direction. She saw no headlights in the distance, but that didn't mean another car wouldn't come barreling around the corner at any second. Her panic grew, and her chest constricted. Her breaths became shallow. Her head grew light and her vision spotty.

A soft glow in the distance caught her attention. If it was another car, there would be no time for her to move out of the way. She tried once more to turn the steering wheel, but it was locked in place. Her trajectory was certain.

As she closed the distance between her and the soft glow, forms took shape. The illumination didn't look like headlights. Instead, it appeared like an invisible lamppost shining its light across the center of the highway.

A figure appeared in the center. Then two. Then three.

Cassie tried once again to slam on the brakes, but instead of slowing down, the car shuddered and barreled down the road with renewed vigor. She leaned forward, squinting, trying to figure out what she was seeing in the distance. And as soon as the figures came into focus, she couldn't control the scream that escaped her mouth.

Her parents stood in the road with blank faces. The light washed out their features, making them look pale and lifeless. They held hands, her father on the left and her mother next to him, but there was no indication they knew what was about to happen. They didn't notice Cassie bearing down on them.

Laura, only five or six years old, stood next to their mother. Unlike her parents, Cassie's little sister could see exactly what was happening. She was crying and clutching a teddy bear to her chest. Her face was a mask of horror and fear. The sight brought tears to Cassie's eyes.

But no amount of turning the steering wheel or slamming on the brakes would slow the car down. The distance between them closed within a matter of seconds, and just as Cassie could see the size of her sister's dilated pupils, just as the car was about to crash into her family, Cassie slammed her eyes shut.

Cassie's eyes snapped open, and for a few seconds, she refused to move. Refused to breathe. Refused to accept she was safe in her bed. That her sister—now a full-grown adult—was safely asleep in the guest bedroom.

The breath she held burned her lungs, and she let the air out in one long go. She wiped the tears from her eyes and sat up, taking several deep, calming breaths. Her heart rate slowed to what resembled normal. Her shaking hands would need a few more minutes.

When Cassie looked to the corner of her room to see if the ghost boy was standing there like usual, his absence disappointed her. Last night's run-in still weighed on her mind, and she wondered if he was instead paying a visit to her sister while she slept.

Cassie flung the bedcovers off and swung her legs to the floor. The clock read six in the morning, and the chilly air sent goosebumps down her spine. But she reveled in the feeling. It was better than the sweat beading across her forehead, left over from the intensity of her nightmare.

She wouldn't be able to rest now, so she made her way to the kitchen, hoping coffee would throw off the last vestiges of sleep. It felt strange knowing another living being—aside from her cat, Apollo—was inside her house. Felt even stranger knowing it was her sister.

Cassie poured her coffee and allowed herself an extra spoonful of sugar this morning. The night before had been...awkward. She and her sister had talked about work and Savannah and what it would be like to go to Charlotte to visit their parents, but after that, the room had fallen silent. Cassie had put on a movie and fallen asleep on the couch.

When she woke up, Laura was already in bed with her lights out.

Today would be different. She'd make sure of it. They had a few fun things planned around the city, and with something to distract them, maybe they'd find more to talk about. She prayed that'd be the case, anyway.

Movement in her peripheral vision caught Cassie's attention. She turned, expecting her sister to be standing in the dining room. Instead, she met the gaze of a strange man with sad eyes and translucent skin.

Cassie reacted involuntarily. She jumped and stifled whatever noise was about to escape her mouth. Unfortunately, she hadn't been able to keep her hands from shaking, and her hot coffee spilled over the edge of the mug and onto her left hand. The pain caused her to let go, and the cup crashed against the floor. Apollo, who had been lurking under the dining room table, bolted to the other room. An angry meow followed in his wake.

The noise didn't affect the ghost. He was tall and bone thin. He looked to be in his late fifties, though age was hard to pinpoint on ghosts, given that they weren't completely solid. Cassie had imagined they appeared in her world by supernatural radio waves. Sometimes that connection was weak and made them glitch and blur like static.

From the waist up, the man appeared unscathed except for the dark bruise circling his neck. From the waist down, however, his legs looked...wrong. They were bent in odd places, and patches of dark blood marked his jeans.

Cassie locked eyes with him again. Remorse filled her, and he moved forward. As he did, his pupils constricted. He opened his mouth, but instead of sound, a wall of burning anger hit her and crawled along her skin like ants. She took an automatic step backward and felt coffee soak into her sock.

The figure in front of her took another step forward, and the heat rose to such a level that she could feel sweat beading along the back of her neck. Her chest constricted; she could do nothing more than take shallow breaths. Her knees shook and spots danced in front of her eyesight.

The spirit froze, and just as Cassie didn't think she could stand another minute of the oppressive heat, he disappeared. Between one blink of an eye and the next, he had left and taken the rising fury with him.

Cassie could breathe again. Her skin returned to normal, and the visceral hatred that hung in the air like smoke faded. She took another breath, slow and deliberate, and the rage dissipated.

Laura emerged from her bedroom. She looked at Cassie, then down at the mess on the floor, then back at Cassie. "Are you okay? What happened?"

Cassie acknowledged the shattered mug and coffee at her feet. One sock was still white, while the other had turned a grayish brown.

When she looked back up at Laura, the fear and confusion in her eyes was still present. "Apollo startled me. I almost stepped on him, then I dropped my coffee."

"That explains why he came tearing down the hallway like that."

Cassie stepped out from the mess and peeled her socks off. "I'm sorry. Did I wake you?"

"No, I was already up. I have trouble sleeping anywhere but my own bed. Then I heard the crash and decided I should check it out."

Cassie laughed. "Thanks. Let me clean this up, and I'll pour some fresh coffee."

"I can help. Where do you keep your broom?"

"No, no, it's fine." Cassie ducked her head as she passed her sister. The less Laura could surmise from her expression, the better. "It'll only take me a minute. Sit down. I'll cook breakfast, too."

"You sure nothing happened?" Laura put a hand on Cassie's arm, forcing her to stop. "You look freaked out."

Cassie forced a smile onto her face, hoping it reached her eyes. "Yeah, it was just Apollo. I got surprised, that's all. Don't worry about me."

Laura wasn't convinced.

5

"I'LL BE READY IN TWENTY!" CASSIE CALLED, BACKING INTO HER bedroom. She waited for Laura to respond before she closed the door and sighed. Her room was a calm oasis compared to the chaos of the kitchen, but her relief only lasted for a moment. The sun had barely risen above the horizon, and today already felt like a test.

She tossed her soggy socks in the laundry. Today, they'd planned to walk around Savannah in the morning, then head to The Pirates' House restaurant for lunch. A little touristy, but Laura hadn't been back in a few years, and the food was delicious. Cassie would have to figure out how to not react to the number of ghosts that usually hung out there.

Though her abilities weren't what they had been before Novak attacked—twice—, they were coming back. Occasionally, she'd see a spirit here and there. Savannah's historical district always provided ample encounters, and a location as historic as The Pirates' House did as well.

She'd also have to avoid thinking about her disastrous date with Jason, keep up the conversation with her sister, and pretend like everything was perfect.

But that was a problem for Future Cassie.

Right now, she had a different mission. Cassie found a cute comfortable outfit and replaced her pajamas. Then, she walked in her bathroom and shut the door behind her. She didn't want Laura to hear any part of the conversation she was about to have.

It had been a couple of months since Elizabeth Montgomery's case, which involved Dr. Langford and William Baker. Cassie had seen a few ghosts since then, but nothing as intimate or jarring as what had just happened in her dining room. Whoever the man was, he was clearly searching for help. The least she could do was reach out to someone about it.

Cassie began to call Detective Harris. They had come to a mutual understanding of each other during the previous case, though they weren't exactly friends. Harris was a good cop, and she'd help if asked, but Cassie didn't want to seem to be pushy.

Better to call someone she had more history with.

He picked up after two rings. "What's wrong?"

"David, really, you have to stop answering the phone like that."

He kept his voice measured with a tinge of humor to his words. "Well, maybe if you called me more often, I wouldn't think there was something wrong every time I heard from you."

"I saw you last Sunday for dinner." Cassie felt lighter just hearing his voice. "You can't guilt-trip me."

"Yeah, yeah. Did you pick up your sister last night?"

"Yep." Cassie leaned against the sink and tipped her head back. "It's going...fine."

"That sounds very convincing."

All of Cassie's worries and fears rushed out of her before she could stop them. "I don't know what to talk about. I don't know how to act around her anymore. We're not the same people we were when we were kids."

"I would hope not." David still sounded amused. "It'd be weird if you were."

"You know what I mean."

"I do, and I'm trying to tell you it's okay. You're not supposed to be the same people. You're supposed to grow and change and find your own paths. That doesn't mean she's not your sister anymore."

"I know." Cassie stared at herself in the mirror. Worry had made her forehead crease, and she worked to smooth it out again. "Everything just feels weird."

"I'm sure it feels weird for her, too."

"You sound like my therapist."

"She's a smart lady. And you and Laura will work through the weirdness. You're both trying. That's the important part."

"Yeah, I guess."

"So, did you call for my sage advice, or is there something else?"

Cassie didn't want to admit it, but she was on a time crunch. "Well, maybe there is something wrong."

"Can't fool me, kid. What's going on?"

"Ghost in the dining room."

"With the candlestick or the revolver?"

"Actually, it was a rope. He had a nasty bruise around his neck. And it looked like someone did a number on his legs."

David inhaled sharply. "You'd think this shit would stop surprising me."

"You have a dead body?"

"Yeah. Male, sixties, strangled to death. Legs crushed."

"He looked like he could've been that age."

"Did you get anything else from him? Any feelings?"

Cassie checked the time before she sat down on the lid of the toilet. Seven minutes left. "He looked sad at first. I also got a sense of remorse. But I've been having these recurring dreams about running my family over with a car—"

"That sounds pleasant."

"—so the remorse could've been left over from that. But that's not the weirdest part."

"Well, don't leave me in suspense."

Cassie rolled her eyes. "He moved closer to me, and then the room felt like an angry oven."

"Did you just say an angry oven?"

"Yes." Cassie could picture the incredulous look on his face. "It's the only way I can describe it. This feeling of intense hatred, this fury, filled the room. It crawled across my skin. Everything got tighter, and hotter, and I had trouble breathing. Then he just... disappeared."

"Has that ever happened to you before?"

"No. I've seen ghosts interact with each other a few times, but this felt different. Like a demon or something."

"Please don't say that, Cassie. My heart can't handle it."

"It's not a demon." Cassie wasn't sure if she believed that or not, but she tried to sound convincing. "But something felt off. This ghost, he didn't look angry. He didn't hurt me or even scare me. He just stood there, took a few steps forward, and then left."

"Okay, we'll mark that down in the column of Things We Need to Investigate."

"What about you? Do you know anything about the body yet?"

"A few things." David paused, and Cassie heard shuffling papers. "We're still waiting on some reports. But that's not the strangest part of this whole thing."

"I never thought I'd hear you say ghosts aren't the strangest part of an investigation."

"The man we found this morning died in the exact way as a handful of other people—from twenty years ago."

Cassie's jaw dropped. "Are you serious?"

"I worked the investigation myself back in the nineties. It was like the past had come back to haunt me."

"Interesting choice of words."

He ignored her commentary. "I don't know if this guy is back in business or it's a copycat, but I'd love your insight. You got some time to stop by later?"

Cassie looked down at her watch. Time was up. "I...don't know."

"Not quite the answer I was expecting."

"I know, I'm sorry. I want to help. Really. But with Laura in town…"

"Of course. I don't want to take you away from her."

"But?"

"No buts." David paused. "*However.*"

"That's just a fancy but."

"However, you know we can't put stuff like this on hold. I promise I won't keep you for long, okay? I just want to see if you can get a read off of anything."

Cassie raked a hand through her hair and stood up. "Okay. Deal. I'll shoot you a text when I'm on my way. But I'll have an hour, tops. I don't want Laura to get mixed up in any of this."

"You got it."

Cassie hung up the phone and took one more look at herself in the mirror. She had bags under her eyes and her hair was frizzy. She didn't want to think about what she'd look like by the time she swung by to see David.

Cassie tossed on a bit of makeup and ran a brush through her hair. It wasn't the sweeping makeover she had hoped it'd be, but it would have to do. She left the bathroom and pulled open her bedroom door, only to find Laura on the other side.

She was standing too close to have been doing anything other than eavesdropping.

Cassie put a hand to her chest. "Jesus, you scared me."

"Sorry. I was just about to knock and see if you were ready."

"Yeah, sorry. I was trying to figure out what to do with my hair."

"And opted for frizzy and disheveled?" Laura's mischievous grin was the same as it had always been.

"You're hilarious." Cassie pulled her door shut behind her, hoping that if Laura had heard anything she'd said, she would forget about it by noon. "Let's go."

6

THE PIRATES' HOUSE IN SAVANNAH WAS OVER 250 YEARS OLD. A historic building from its age, but the ghost stories made the restaurant more intriguing for locals and tourists alike. Most of the stories weren't true. Simple explanations could explain away creaking floorboards, cold gusts of wind, and a strange feeling of being watched.

But some legends were based in fact. And some ghosts were very real.

Laura had suggested the venue for lunch, and Cassie said yes to please her. But she had never felt comfortable inside the walls of the restaurant. The owners had kept up the tradition of painting the shutters and doors faint blue, but it didn't work to keep the spirits away as much as Cassie would've liked.

As soon as the host seated them, a chill passed down Cassie's spine. She kept her eyes forward, hoping that if she ignored the restaurant's supernatural guests, they would repay her in kind. All she wanted to do was eat and get out of there.

"Are you okay?" Laura asked.

Cassie flinched. So much for not being obvious. "Yeah, why?"

Laura shrugged. "You look worried about something."

"I'm always worried." Cassie laughed because it was the truth. "Just hoping I don't run into anyone I know, that's all."

"Don't want to be seen with your kid sister?"

"I have a reputation to uphold, you know."

"Oh, yeah, your sister's a psychologist. What horror. What embarrassment."

"Ew, science." Cassie crinkled her nose. "Art is the superior field, obviously."

Before Laura could respond, their waitress seemed to materialize out of thin air. "Good afternoon, ladies. My name is Cara. What can I get for you today?"

Cassie opened her mouth to relay her order, but when she looked up at the server, her jaw went slack. The woman herself looked normal—mid-twenties, short hair, heavy eyeliner, and a piercing in both her nose and one of her eyebrows—but the shadow that hovered over her shoulder was out of place.

Cassie had only seen this once before and had never dealt with one directly. She wasn't sure what it was. A ghost of some sort? A darkness that twisted and curled like it was alive? The woman must've gone through something truly horrific to have attracted it.

"I can come back," the woman said. "If you need a few more minutes?"

"No, we're ready." Laura shot Cassie a look and then pointed to her menu. "We're going to share the fried calamari. And then I'm going to get the tropical chili glazed shrimp as my entrée."

"Sounds great." The waitress made a note and then turned back to Cassie. "What about you?"

Cassie had recovered enough to talk, but she read straight from the menu so she didn't have to make eye contact with the woman. "I'll get the chicken gumbo, please."

"All right, you want shrimp added to that?"

"No, thank you." Cassie closed her menu and handed it to the woman without looking up.

"Perfect. I'll get that right in for you."

"Thanks." Laura waited until the waitress walked away before she shot Cassie a look. "What was that about?"

Cassie took a long sip of her water. "What was what about?"

"Why'd you freak out?"

"I didn't freak out."

"You freaked *her* out."

"I thought I saw something."

"Something like what?"

Cassie cleared her throat and attempted a mischievous smile. "You know this place is haunted."

Laura rolled her eyes. "I know you don't believe in that crap."

The words stung more than Cassie expected. "Hey, you never know."

"I deal in science, remember? There are no such things as ghosts."

"Speaking of—the science part, I mean—how's work been going?"

"Oh, you know, it's going."

Laura launched into a long explanation of the trouble she'd been having with one of her bosses refusing to assign her new clients, despite her excellent track record. It sounded less about Laura's performance and more about trying to butter up one of her male colleagues, who was the nephew of some B-list celebrity.

Cassie listened with one ear, but her mind wandered. She'd planned on keeping Laura as far away as possible from any business of murder or ghosts, but a part of her must've still hoped that their attempt to reconnect would come with a chance to be open and honest about everything going on in her life. Bitter disappointment rose like bile in her throat.

"What about you?" Laura asked after a long pause.

"Me?"

"Yeah, what's been going on in your life? How's the museum?"

"The museum's great. I love it there. A lot of work to do, but I don't mind."

"What's the oldest, weirdest thing you've handled?"

Cassie laughed. "I don't deal with a lot of the older pieces. I'm mostly working with modern art. I just finished redesigning the 19th and 20th century photography exhibit, but now that it's done, I need to clear space for a new installation. Less artwork and more organizing."

"That's too bad."

"Why?"

"You always liked the old stuff. I remember how obsessed you used to be with Greek mythology and architecture and stuff. It's too bad you're not working on that."

"I told them I wanted to work on modern pieces." Cassie sounded defensive, but she couldn't help it. "That was my choice."

"Oh, okay." Laura looked confused. "As long as you're happy."

"I am."

The appetizer's arrival saved the sisters from more tense conversation. The shadow still hovered over the young woman's shoulders, but instead of looking away, Cassie offered the server an enormous smile as she thanked her for the food.

Laura gave Cassie a look but said nothing as the server went to check on one of her other tables. "Oh my God, I'm so excited for real seafood."

"You live in California. They have real seafood there."

"Not like this." Laura spooned a couple of pieces of calamari onto her plate. "Nothing like this."

A few minutes later, their meals arrived, and they spent the rest of the lunch talking about how incredible everything was.

Cassie was glad for the superficial conversation. The longer she spent in the Pirates' House, the more in tune she felt with the building. She didn't see any other shadows, but there were a few figures passing through doorways or standing against walls she knew no one else could see. Her attention fought between trying to respond to her sister when appropriate and keeping eye on the rest of the dining room.

Luckily for her, older spirits like the ones found in the Pirates'

House seemed to be mostly harmless. Sometimes, they were stuck in a time loop they couldn't get out of. They'd repeat the same actions day after day, unaware they were dead. Cassie often wondered how conscious they really were. Maybe they were just reflections of their former selves, more like a fingerprint left behind than anything that could talk or move on their own.

Cassie watched as their waitress made her rounds. The shadow didn't seem to move independently, and it didn't seem to be actively hurting her. But Cassie could feel the sadness emanating off it from across the room. Whatever it was—whatever had created it—Cassie didn't envy the girl for having to carry that around with her.

"You about ready?" Laura snapped Cassie out of her thoughts.

"Yeah, let's go."

Cassie signed the check, giving the girl a hefty tip. Money wouldn't make the shadow go away, but maybe it could help alleviate the girl of some stress. It was the least she could do.

"What do you want to do now?" Laura asked. "Honestly, I'm kind of beat."

Cassie pulled out her phone and pretended to read a text message. "Oh, you know what? I just got a message from my boss. They need me to sign off on a few things so they can get the ball rolling on a few projects. It shouldn't take long."

"Oh, okay. Do you want me to go with you?"

Cassie's heart pounded. She hated lying. Most of all to her sister. "No, no, that's fine. I'll be quick. I can just drop you off at home, and I'll be back as soon as I can."

"Sure." Laura sounded apprehensive. "That's fine."

"Great."

Cassie couldn't shake the twinge of guilt over lying to her sister.

7

WHEN CASSIE ARRIVED AT THE PRECINCT, AN OFFICER MET HER AT THE front desk and led her back to a meeting room. He knocked on the door, a muffled voiced responded, then he gestured for Cassie to enter on her own.

The room was nothing more or less than what she had experienced in the past: white walls, stale air, and just small enough to feel like the walls could press in on you at any second.

David sat at the head of a rectangular table covered in boxes full of paperwork and evidence bags. Cassie let the door swing shut behind her and it clicked closed. David let out a long breath of air, like he had finally allowed himself to release the pressure that had been building up inside him.

"What've you got for me?" Cassie asked.

David leaned back, linking his hands behind his head. "Don't even get a hello first?"

"Hello." Cassie set her purse in a chair and placed her hands on the back of it. She leaned forward and arched an eyebrow. "What've you got for me?"

"You used to be so nice, Cassie." He tucked his chin to his chest while shaking his head. "So pleasant to work with."

She tried not to laugh, but it was useless. "My sister thinks I'm at work. I don't have much time."

David looked serious now. "Why'd you lie to her?"

Cassie shrugged. "She's my little sister. I don't want to get her mixed up in all this."

"But she knows you've worked with the police in the past."

"Kind of different talking about it in the abstract than having to say, 'Hey, I'll be back in a couple hours. Gotta go check out a dead body.'"

"She'd understand."

"I'm sure she would." Cassie struggled to control the rising frustration in her voice. "But I just need her and this case to have separation. At least for now. I'm not ready to talk to her about it yet."

"You mean you're not ready to talk to her about the ghost stuff just yet."

"Yeah, the ghost stuff." Cassie used air quotes as she wound her way around the table until she was standing over his shoulder. "Come on, catch me up."

"Yeah, yeah, hang on. Let me find the beginning of the thread."

David pulled one box closer, shifting through files and papers and bags. Cassie couldn't see anything in particular, but she let her mind wander. Sometimes her abilities came to her unexpectedly. Other times, she could help them along an inch at a time. It was like defocusing your eyes to see a shape pop out of those *Magic Eye* books. If she could defocus her mind, let it wander a little, sometimes she could get a read on the situation.

"Here we are." David's voice snapped her back. He had pulled a file out of the box and placed it on the table in front of him. There was a name along the top. "Robert Shapiro."

"Is that the guy you found?"

He nodded and flipped open the cover. Inside was a coroner's report and a 4x6 picture of the dead body from the chest up. "Sixty-three years old. First, someone crushed his legs and then strangled him to death. We're still waiting on some final reports, but I'll bet money someone pumped him full of heroin, too."

"Like the other victims? From the nineties?"

"Exactly."

Cassie leaned closer. "How do you know it's not a drug deal gone wrong?"

David chuckled, and when Cassie shot him a look, he held up a hand. "They've been saying that for over twenty years. All the victims we found had died the same way, and all of them full of heroin. But it never made sense. Most drug dealers don't kill their best customers. They give them a warning."

"Maybe they ran out of warnings?"

"There was also way too much heroin in their system. The killer must've forcefully injected that much and killed them, anyway."

Cassie ran a hand through her hair. "And what drug dealer would waste his product like that?"

"Right." David pointed at a section of the coroner's report. "The killer likely crushed their legs so the victims couldn't get away."

"So, the drugs had nothing to do with it."

"They were sending a message." David looked up at her. "Although I don't know who they were sending it to."

Cassie tapped the photo. "Not to complicate matters, but that's not the guy I saw this morning."

"You're sure?"

"Positive. My guy was a little younger. A lot bonier. Definitely not Robert Shapiro."

"Perhaps there's another victim."

"Or he could be one of the original victims?"

David held up a finger and leaned forward. He grabbed another folder and flipped through it. When he didn't find what he was looking for, he tossed it to the side and scanned through two more.

"Here we go." He looked up with a sheepish grin. "Sorry, we're still getting set up. I'm not organized yet."

Cassie gestured to the boxes strewn across the table. "Is someone gonna help you with all this?"

"Harris got to the body first, but she's deferring to me. She's got her own crap to work on. I have a couple rookies, but I don't trust them to do things the right way."

"You mean *your* way."

"Yeah, the right way." He opened the folder and pulled out seven 8x10 photographs, spreading them out across the table. "These are the original victims. All male. Ages anywhere from their mid-twenties to late fifties."

"So, Shapiro isn't outside the typical victim pool."

"Other than being two decades late to the game. At first glance, he looks like he could fit right in."

"May I?" Cassie asked. David gave his chair over to her, and she took her time looking at each photograph, touching and holding each, trying to defocus her mind enough to get a read on any of them.

After ten minutes, she looked back up at David. "Nothing."

"Really?"

"Really." She turned back to the pictures. "None of these guys match the guy I saw this morning. And I'm not getting any readings off the photos."

"Think there's a reason for that?"

Cassie sighed. She was always trying to figure out a reason for everything that happened to her. "There could be, but I doubt it. My abilities are still coming and going. It's like I've got a crystal-clear picture with the ghosts, but the psychic flashes are mostly static."

David started pacing the length of the room. "So, we've got a dead body without a ghost and a ghost without a dead body. Both died the same way, mirroring a case from over twenty years ago. There's a lot to get through, so where do we start?"

Cassie pointed to the picture of Robert Shapiro. "With him. He's the only tangible evidence we have. If we follow his trail, then maybe my new friend will pop up again, and we'll be able to connect the dots."

"And what if your *new friend* isn't too happy about that?"

"That'll be my problem to deal with." Cassie thought back to the strange interaction from earlier. "The feeling I got from this morning was uncomfortable, but it didn't feel directed toward me."

"Right. The angry oven."

"As soon as I come up with a better name, I'll let you know and give you the naming rights. You can put it on a t-shirt and sell it on Amazon." Cassie shook her head. "But we'll figure that out, eventually. What do you know about Shapiro so far?"

David pinched the bridge of his nose and blinked hard. "Seems like a regular guy. No immediate family. His wife, Susanna, died years ago. They didn't have any kids. He was a postal worker. The only strange thing is he didn't have a criminal record."

"That's strange?"

David walked back over to the table and tapped a photograph of one of the original victims. "Every single one of these guys had been to prison for drug-related crimes. Some of them served months, others served years. It's the one thing they had in common. Each of them died within a few weeks of being released."

"So, it's not just a question of why *now*." Cassie picked up the photo of Robert Shapiro. "But why *him*?"

There was a soft knock on the door.

"Come in," David called out.

The officer that had led Cassie to the room earlier popped his head inside. "We're ready to search the house, sir."

"Got it. Be there in a minute." David waited until the door shut again before he turned to Cassie. "Want to come with?"

Cassie checked her phone. She'd been gone for almost ninety minutes. "I should get back to my sister."

"You sure? We could use your eye."

"Maybe next time." Cassie grabbed her purse and swung it over her shoulder. "I'll let you know if I see anything else."

"Want me to keep you updated?"

"Sure."

She was part of this now, whether she liked it or not.

8

CASSIE OPENED THE FRONT DOOR AND WAS SURPRISED WHEN APOLLO didn't greet her. The house was dead silent other than the slight static of a TV from somewhere in the back. After tossing her purse on the bench and slipping off her shoes, she made her way to the guest bedroom. She knocked gently on the door.

"Come in."

She pushed the door open and found who she was looking for. "Ah, we have a traitor in our midst, I see."

Apollo looked up from Laura's lap with lazy eyes. He was purring so loud that when he meowed, almost no sound came out. He put his head back down when he saw Cassie didn't have any food in her hands.

Laura looked comfortable herself. She had a mountain of pillows propping her up in bed as she flipped through the channels on the small TV sitting on the dresser. She hadn't even looked over when Cassie walked in.

"Interesting choice of words," she said.

Cassie's eyebrows pinched together. "What do you mean?"

"Having a *traitor in our midst*."

"You're gonna have to be more specific—"

"Where were you?"

Cassie felt the heat rise in her face. "I told you, I was at work."

"I called your work."

"You did what?"

Laura finally faced her, and Cassie could see how hard her eyes were. "I called the museum."

"Why would you do that?"

"You were acting really weird earlier. I felt like you were lying, but I wanted to make sure."

Cassie couldn't keep the anger out of her voice. "Wow, how very trusting of you."

"You can't be mad at me for thinking you were lying when you actually were. You're the one who did something wrong here."

"What I do in my free time is my business, Laura."

"Yes, it is. But don't lie to me about it."

"Who did you call at the museum?"

"Relax, I just called the front desk and asked for you. Whoever answered just said you weren't working today."

"Tonya?"

"Yeah, I guess." She shot Cassie an ambivalent look. "Does it matter?"

Cassie threw up her arms and walked out of the room. "Yes, it matters. I don't need my little sister checking up on me."

A thud told her Apollo had jumped down off the bed, and a second later, the squeak of the mattress revealed that Laura had followed suit.

"Maybe you need people to check up on you, Cassie. You're not great at staying out of trouble."

"We spent the last few years barely talking, and I've been fine."

Laura grabbed Cassie's arm and spun her around. They now stood toe to toe in the kitchen. "Fine? You think you've been fine? Look at what happened to you."

"I'm well aware of what happened to me."

"Then how can you say—"

"What else am I going to do?" Cassie's voice was loud now. But she didn't care. "Huh? Hide in my bedroom every day? Refuse to go out? Refuse to go to work? I can't live my life that way."

"I'm not asking you to." Laura took a deep breath, and when she spoke again, her voice was much softer. "Cassie, I was worried about you, okay? I didn't mean to cross any boundaries. Didn't mean to cause any trouble. I didn't want to accuse you of anything without evidence to back up my claims."

Cassie had better control of her voice now, but there was still a bite. "So, what are your accusations?"

Laura rolled her eyes. "Poor choice of words. I'm not accusing you of anything. I know you didn't go to work today. I worried about you the entire time. You don't have to tell me where you went, but I would like to know why you felt like you had to lie to me. That hurt my feelings."

She wasn't sure if Laura had done it on purpose, but her sister's words achieved the desired effect of washing away the rest of Cassie's anger. A pang in her chest replaced it. "Believe it or not, I lied to you because I *didn't* want you to worry about me."

"Well, you failed on that account."

Cassie's laugh was a little watery. "Yeah, I guess so. I'm sorry, okay? I wasn't trying to hurt your feelings."

"I know." Laura leaned in and Cassie returned the hug. When they separated, Laura had a smirk on her face. "So, are you going to tell me where you were?"

"I thought you said I didn't have to?"

"You don't. But now I'm curious."

Cassie leaned against the kitchen counter. Less than twelve hours earlier, she and her sister had been in this same room under quite different circumstances. There was no evidence of the shattered coffee mug or the strangled ghost, and yet Cassie wished she could rewind the clock. Dealing with the spirit world was much easier than dealing with her sister.

"I was at the police station downtown."

"The police station?" Laura stood up a little straighter. "Why? Is everything okay? Are you in trouble?"

"See? This is why I didn't want to tell you."

"I'm allowed to worry. You don't have a good track record in the Everything-Is-Fine category."

"Everything *is* fine." When Laura frowned, Cassie carried on. "Really, it is. I'm not in any kind of trouble, I promise. I have a friend who's a detective. He wanted me to check out some details about a case he's working on."

"And you couldn't tell me this?" Laura's entire face lit up. "Wait, is this detective your secret lover? Do you have to keep your relationship quiet so the criminals he puts away won't target you when they get out of jail?"

"Whoa, whoa, whoa. What are you talking about?" Cassie couldn't keep from laughing. "My life isn't some lame romance novel."

Laura shrugged her shoulders. "Doesn't have to be a romance. Happened to Batman all the time."

"David is not Batman."

"You don't know that. But you're getting sloppy—you said his name."

Cassie covered her face with her hand. She couldn't decide if she wanted to laugh or groan. "His name is David Klein. He's a detective, not Batman. He's also twenty-some years older than me and married with kids. He's got grandkids. He is not my secret lover."

Laura deflated. "Okay, then I really don't understand why you didn't tell me."

It was Cassie's turn to shrug now. Did she have a suitable answer? "I didn't want you to worry. And I didn't want you to get involved in a murder case."

"Who said I'd get involved?"

"I know you. You're too curious for your own good. You like helping people. I don't need you to stick your nose in this one."

Laura held up her hands in surrender. "I promise I won't go sticking my nose anywhere you don't want it to be. But I think you should tell me about the case."

"No." Cassie grabbed a pair of coffee mugs from the cupboard. "Absolutely not."

Laura groaned. "Fine, but will you at least tell me how you help them? How'd you even get started with this? You never told me. And before you say anything, I'm not trying to weasel my way into anything. This trip was about bonding, right? This is a big part of your life, it seems. I'm curious."

Cassie finished pouring the coffee and then led her sister to the dining room table. "I'm sure you are."

"I'm serious." Laura's eyes were pleading as she sat down. "I really want to know more about what you've been up to. What interests you?"

Cassie didn't want to lie to her sister again, but she had to figure out a way to be truthful without painting the full picture. "I know a lot of the cops around Savannah. I don't remember how I met half of them, to be honest. They figured out I had a talent for, uh, picking up on details other people missed."

"Like *Monk*?"

The question was so genuine, so innocent, that Cassie burst into laughter. "No, not like *Monk*. I don't have OCD."

"More like *Psych* then?"

"Oh." Cassie hadn't expected Laura to hit so close to home, even if it wasn't a bullseye. "Yeah, I guess it's a bit like *Psych*."

"That's pretty cool." There was a beat of silence. "Does it ever bother you?"

Cassie took a sip of coffee and felt the heat slide down her throat. "Does what bother me?"

"Looking at murder cases? Being that close to death. That close to serial killers."

"They're not all serial killers," Cassie said. "But yeah, sometimes it bothers me. Sometimes it brings up terrible memories. Sometimes it gets scary. But it feels good to help people. They can get closure. They can move on."

Cassie didn't mention that sometimes those *people* were really ghosts.

"Well, I'm happy for you," Laura said. "Really. But I just hope you'll be careful."

"Always." Cassie laid a hand on Laura's arm. "You don't have to worry about me."

"I'm always going to worry about you," Laura said. "You'll just have to live with that."

9

CASSIE GRIPPED THE STEERING WHEEL UNTIL HER KNUCKLES TURNED WHITE *and her hands ached. Her headlights illuminated the road in front of her, and the rest was so dark she felt like she was driving through a void in space. She could sense, rather than see, the trees whipping by as she sped down an empty highway.*

Her foot slid off the gas pedal, but the car didn't slow down. She slammed her foot on the brake, and it went right to the floor with no resistance. The car didn't shudder or stop, no matter how many times she pressed her foot against the pedal. There was no slowing down.

Cassie looked around, wondering if she could use something—anything —to help her slow down and stop. There were no guardrails, and the inky blackness scared her more than the road ahead. If only she could find an exit and maybe an empty field to help her slow down.

An itching sense that she had been here before grew at the back of her neck. She didn't know exactly what was coming, but she didn't like it. This wasn't going to be good.

The car drifted to the left, but no matter how hard she yanked the steering wheel to the right, she couldn't change directions. She saw no headlights in the distance, but that didn't mean another car wouldn't come barreling around the corner at any second. Her panic grew, her chest constricted. Her breaths became shallow. Her head grew light and her vision spotty.

A soft glow in the distance caught her attention. If it was another car, there would be no time for her to move out of the way. She tried once more to turn the steering wheel, but it had locked in place. Her trajectory was certain.

As she closed the distance between her and the soft glow, forms took shape. The illumination didn't look like headlights. Instead, it looked like an invisible lamppost shining its light across the center of the highway.

A figure appeared in the center. Then two. Then three.

Cassie once again slammed on the brakes, but instead of slowing down, the car shuddered and barreled down the road with renewed vigor. She leaned forward, squinting, trying to figure out what she was seeing in the distance. And as soon as they came into focus, she couldn't control the scream that escaped her mouth.

Her parents stood in the road with blank faces. The light washed out their features, making them look pale and lifeless. They held hands, her father on the left and her mother next to him, but there was no indication they knew what was about to happen, no indication they could even see her bearing down on them.

Laura, only five or six years old, stood next to their mother. Unlike her parents, her little sister could see what was happening. She was crying and clutching a teddy bear to her chest. Her face was a mask of horror and fear, and the very sight brought tears to Cassie's eyes.

This is what she had feared. This is what she had known was coming. And that awareness was all she needed. This had happened before, and she refused to let it happen again. She grabbed the steering wheel and pulled it as hard as she could to the left. Her hands burned and her arms shook, but she refused to let go. Refused to give up.

Adrenaline gave her superhuman strength. Foot by foot, the car drifted. The darkness whipped by and the illuminated section of the road grew closer with every second. She changed her trajectory enough to miss hitting her sister, but it wasn't enough to save her parents. Right before the colli-

sion, she locked eyes with her mother. Years of silence had caused a mountain of regret to form between them. And now, Cassie didn't have enough time to say she was sorry.

She forced herself to keep her eyes open as the car collided with her family.

CASSIE BOLTED UP IN BED, clutching her sheet to her chest. Sweat and tears soaked through her pajamas. Her breath came out rough and ragged. It took her a moment to realize the inky blackness around her was not the same as the one in her dream. She was safe in her bed. And, most likely, so were her parents and her sister.

Just like the night before, Cassie swung her legs over the side of her bed and plodded into the kitchen. Unlike yesterday, however, she took a moment to cast a glance over her shoulder to the dining room.

The same ghost from yesterday waited for her.

She didn't have a coffee cup to drop this time, but it wouldn't have mattered. She had expected him. The adrenaline in her system subsided, and she didn't care what happened next. She refused to be afraid.

Like any good ghost whisperer, she walked straight up to him.

"Can you talk?"

The ghost looked down at her but didn't open his mouth.

"Can you show me who you are? A name? A house? Anything for me to help you. This is a two-way street, you know."

The figure in her dining room blinked twice before shaking his head side to side. It was subtle, almost imperceptible, but Cassie had caught it.

"Are you afraid to talk to me?"

The ghost said nothing.

"Is someone stopping you from talking to me?"

The instant the words left her mouth, a fiery anger crawled across her skin. Just like yesterday. Instead of giving in to her fear, Cassie pushed back. She closed her eyes and reached out with her mind.

She had an ability few people possessed. If anyone could figure out what was going on, it was her.

She realized the anger didn't emanate from the spirit in front of her. He was a cool breeze on a hot summer day. He was static and calm. But the rest of the room was a furnace. Was this what hell would feel like? Was the Devil knocking on her door?

An electric tingle struck the tips of her fingers and worked its way up her arms and shoulders, to the top of her head. A feeling she rarely experienced these days, except when she was closest to the other side.

But before she could channel the energy, it sparked and fizzled out of existence. The cool breeze in the center of the room dissipated. The surrounding heat was slower to recede. However, Cassie had gotten her first real answer.

The fiery anger was separate from the ghost that had now visited two days in a row. In fact, it was trying to control the spirit and keep it from talking to her. But why? What would it gain from not allowing Cassie to solve the mystery man's case?

Cassie opened her eyes and found herself alone in her dining room. The encounter had been so short, but she'd gained insight into the case. This was the information David wanted from her. It wouldn't be much for now—most likely it would make things more confusing—but it could eventually nudge them in one direction over another. And those were the decisions that helped solve a case.

Ignoring her need for coffee, Cassie ran back to her room and grabbed her phone. It was four in the morning, but she couldn't wait to text David. Besides, he was an early riser. One hour wouldn't be the death of him.

Two entities. Mystery victim is cool and calm. Seemed afraid to talk to me. As soon as he tried, a second entity appeared. The angry oven. Couldn't see it, but it filled the room again. Doesn't want me communicating with the victim. Don't know why. I'll let you know if anything else happens.

Cassie read over her text twice, making sure she left nothing out. There wasn't much to say. She had no concrete information about the victim to tell who he was or when he died, and the red-hot entity was, at least for the moment, invisible to the naked eye.

Some ghost whisperer she was.

But an unread text distracted her from her self-loathing. From someone unexpected. She didn't think she'd hear from him anytime soon. If ever.

Jason Broussard, the security guard from the museum, had sent her a message. Cassie's heart hammered as she clicked on his name. Part of her couldn't get to the text fast enough, and part of her wanted to throw her phone out an open window.

I know it's late, so I hope this doesn't wake you up, but I've had two beers and apparently, I'm a lightweight these days. For what it's worth, I had a great time on our date. It was a complete disaster and ended with me getting sucker punched, but I still had a good time. I know you've been avoiding spending more than 30 seconds with me at a time, so I just wanted to apologize if I did anything wrong. If it's because you decided you actually hate me, that's fine. But if it's out of embarrassment, I hope maybe I can take you out again sometime. It can only get better from here, right? No pressure. Hope you have a good time with your family. See you at work.

Cassie groaned and fell back onto her bed. She'd been avoiding even thinking about her date with Jason for the last few weeks because it had gone up in such spectacular flames. She'd been so distracted by the revelation that the little boy ghost in her bedroom had spoken the name of her childhood friend, Sarah Lennox, that dinner at The Pirates' House had been a quiet, uninteresting affair. Even a room full of spirits hadn't been enough to rouse her from her thoughts.

But after that, Jason had wanted to walk to get ice cream and eat it in Warren Square. The ease of their relationship from work had disappeared. Finding something to talk about had been excruciating. Cassie had overcompensated by going into detail about what she'd been cataloging at the museum, even though she'd promised herself she'd leave work behind for the night.

They had to have more in common than just that, right?

But she couldn't be sure. She barely remembered what he'd spoken about at the restaurant, and their conversation in the square was a blur of anxiety and confusion. By the end of the night, she'd tripped over her own feet, and he tried to catch her at the same time she flung out her arms to stay balanced. That's when she'd accidentally sucker punched him in the face. He'd said he was fine, and she hadn't given him a bruise, but she was so embarrassed that she asked him to take her home. She didn't even look at him as she said goodbye and got out of his car. She bolted to her house and a large glass of wine.

Then she spent the last several weeks trying not to be in the same room with him. Magdalena thought she was being stupid—and she was right—but Cassie didn't know what else to do. Although she'd rather crawl into a hole and die than see him again, she did still like Jason. A lot. He was kind and funny and smart and insightful. He had the self-assurance she was still trying to find in herself, but he also understood anxiety and fear and how much the world could suck sometimes.

She looked back at her phone but couldn't find any words that would explain her feelings. Was it worth going on a second date to see if it could be worse than the first? She appreciated Jason's optimism, but she didn't share the sentiment. Maybe it was better to salvage the friendship than try to pursue anything romantic.

She could at least handle that, right?

Cassie tossed her phone onto the nightstand and crawled under her covers. That was a question better reserved for daylight hours. For now, she'd try to get at least a couple more hours of sleep. If she could achieve that, she might gain a modicum of energy for the day to come.

10

DAVID SAT IN THE SITUATION ROOM AND STARED AT CASSIE'S MESSAGE for the third or fourth time that day. Like most conversations he had with her, he didn't know what to make of it. The ghost she saw was obviously connected to the case, but until they found the ghost's physical body, they had no usable evidence. A chill passed through his body that had nothing to do with the fact that someone had recently cranked up the AC by a few degrees.

And this other entity, the "angry oven"? David still didn't understand what Cassie did or how it worked, but this wasn't a good sign. If another spirit kept the victim from communicating, then the case was as big and complicated as he had feared.

David leaned back in his chair and looked around the room. It had transformed since the last time Cassie had been in there. Boxes and papers were still strewn about the table in an organized chaos. A board at the front of the room held pictures of the known victims, including Robert Shapiro, along with a map showing where the police had discovered them.

The table held personal effects, additional evidence, and paperwork, grouped according to each victim. The detectives had gathered copious amounts of evidence, yet still didn't have enough to solve the case.

Technology had come a long way since the nineties, and it would be interesting to see if revisiting the case in the modern era would drum up anything new. Then again, technology went only so far when the bodies were decayed and the evidence damaged.

But every time David felt like the mystery was insurmountable, he remembered Cassie's advice to start with Shapiro. Their new body was the reentry point. It was another inch of thread leading them in the right direction.

A sharp knock sounded on the other side of the door, and instead of waiting for an answer, a man pushed his way inside. He was big— at least a head taller than David—and older and rounder, too. He wore a handlebar mustache and a scowl.

Huck Crawford was part of the old guard. He was ten years David's senior, but hadn't moved up the ladder as quickly. The two of them were never friendly, but sometimes the job had to get done, with or without being friends. Crawford enjoyed the power he wielded more than the work required to get the power.

"Let's make this quick, Klein. I've got about thirty-two things to get done today."

"The faster the better." David had learned over the years that keeping his cool and sticking to the point was the best way to deal with people like Crawford. "You heard about the case I'm working on? Murder victim by the name of Robert Shapiro?"

Crawford hovered in the doorway, like he couldn't wait to leave. "'Bout the only thing people are talkin' about around here."

"And how it connects back to that case we worked on in the nineties?"

"The one with all the addicts who were strangled to death. Yeah, I remember. Got a point you're gonna get to anytime soon?"

"What do you remember of the case?" David's tone was still even, but he could feel his blood pressure rising. "Any details that jump out?"

Crawford pointed to the mess of papers on the table. "The records are gonna remember better than I can."

"Humor me?"

Crawford blew out a breath and finally let the door swing shut behind him. The office chair squeaked as he sat down. "Was a long time ago."

"These cases stick with you, especially your first ones."

"Eh, it was *your* first big one. My second or third by that time." Crawford sounded somewhat wistful. Haughty. "Still, those bodies washing up on the shore weren't fun to deal with. Had everyone in a panic. Word got out real quick that it was a serial killer."

"I remember hearing that word everywhere back then."

"Wasn't new terminology but wasn't as common as it is now."

"What did you think when you first saw them?" David asked. "The bodies, I mean."

Crawford leaned back in his chair with a grunt. "Three of them at first. Crushed legs, strangled throats. Figured they were a bunch of poor sons of bitches who were in the wrong place at the wrong time. Then we started digging. Found out they were addicts. Made sense."

David's eyebrows pinched together. "Made sense?"

"Addicts are always addicts. They'll do anything for their next hit. Figured that's what happened. Didn't think much of it after that. Seemed like a waste of money to me."

David had to work to keep his fist from clenching. "What do you mean, a waste of money?"

"Seemed cut and dry, is all. Lot of shit was going down back then. Missing kids. Dead women. We had bigger fish to fry than a guy killing off addicts."

"I think the families of the victims would disagree."

Crawford laughed. It was loud and obnoxious and devoid of any real humor. "What families? Most of them didn't have anyone, and the ones who did had been disowned. If they had been married, their wives had left them. If they had kids, they had taken away their custody."

"So, they didn't deserve to have their cases solved?"

"I'm not saying that. Don't put words in my mouth." Crawford thumped his fist on the table. "You know as well as I do that the higher-ups prioritize some cases over others. This was a low-priority case."

David didn't know what to say. Crawford wasn't wrong. David had seen it happen hundreds of times over the years. Some victims fell in the cold case files simply because they had a bigger crime to solve. Because the department didn't have enough money. Because the dead didn't have anyone who cared enough to keep asking.

But none of that made it right.

"You're right, I'm sorry." David cooled his tone. He needed Crawford's cooperation more than he needed to let him know he was a jerk. "I'm trying to think if that changed after we found the next bodies?"

"The ones in the woods?" Crawford shook his head. "Not really. The Captain was angry as all hell that he had to send us back out to investigate that."

"I do remember that," David said. "I was out in those woods every day for a week."

Crawford guffawed. "Yeah, well, Cap liked to bust your balls, didn't he? You were always asking so many damn questions."

"Guess that's why I became a detective."

"You're no better than the rest of us, Klein. The world needs cops like me and the boys to keep 'em in line."

"You're not wrong." David wondered if his laugh sounded as forced to Crawford's ears as it did to his own. "What happened after that? I just remember one day we were working the case, and the next day someone shoved it to the back of some drawer."

"We weren't getting anywhere. It was a dead end. We didn't have any evidence. There were no leads. What else were we going to do? We had other cases to solve."

"Yeah, I guess you're right. Cap was happy about that."

Crawford eyed him, and his scowl deepened. "I know what you're doing, Klein."

"What am I doing?"

"You're trying to get me to turn on Cap."

"No, I'm not." David paused, weighing his options. He went for the riskier move. "But it doesn't matter. Cap's retired. If you know anything else about the case that can help us now, then—"

Crawford stood up, bumping the table and nearly knocking over his chair. He jabbed a finger at David. "A cop never retires. You damn well know that. I've got nothing to say to you."

David stood up. "Huck, come on."

"No." He was red in the face now. "No. Cap was a good cop. He did all he could for those people. He did his best with what he had. At some point, you've got to cut your losses. They were a bunch of addicts, a bunch of deadbeats. They drained resources when they were alive, and they drained resources when they were dead. Now, I'm sorry their families never got closure, but that's just how it goes sometimes."

David opened his mouth to speak again, but Crawford waved him off. Without another word, he left the room and slammed the door behind him. David could hear him barking at people to get out of his way as he walked down the hall.

Crawford hadn't been as insightful as David would've liked, but he had proven useful. If nothing else, it had convinced David he needed to reach out to his old boss.

It was time to track down Captain Phillip Stockton to see what he had to say.

11

CASSIE YANKED AT THE HEM OF HER SHIRT AS A GENTLE BREEZE RUFFLED her hair. They were standing outside a café, but for all she knew, she could've been on stage with three spotlights trained in her direction. "I'm nervous. Are you nervous?"

"No," Laura replied. "Why would I be nervous?"

Cassie tried rubbing the sweat from her palms. "We haven't seen him in, like, fifteen years."

"Yeah, that's why we're meeting him for brunch."

"Why aren't you nervous?"

Laura put a hand around Cassie's shoulder. "There's nothing to be nervous about. It's going to be the same old Michael."

The Michael she remembered was hilarious but cutting. He didn't beat around the bush. He was kind and generous and loved with his entire heart, but that often got him into more trouble than he could handle. "That's what I'm nervous about. Same old Michael. A lot has happened to me in the past decade. In case you forgot."

"I didn't forget." Laura gave her one more squeeze and let go. "Besides, you're the one who wanted to do this."

"Doesn't mean I'm not allowed to be nervous."

"Well, it's too late to back out now." She gestured with her head. "There he is."

Michael was hard to miss. He was six-foot-three with blond hair and blue eyes. He had the body of a dancer—muscular but lean—and wore a Hermes scarf with just about every outfit. Cassie had never seen him wear anything she'd consider a faux pas, and he looked both put together and casual.

"Ladies, ladies." Michael hugged Laura and gave her a kiss on the cheek and then did the same to Cassie. "You both look incredible, holy shit. California is treating you well, Laura, but where's the tan?"

"I'm Irish, Michael. I only have two settings—undercooked and overdone."

He threw his head back and laughed. Several people turned around. "Oh my God, I missed you girls."

They entered the Funky Brunch Café and asked for outdoor seating. Once they had their spots and ordered their breakfast, Michael leaned forward and put his chin in his hands. "Okay, tell me everything."

"What's the last thing you remember?" Laura asked.

"Oh, God. Graduating high school, I guess? Cassie, you stayed here for college. We met up a couple times. Laura, you came back from California once or twice. It's been at least ten or fifteen years."

"Definitely more than ten," Cassie said. She broke her life into two parts—Before Novak and After Novak. Michael fell squarely in the Before Novak era. He seemed to pick up on the reference, but kept his mouth shut. Maybe she'd be able to get through this meeting without reliving everything.

"Yeah, closer to fifteen." Laura sounded wistful. "Let's see, what's happened to me? Went to college. Changed my major three times. Landed on psychology and had to take an extra year. My parents weren't too happy about that, but they would never say that to my face. Got my master's and a job right out of college. I've been practicing ever since. I have a gig at an established clinic. Pays the bills and then some. Kind of a dick boss, though."

"Oooh, that sounds amazing. Have you had anyone crazy come through? Any Jokers to your Harley?"

"No." Laura laughed and brushed her curls over her shoulder. "I mostly deal with people who have anxiety and are recovering from a trauma."

Cassie stiffened. She hadn't known that was her sister's area of expertise.

"Oh, come on. You've got to have some juicy stories. Everyone in California is crazy."

"Including me?"

"Including you. There's just the good kind of crazy and the, you know, clinical kind."

The arrival of their food interrupted them, and Cassie breathed a sigh of relief. Did Michael think she was crazy? She had anxiety and depression and PTSD, but she had spent years working through them. She understood they were an illness, but that didn't make her weak or worthless.

Still, it hurt to think maybe Michael didn't see her the same way.

"What about you?" Cassie asked, realizing she'd been silent the entire time. "What've you been up to?"

"Oh, God. Let's see. Well, moved to New York City to make it big. Failed miserably."

"You did not." Laura smacked his elbow. "You were on *Broadway*."

Michael waved her off, but he was smiling. "I did a few things here and there. Mostly ensemble work. Nothing like dreaming about being the leading man and ending up in the chorus."

"You did a great job." Why did Cassie's voice sound so quiet, so meek? "I saw a few clips of you online. You were really good."

Michael's eyes softened. "Really? You looked me up?"

"Of course. We were best friends in high school. That doesn't go away just because we haven't talked in a while."

"You still dating Steve?" Laura asked.

"Yes." Michael rolled his eyes. "Six years this December. He's so annoying."

"Oh no, how come?"

Michael threw up his arms. "Because he's perfect. He's kind and considerate and has excellent communication skills. He's open and trusting. My mother loves him. He talks about cars and fishing and sports with my father. He's got a good job and a huge future ahead of him as a lawyer."

"Oh, yeah, this sounds awful." Cassie smirked. "How can you stand it?"

"You laugh, but you guys know me. Tinkerbell needs applause to live. I need drama. Please tell me you have some juicy stories to share."

Michael looked right at Cassie when he said this.

"I lead a pretty boring—"

"That's a lie, and we all know it." Michael put down his fork and stretched his arm across the table. "I didn't want to be the one to point out the elephant in the room, but we both know you've been through some shit. I'm not going to make you talk about it if you don't want to, but let's not pretend it doesn't exist. That's not healthy for anyone, least of all you."

Cassie was stunned. She opened her mouth to say something, but no words came out.

Laura came to her rescue. "I feel like this is a three-sheets-to-the-wind conversation, not a brunch conversation."

Michael retracted his arm and dug back into his omelet. "Okay, fair enough. So, we'll avoid the serial killer topic for now. What's one step down from that?"

Cassie searched her brain for something—anything—that would satisfy Michael and not feel like she was bearing her soul to someone who was practically a stranger these days. "Uh, I've been having these strange dreams lately."

"That's, like, *several* steps away from serial killers, but I'll take it. Let's hear it."

Cassie turned to Laura. "Actually, you're in them. So's Mom and Dad."

"Really?" She looked flattered. "Good dreams or bad dreams?"

"I would classify them as nightmares." Cassie took a bite of her sandwich to allow herself a few seconds to think. She covered her mouth and continued in between chewing. "Basically, I'm in a car I can't control, speeding toward you guys. The weird part is that you're, like, maybe five years old or so?"

Laura took a thoughtful bite of her pancake. "That is weird."

"Okay, okay. Let's think about this." Michael put his fork down and steepled his fingers in front of his face. "Not being able to steer the car could mean you feel like your life is out of your control. Does that track?"

"What are you, Morpheus, the God of Dreams now?"

"Answer the question."

"I mean, maybe?" Cassie hesitated. "Honestly, I feel like I'm finally getting things under control. Work is going well. My dating life isn't great, but that doesn't keep me up at night."

"We'll circle back to the dating life thing." Michael gave her a knowing look. "Well, this seems specific to your family, so how are things going there?"

Laura and Cassie exchanged looks. Cassie shrugged. "Better? We're working on it."

"Hmm."

Cassie rolled her eyes, then turned to her sister. "Please tell him dreams don't mean anything."

She left out the part where her dreams were often prophetic. Neither one of them needed to know that.

"Actually—"

"You're kidding me."

"*Actually*, they can have meaning. Dreams are just your brain's way of sifting through what's been on your mind lately. They can help store information. They help with memories, too."

"Memories." Michael clapped his hands together. "Okay, maybe it's related to memories. Now we're getting somewhere. Did anything happen to you guys when Laura was around five?"

Cassie was about to tell Michael she had no idea when Laura laughed and looked between them like they were crazy.

"What?" Cassie asked.

"Seriously, you don't remember?"

Michael shrugged and Cassie said, "Remember what?"

"That was about the time Sarah Lennox went missing."

12

CASSIE DROPPED HER FORK, AND IT CLATTERED AGAINST HER PLATE.

"Oh my God, you're right." Michael's voice carried across the outdoor patio, and a few heads turned in their direction. "How could I forget that?"

"Did you say Sarah Lennox?" Cassie asked. It felt like the entire universe had been blotted out except for the three of them. She got tunnel vision as her ears turned hot.

"Yeah, why?" Laura's eyebrows pinched together. "Are you okay?"

"Yeah, I'm fine." Cassie swallowed back some bile. "I've been thinking about her a lot lately."

"That could explain your dreams, then."

"But I don't remember much about that time. And why would I be dreaming about Laura instead of Sarah?"

Laura shrugged. "No idea. Our brains make weird connections sometimes. Could just be random."

"Or maybe not." Michael waggled his eyebrows. "How intriguing."

Cassie had a sinking feeling Michael was hitting closer to home than her sister. The ghost of the little boy had been the first one to utter Sarah Lennox's name in close to two decades. She'd first seen him out of the house when Laura had called about her mother's brain tumor, but that hadn't been the only time he'd appeared outside her bedroom. Were the other times connected to her sister too? She'd been talking about the dream in her therapy appointment. And he'd shown up in the parking garage when she'd gotten Laura from the airport.

Cassie cleared her throat and tried to be nonchalant. "What do you guys remember from back then?"

"I didn't know you two yet." Michael brushed his hair back from his eyes. "But I remember when she went missing because we'd just moved here from Atlanta, and my mom kept saying we should've stayed where we were. But I guess I didn't really understand what missing meant. I just thought she'd gotten lost in the store or something and that they'd find her soon. I didn't know why my mom was so worked up about it."

"She wasn't the first one to go missing," Cassie said.

"Or the last." Laura turned to Cassie. "You were pretty good friends with her. I remember her coming over to the house a bunch of times."

"Oh my God, are you serious?" Michael leaned forward. "Tell me everything. Did they ever figure out what happened to her?"

"I'm not sure. I didn't understand a lot of what went on back then either. Sarah and I were best friends. We were about ten years old, maybe? She'd come over a couple times a week. Her family was poorer than ours, so Mom would feed her whenever she could. She was so tiny for her age."

Laura nodded. "Yeah, I remember that, too. We always had the best dinners when she was over."

"Then, one day, Mom and Dad sat me down and said they didn't know when Sarah would come over again. They said someone took her, and her parents were trying to get her back. I knew it was bad, but I don't think I knew to be afraid."

"I remember getting upset we couldn't play outside like we used to."

Cassie turned to Michael. "Our parents were pretty relaxed. They let us play in the neighborhood wherever we wanted if we were home by dinner. But after Sarah went missing, we could only play in the backyard and only when one of them was around to watch us."

"Wow." Michael looked between the two sisters. "Do you remember anything about what happened to her?"

Cassie shook her head. "It's weird, but I don't remember anything after she went missing. I don't know if I just didn't think much about her after that or what."

"That could be a response to the trauma." Laura took a long sip of her drink. "I don't think you handled it that well."

"What do you mean?"

"Well." She looked at Michael and then back at Cassie. "You kept saying you were going to go outside and play with her, even after she disappeared."

"What?"

"Yeah. I remember getting excited because I thought that meant we'd be able to play with our friends again, but then Mom and Dad would say Sarah wasn't back yet. I was so confused. But you'd tell them she was waiting for you out back. You'd drag us all out there, but no one would be around."

Michael's eyes widened. "Okay, that's spooky."

A shiver went down Cassie's spine. She didn't remember any of this.

"But you were always doing weird stuff like that."

Cassie snapped back to attention. "What do you mean?"

"You were always talking about people who weren't there. The kids at school would pick on you for having imaginary friends at your age, and you'd come home from school and be pretty upset. I'd always give you my teddy bear to make you feel better."

"I remember that part. The teddy bear, I mean." Cassie's mouth was suddenly dry. "But I don't remember the imaginary friends."

"You were always kind of weird." Michael didn't say it like an insult. "That's part of the reason I like you, though. You're *interesting*."

Cassie felt her face warm. "What do you mean I was weird?"

Laura and Michael exchanged glances. Her sister spoke first. "Well, you know."

Cassie looked between the two of them, and her embarrassment turned to anger. "No, I don't know."

Michael leaned back in his chair. His voice was light. "I always thought you had a certain aura about you."

"An aura?" Cassie realized the irony of sounding incredulous considering *she saw ghosts*, but she didn't care. "What does that mean?"

"You've always been intuitive." Laura stabbed at another piece of pancake, pushing it around in syrup instead of eating it. "You'd know things I swear no one told you. You used to have the craziest dreams."

Cassie felt the ground shift under her feet. "I don't remember any of this."

"I think the Sarah Lennox stuff hit you harder than you thought it did. I mean, you guys were best friends. You used to ride the bus together, go to school, and sometimes she'd get dropped off at our house afterwards. She slept over a bunch, too."

"So, what? Her disappearance wiped my memory?"

"I mean, I don't know for sure, but that's a possibility." Laura shifted in her seat, so she was facing Cassie. "Memory loss is a natural defense mechanism. Our brains do that to help us survive. If you couldn't handle your best friend disappearing, possibly getting murdered, then it makes sense that, as a kid, you sort of blocked all the terrible memories."

"Do you remember anything else that happened?" It scared Cassie to know the answer to her question, but she couldn't stop herself from asking. "Anything that would've caused that kind of memory loss?"

Laura twisted her mouth to the side as she thought. "No, I don't think so. But Mom and Dad kept me sheltered, you know? If something did happen, they wouldn't have told me about it. I was pretty young at the time."

"Do you think someone murdered her?" Michael asked. His voice was low for the first time since they'd sat down to breakfast. "I always figured someone kidnapped her and forced her to live with another family or something."

Laura shrugged. "I'm not sure. I never thought to go back and look. I haven't thought about her in years."

"Kind of tragic, if you think about it. Being forgotten like that."

"Well, her parents haven't forgotten, that's for sure. And I think she had a sister, too? Older than Cassie."

"I'm going to look it up." Michael pulled out his phone and started typing away. "God, if she was murdered, I'm going to feel so bad."

"It's not like kidnapping isn't also a terrible crime."

"Yeah, but you know what I mean." Michael gasped and looked over at Cassie. "What if you saw her ghost?"

Cassie froze. "What?"

"Laura said you used to talk to her like she was still there, right? What if you were talking to her *ghost*? They say kids can see things like that."

Cassie was on her feet before she even realized she was moving. Michael and Laura both looked up at her in shock. A few heads turned in their direction, but Cassie ignored them. She dug around in her purse and pulled out a handful of twenties.

"Breakfast is on me."

"Cassie, what—"

"I need to go make a phone call. I'm sorry." She pulled out her phone and started walking away without waiting for their reactions. "It's important. I'm sorry."

She heard Laura yelling after her, but Cassie was already through the door and making a beeline for her car. She felt guilty making Michael take Laura home, but Cassie needed to be anywhere but there. And she wasn't ready to go home yet.

She dialed David. He picked up on the first ring.

"I've got some free time. Need my help?"

13

CASSIE PUT HER CAR IN PARK AND DOUBLE-CHECKED THE ADDRESS ON the mailbox in front of her against the one David had texted her. They matched. Seafoam green shutters stood out against the white siding of a modest colonial home. A shiny, black pickup truck sat in the driveway.

Less than a minute later, a black sedan pulled up behind Cassie. She opened her door as soon as David got out, letting the breeze cool her anger.

"Hey." He waited until they were closer. "Everything okay? You sounded worked up on the phone."

"I'll tell you later." When David gave her a dubious look, she rushed on. "Some weird shit just came to light. It's unrelated to the case. I need to process it for a minute first."

"All right, I won't push. As long as you're okay?"

"I'm... coping." It was a welcome relief to be truthful about how she was feeling. "Let's just do what we're here to do."

David looked up at the house. "First, some background for you. We're here to see Captain Philip Stockton. He's retired Savannah PD.

Used to be my boss. He was the lead on our original case back in the nineties."

"You think he'll have some insight into what's going on?"

"No idea." David ran a hand down the side of his face brushing down sideburns he hadn't grown in a couple decades. He looked tired. "Earlier today, I had a conversation with one of my esteemed colleagues."

"When you say it like that, I kind of think you mean the opposite."

David smiled. "Crawford is a bit of a dick. He was never that ambitious. But I always felt like he did his job, you know? At least didn't screw up too often."

"But?"

"The way he talked about the case made me uneasy. Kind of sounded like they never gave a shit to solve it. I remember hitting a lot of roadblocks back then. I remember a lot going down and this case getting pushed to the side. It's unfortunate, but it happens. But after talking to Crawford, it seems maybe that was on purpose."

"And you want to see if Captain Stockton affirms your suspicions."

"Bingo."

"Do I need to know anything about him before going in there?"

"He was a hardass when he was on the force. Real serious type. Not much for the hijinks a lot of us rookies got up to back in the day. But he was a good one. Always did his job. Stayed active in the community even after his retirement. I haven't actually talked to him in years, though, so we could be walking into a hornet's nest."

"Wonderful."

"Just follow my lead." David started walking up the driveway, and Cassie followed close behind. "I'll do most of the talking. I want you to keep your eye out for anything weird."

"My specialty."

David didn't answer. He pressed his index finger against the doorbell. A muffled ring came from inside. A dog barked. A man spoke.

The barking ceased. Then the handle twisted, and the door swung open.

The man on the other side matched the description Cassie had created in her head. He was in his eighties, with shockingly white hair and a mustache to match. He was just a few inches shorter than David, only because he had a slight hunch. And even though he carried a cane, he still looked solid. His eyes were sharp.

"Well, I'll be damned." The man stuck out his hand. "David Klein."

"Sir." David shook his hand, then gestured to Cassie. "This is my colleague, Cassie Quinn."

"The officers are getting prettier, aren't they? How do you concentrate with this one around?"

Cassie couldn't help the grimace that found its way to her face, but she stopped herself from cringing when he reached out to shake her hand.

"Oh, no, I'm not an officer, sir. Just a friend."

"A consultant for the department." David's voice was firm but kind. "We're here on official business. You got a minute?"

"I'm not in any sort of trouble, am I?" His voice was light, but his eyes were hard.

"No, sir. None. I just wanted to pick your brain about an old case."

"All right, all right, come on in. I'll see if I can help you out. Make sure you take your shoes off."

David let Cassie enter before him, and she slipped off her flats at the door. After a long hallway covered in pictures of Captain Stockton in uniform, they entered a living room where a German Shepherd was sitting at attention on a soft dog bed. It smelled like cigars and disinfectant.

"Colonel, barracks."

Without hesitation, the German Shepherd got up and trotted down the hallway, ignoring the new guests. He left through a door, and Cassie could hear his footsteps as he bounded upstairs and headed off to what she assumed was his bed on the second floor.

Stockton settled into a well-worn recliner and leaned his cane against an end table. He pointed to a love seat across from him. "You two can sit there." He checked his watch. "I may be old, but I'm not dead. Time is of the essence, Klein."

"I understand, sir. I'll get right to the point. Did you hear about the dead body found under the Harry S. Truman Parkway?"

"I did."

David waited for him to elaborate, but the other man just stared him down. "Did you hear how the man died?"

"I did."

Another pause. "Do you think it's related to the crimes we investigated in the nineties, sir?"

"Isn't it your job to figure that out?"

Cassie could sense David's growing frustration, but her friend kept a neutral expression locked in place. She wanted to chastise Captain Stockton for being difficult, but her gut told her that would make the situation worse.

"The man's name was Robert Shapiro. Someone broke both his legs and then strangled him. Just like before."

Cassie tuned David out as he went over the details of the case. Her job wasn't to listen to their conversation. It was to figure out if anything supernatural was going on.

It was easier if Cassie closed her eyes, but Stockton seemed like the observant type, and she didn't want to give him any reason to suspect she was more than what David had introduced her as—just a colleague. She defocused her mind, let the buzz of David's voice fade, and tuned into the house as best she could.

In her experience, ghosts came and went as they pleased. She had no control over it, and any belief to the contrary had led to sheer disappointment. The psychic abilities she possessed were even more temperamental. If she concentrated, sometimes she could pull them to the forefront. Other times, they caught her by surprise. And on several occasions, they refused to come out and play at all.

As Cassie relaxed her body and tried to drown out the

surrounding chaos, she reached out with invisible tendrils, testing the waters. Did anything seem out of place? Did anything seem important?

This was easier when she had a physical object in her hand, like a picture or an item from the victim, but sometimes she could get gut feelings to pull her in one direction or another. Laura had said it was a strong sense of intuition, but now she knew better.

That singular thought broke her concentration.

The embarrassment and anger and fear from breakfast returned in full force, and she lost any psychic connection she might've had to the world around. She had felt nothing significant, but she wasn't about to bet her life on that conclusion after only a few seconds of trying.

"Was Robert Shapiro ever a suspect?"

Cassie turned to David with raised eyebrows. That wasn't a line of thinking she'd been expecting.

Captain Stockton's reply was terse. "I'm better with faces than names."

David leaned forward and handed him two glossy photos—one of Shapiro when he was alive, and one of him taken in the morgue.

Stockton's eyes glanced over them for a fraction of a second before he handed them back. "I don't recognize him. As far as I can recall, he wasn't a suspect."

Cassie noticed David choose his words carefully. "He fits the description almost exactly. He would've been in his forties in the nineties. His wife was killed in a car accident about ten years prior. The person driving that car was an addict who'd recently gotten out of prison. Shapiro was a postal worker and knew Savannah well. He'd be able to navigate easily without getting lost. He'd also be able to avoid suspicion if he were driving a mail truck."

"I don't know what to tell you, Klein." Stockton grabbed the head of his cane but didn't move out of his chair. "He wasn't a suspect. I never interviewed him. Do you have any evidence that he could've been our killer? Anything concrete?"

"Not yet." David's tone was harder than it had been. "But I have a feeling it'll turn up sooner rather than later."

"Feelings don't mean shit." Captain Stockton leaned forward and used his cane to steady himself as he got to his feet. David and Cassie stood as well. "You need evidence. That's what makes a great detective."

Cassie couldn't help herself. "David *is* a great detective."

"Oh, I'm sure he is. And I'm sure you're a great *colleague*. And it seems like you've done a better job than I did on this case, so I'm not sure why you've made it a point to disturb my morning."

"Captain Stockton." David's voice sounded more controlled now. "I didn't mean any disrespect. I know what it was like back then. I remember—"

"You don't remember. You were too green. You had it so easy. The pressure we were under back then? Kids going missing left and right. Murders every other week. And a bunch of addicts wind up dead? We did the best we could."

Cassie could tell Stockton had stopped himself from saying what he really wanted to say. So, she finished it for him. "*Good riddance*, right? A serial killer who was cleaning up the streets? One less thing to worry about."

She expected David to chastise her, but he kept a steady gaze on Stockton, whose face grew redder by the minute. His words were serious.

"Get out."

"Sir—"

Stockton's voice boomed as he called for his dog. "Colonel. Battle stations."

A thump from upstairs was followed by loud footsteps on the stairs as the German Shepherd rushed to his owner's side. He stood at the ready. He wasn't growling and didn't appear aggressive, but Cassie wasn't interested in testing his limits.

"Captain—"

"I've answered your questions. It was very nice to see you, Detective Klein. You've come a long way. You've done good for yourself. Try not to ruin anyone's legacy on your way out the door. Us old geezers aren't too forgiving these days."

David looked from Stockton to the dog and back again. "Yes, sir."

When David turned on his heel and walked to the door, Cassie had no choice but to follow. The pair of them slipped on their shoes and exited without a goodbye. Cassie heard Stockton call out a command for Colonel to shut the front door, and it slammed shut behind them with a finality that rattled her teeth.

14

CASSIE HAD TOLD DAVID SHE WASN'T READY TO GO HOME, AND without asking questions, David told her to follow him. She wanted to know where they were going, but when she looked back at Stockton's house, she could see him looking through the front window with Colonel by his side. He wasn't trying to hide.

Half an hour later, Cassie found herself outside Savannah in Black Creek, Georgia. David pulled into the driveway of a small, beige ranch-style home. She slid her car in behind him and put it in park. Goosebumps erupted across her skin, and when she met David at his car, he confirmed her suspicions.

David removed his sunglasses. "Robert Shapiro's house."

Her stomach turned, and she felt a bitter taste in her mouth. "You really think he's the original killer?"

"I'll answer your questions if you answer mine."

Cassie rolled her eyes. "Fine."

David leaned back against the hood of his car and folded his arms. "I don't know for sure, but if I had been running the case back then, he would've been my prime suspect."

"Do you think Stockton just missed him?"

"Oh, absolutely. But I don't think he was really looking." David shrugged as if to say *it is what it is,* but he looked sad. "I don't know, maybe I'm being too hard on him. He wasn't lying when he said a lot of shit was going down back then. A lot of people said he was on track to become Chief of Police in Savannah, but he didn't want it, I guess. I think he enjoyed hovering around in the middle. Just enough responsibility to garner respect without having to stick his neck out too often."

"Can't really blame him for that."

"I guess."

"That was convincing."

David chuckled and then grew serious again. "God knows I've made mistakes in my career. I've looked the other way when I shouldn't have. I've gone out on a limb for people who didn't deserve it. I followed my gut and wound up walking in the wrong direction. I hurt people because of the actions I've taken."

"A lot of people have those same experiences."

"But it means something different when you carry a badge and a gun. We can't forget our responsibility to protect and serve. We can't dismiss that. Not ever."

"You think Stockton dropped the ball."

"I do." David's voice was full of controlled anger. "And I'd be a hypocrite to say I never made a bad call in a tough position, but I won't let my pride get in the way. It doesn't matter who those victims were, they deserved better. Their families deserved better."

Cassie looked at the house before her. Its presence felt dark and heavy. Hot and angry. The goosebumps she'd felt in the car had transformed into beads of sweat on the back of her neck. And it had nothing to do with the heat of the day.

"So, I have a working theory," Cassie said.

"Let's hear it."

"I think he's the second entity I've been feeling. And if that's the case, then I think you're right to assume he was the original killer."

"What makes you say that?"

Cassie pointed to the house. "I can feel him in there. Not as strong as when he came to me in my house, but I think once we walk through those doors, it's going to get interesting. You've been in there already?"

"Yeah. Not much to see. Nice and tidy. Didn't find a smoking gun if that's what you're wondering. But that's what I have you here for. To see if we missed anything."

"Shall we?"

David pushed off the car and started toward the house. "Sure, but you've still got questions to answer."

Cassie blew hair away from her face. "Fair is fair, I guess. What do you want to know?"

"What happened this morning?"

"Went out to breakfast with my sister and a friend we knew back in high school. Long story short I found out my abilities didn't originate from the run-in with Novak like we thought."

David had the key halfway to the door when he turned around with his mouth wide open. "Seriously?"

"Seriously. They were talking about things I don't remember. So, it sounds like something happened when I was a kid. Does Sarah Lennox ring a bell?"

David shook his head. "Should it?"

"It was a long shot. She was a little girl who went missing when I was about ten. A couple years after these murders. She wasn't the only one. Apparently, I used to say she was hanging out in our backyard even after she was kidnapped."

"Her ghost?"

Cassie nodded. "Seems like it."

David whistled and finished opening the door. When Cassie stepped across the threshold, a wall of hot, stale air hit her square in the face. The sweat beading on her neck dripped down her back, but when she looked over at David, he seemed comfortable.

"Definitely something going on in here."

David freed his weapon. "Let me know what direction you want to head in."

"You know that won't make a difference against a ghost, right?"

"I know that." A beat of silence. "It just makes me feel better."

Cassie pointed toward the kitchen to their left. "There."

David led the way and cleared the room. Cassie stayed close behind. The house was empty of any human threats, but she felt on edge and nervous. And it was transferring to David. He was calm and steady, but she saw his eyes darting around to every nook and cranny in the room.

It was harder to breathe in the kitchen. Like someone had thrown her into a sauna with all her clothes still on. The air was thick with humidity, and the sweat rolling down her back was getting uncomfortable.

To distract herself, she kept talking. "I got so upset at breakfast, I just threw down money and walked away. I left Laura with Michael and hoped he'd take her home."

"I'm sure he did. I'm sure everything is fine."

"I'm not doing a very good job of reuniting my family."

"You're doing the best you can." He spoke in his most fatherly voice.

"No, I'm not." Cassie pushed past David and walked into the hallway on the other side of the room. She heard his protests, but the sound of her own blood pumping in her ears muffled it. "I spent years ignoring my family. Years thinking they'd have me institutionalized if they knew the truth. Years thinking they would hate me. And all my sister has been doing is trying to get to know me and trying to be part of my life."

"Hey, hey, hey." David turned Cassie to face him. "What's going on here?"

Cassie took two shuddering breaths. She touched her face and realized it was wet. When had she started crying? "The rooms are getting hotter. It's making me anxious and angry and sad all at once."

"The sooner we get out of here, the better, okay?"

Cassie let a sob escape. "I just want my family back."

Realization dawned on David's face. "I'm sure that's how Robert Shapiro felt, too. He lost his wife in a car accident."

"Down the hall and to the left." Cassie pointed the way forward. "That's the room."

David nodded and crept along the hall. "A heroin addict killed his wife. I don't know the whole story, but that's enough to understand the connection between Shapiro and the murders he committed."

With every step, Cassie felt as though iron boots were wrapping around her feet and legs. She tried to pay attention to what David was telling her, but she couldn't focus on the words. Her thoughts raced, jumping from one half-formed revelation to the next. One minute, she was sure her sister would never speak to her again, and the next, Cassie was wishing Novak had finished the job, so she didn't have to worry about fixing their relationship.

That last thought made Cassie groan and grab her head. She pulled at her hair and rocked back and forth. She didn't want that. But Shapiro's influence was getting stronger and stronger, and the more time she spent in the house, the worse it would get.

David wrapped his arms around her. "Come on, we're almost there. I need you to tell me what's in this room."

"I don't know. I don't know." Cassie could do nothing but repeat those words over and over.

But David wouldn't let her give up. He grabbed her arm and put it over his shoulder so he could hoist her up and half carry, half drag her down the hallway. When they reached the room, Cassie could barely stand on her own. Sweat matted her hair, and her breathing was shallow and rough.

"Master bedroom," David said. His voice sounded so far away. "What are we looking for?"

Cassie forced her eyes to scan the room, and even though they were heavy with exhaustion, she could make out a blurry red figure in the corner. He was radiating anger and hatred like flames from a dragon destroying a hamlet.

She managed to lift her arm and point at him before she passed out.

15

CASSIE COULD TELL THE SECOND DAVID HAD CROSSED THE THRESHOLD and carried her outside. The cool breeze dried the sweat on her brow, and her limbs felt a hundred pounds lighter. She opened her eyes, and the brightness of the sun greeted her kindly. Its heat felt gentle and regenerative, rather than oppressive and lethal.

David set her down on the front stoop and leaned her against the wall. "Do we need to get farther away?"

"No, this is fine."

"I'll be right back."

Cassie watched as David darted inside, presumably to return to the room and see if he could find anything new. The ghost of Robert Shapiro hadn't affected him, but Cassie still didn't like the idea of him going in alone. Then again, she wouldn't be of much help.

She closed her eyes and soaked in the sun until David returned fifteen minutes later.

"I half tore the room apart, but I found something."

Cassie's eyes snapped open. "Found what?"

"Letters." David sat down next to her and held up a thick stack of folded pieces of white semi-translucent paper. "Well, carbon copies of letters. They're all addressed to Coastal State Prison, and a few of the names match up with some of our victims. Looks like he was writing to them while they were still in prison. This is the evidence we were looking for."

"Would've been useful twenty years ago."

"Now you sound like me." David rubbed a hand across the back of his neck. "I don't think anyone knew Shapiro existed back then. I think Stockton was telling the truth—he wasn't on our radar. Were we even looking at the radar? Maybe not. But the past is in the past, right? We have the letters now. Presumably, we can put those souls to rest."

"Where were the letters?"

"The corner of the room you pointed at before you passed out. I'd searched the room last time we were here and didn't come up with anything. I thought this was a longshot, but you pulled through once again. I gotta stop doubting you." He patted her on the shoulder. "He'd slipped them behind a baseboard. I wouldn't have bothered to pry it off if I wasn't so sure you were onto something in there."

"You think the letters will be helpful?"

"Don't know. I'll have the team look through them first. Could be all sorts of information in here. If nothing else, it might paint a better picture of what he was thinking. What his motive was." David looked down at her with an arched eyebrow. "What happened back there?"

Cassie kept her eyes closed. The faintest hint of a headache came on. "He was strong. Angry. Didn't want us finding those letters. He was a bad man. Maybe not from the beginning, but by the time he died all that was left was pure evil. His aura was a dark, angry red. I could barely even look at him without being overwhelmed. I've never felt anything like that before."

"Well, I don't suppose you get many ghosts of serial killers knocking at your door."

"No, I guess not."

"What about the rest of it?"

"Rest of what?"

"The stuff about your sister."

Cassie scrunched up her face. "A moment of weakness?"

"Something tells me you meant at least some of it."

"There was an ounce of truth to it." Did she really want to avoid dealing with her relationship with Laura so badly she'd rather be dead? No. Would it be nice to not have to worry about what she was going home to? Yes. "I'm glad Laura and I are reconnecting."

"But?"

"*However*, it's hard." She shrugged. "It's a lot harder than I thought it would be. We're two grown adults. We don't *need* each other. We haven't relied on each other in years. And yet, there's still a piece of us that's stuck back in our childhood. I want to be the big sister and protect her, and she wants to prove she can handle anything I throw at her."

"Maybe you should give her a chance."

Cassie cracked an eye open and glared at David. "Way to take her side, *Dad*."

He chuckled. "I'm not taking anyone's side here. But you're right, you're both adults. You can each handle more now than you could as kids. Both of you need to trust each other. And both of you need to be vulnerable with each other."

"Yeah, but I hate rejection."

"Who doesn't? But what makes you assume she's going to reject you?"

Cassie opened both her eyes now and pointed an index finger at her face. "Talks to ghosts, remember?"

"You can ease her into that part. Remember, she's here to get to know you. She's ready to accept you if you give her the chance."

"I'm so glad you're old and wise."

David scowled. "Easy on the old part." A distant look crossed his face. "My father and I didn't have the best relationship. We were always at odds. He was a selfish, materialistic man. I just wanted to help people. He wanted me to be a lawyer."

Cassie scoffed.

"My reaction exactly. I had no interest in that. He figured I'd make a shitload of money and then he'd be able to live out his retirement in peace, away from everyone and everything."

"What happened?"

"He drank himself into an early grave. My mother stayed by his side the entire time, but he was ungrateful to all of us. He was angry I became a cop. Said I was wasting my life. Even told me once that he hoped a bullet put me out of his misery."

Cassie sat up. "That's awful. I'm sorry your dad spoke to you like that."

David shrugged a shoulder. "I've worked through all of that. I regret not trying harder, though."

"Really? Even though he said stuff like that?"

"Not for his sake. For my mom's. It always hurt her to see us at each other's throats. She died not long after he did, and more than anything I wish she could've seen us be a family again. It's all she ever wanted."

Cassie blew out a deep breath. She knew what David was trying to tell her. *Change things before it's too late.* Luckily for her, Laura was willing to meet her halfway. She'd told Cassie how hard it was that things had been rocky between them, but she'd also told Cassie that she wanted to work on changing that.

"I should get home. I think I owe my sister an apology."

David smiled. "That's good to hear. You know, I was a real emotional kid. Drove my dad nuts. I'd cry and scream and get angry at the drop of a dime. I've gotten better at controlling it over the years, but it's not always easy. We must own our reactions. We can't make excuses for them. But my mom always told me we shouldn't feel guilty for them either. That's us at our rawest. Our most honest. The most important thing to do after the fact is to own them and work toward being better. I think Laura will understand she upset you.

Now it's up to you to explain to her why and to promise to do better next time."

Cassie felt tears forming, and she blinked them away. "What about you? What are you going to do?"

David held the letters up. "I'm going to solve a twenty-year-old cold case."

16

CASSIE PULLED UP IN FRONT OF HER HOUSE WITH A PIT IN HER STOMACH. It was nearing dinnertime, and she hadn't heard from Laura since she'd left her behind at the restaurant. She didn't even know if her sister would be home, and she couldn't figure out which option was better—facing her now or later.

But as soon as she pushed open the front door, she sensed Laura's presence. She could hear the TV in the back bedroom, and the kitchen light was on. The smell of fresh coffee wafted through the air.

She heard a thud followed by happy meows as Apollo ran to meet her. Cassie knelt and stroked his back, allowing his purrs to relax her. He flopped down by her feet and rolled back and forth in what she had christened his happy cat dance. Maybe he'd sensed the tension in the house and wanted to alleviate what he could.

Laura emerged from the back bedroom with her arms crossed over her chest. She stayed silent.

Cassie tossed her purse on the ground and made a beeline for the coffee. "Thanks for making a fresh pot."

Laura's words were curt. "You're welcome."

Cassie didn't know how to start, so she jumped right into the middle. "Was Michael mad at me?"

"No, he was worried he upset you. I spent half an hour reassuring him he did nothing wrong, and that you had a lot going on."

"Did you tell him anything?"

Laura threw up her hands. "What would I have told him? I have no idea what's going through your head, Cassie, because you're not sharing that with me."

Cassie stirred her coffee with a spoon, but she'd suddenly lost any taste for it. "I'm sorry."

Laura tipped her head back in exasperation. "Sorry for what? Running out on us? Making Michael go out of his way to take me home? Scaring me half to death?"

"All the above?"

"Don't be cute. I was worried."

"You could've called or texted."

"And would you have answered?" Laura crossed her arms over her chest.

They both knew she wouldn't have, but she wasn't about to admit that out loud.

"Exactly." Laura crossed the room and put her hands on her hips. "Where did you go?"

"You know, you look just like Mom when you do that."

"Answer the question."

Cassie threw up her arms. "I called my friend, Detective Klein. We went to his former Captain's house to ask him if he'd purposefully looked the other way when a bunch of addicts were being murdered back in the nineties. He kicked us out, so we went to a dead serial killer's house to poke around to see if we could find any evidence corroborating our theory. Turns out, we did. Then I came straight home, I swear."

Laura's jaw went slack. "Are you serious?"

"Yes. Now, can you stop yelling at me so I can apologize properly?"

When Laura nodded, Cassie led her over to the sofa in the living room. "I'm sorry I ran out on you at breakfast. That was wrong, and I regret doing it. I was overwhelmed and afraid, and it was an automatic reaction."

"Why were you afraid?"

Cassie chose her words carefully. She wanted to be truthful without painting the entire picture. "I don't remember a lot about Sarah's disappearance. You talk about things that I should remember, but they're blank spaces in my head."

Laura crossed her legs and leaned forward. "Why does that make you afraid?"

Cassie couldn't stop the laugh that escaped her mouth. "All you need is a pen and a notebook. Want me to get you one? What's your hourly rate?"

Laura tossed her curls over her shoulder. "You couldn't afford me."

"That's true." A grin broke out over her face. "Hey, if you ever go back to school, you'll have to go by Dr. Quinn."

"You know, you're not the first person to make that joke. You're not as clever as you think."

"*Dr. Quinn, Therapist Woman* just doesn't have the same ring to it."

"You're very well-practiced at being avoidant, you know."

Cassie did a little half bow in her chair. "Thank you."

"That wasn't a compliment."

"I know." She turned serious before Laura got mad at her again. "It scared me because I don't enjoy being out of control. Realizing something may have happened to you when you were a kid to cause your brain to erase memories is frightening. I remember everything Novak did to me, so it's concerning to think this could be worse."

"Maybe. But you were only a kid. Having your best friend disappear is traumatizing enough. Your brain might not have been able to process it fully. Doesn't mean something worse than that happened."

Cassie wasn't convinced.

"Not to go all therapist on you again, but have you fully processed what happened to you?"

"You mean with Novak?" Cassie considered the question for a minute before she was sure she'd found the right words. "Yes. I've been through years of therapy. I still struggle. Still have nightmares sometimes. Still have anxiety. I'm afraid a lot. But I've learned to work through it. I know when to push myself past that fear and when to allow myself off the hook."

"That's great." Laura's smile was genuine. "You should be proud."

"I am. But talking about it with other people is harder. Talking to you about it is hard."

Now Laura looked confused. "Why?"

"You're my baby sister. I'm supposed to protect you." When Laura opened her mouth to argue, Cassie held up a hand. "I know, you don't need protecting. We're both adults. But old habits are hard to break. I'm really trying here. I promise I am. But it's going to be a bumpy road."

Laura got up, crossed the room, and smothered Cassie in a hug. "I can handle bumpy roads. Just need you to let me come along for the ride."

"I promise I will. Thanks for sticking it out with me."

"That's what sisters are for." Laura let go and stood up straight. "But you should text Michael."

Cassie slapped a hand to her forehead. "God, I was so awful. He's never going to forgive me."

"Are you kidding? He lives for drama like this. You should've seen his face. I've never seen someone so conflicted. He was caught between desperation and absolute elation. It would've been hilarious if I hadn't been so damned worried about you."

"He did ask for drama."

"That he did." Laura cocked her head to one side. "You were serious about that serial killer stuff?"

Cassie nodded. "Yep. Might've helped David solve a twenty-year-old cold case, too."

"That's pretty awesome." Laura's eyes sparkled. "I'm kind of jealous, actually."

"Really? I didn't think you were into that kind of stuff."

"Are you kidding? I've watched every episode of *Criminal Minds*, plus *CSI* and *NCIS*. All of them."

Cassie felt the tickle of inspiration in the back of her head. "Are you up for some sister bonding time?"

"Always. What did you have in mind?"

"Let's bake cookies and do something weird."

17

CASSIE PULLED UP TO THE FRONT OF THE BUILDING AND PARKED HER car. She ignored the way her heart beat faster at the thought of what they were about to do. Instead, she waited until she had Laura's full attention. "Are you sure you want to do this?"

"I already said yes."

"You can back out any time."

"I'm not going to back out."

"I know. But you can. If you want to."

"I don't want to." Laura unbuckled her seatbelt but didn't open the door. "At least now I can cross Visit Morgue off my bucket list."

"Going to the morgue was on your bucket list? Maybe you are my sister after all."

The two women exited the vehicle, and Laura held the door open for Cassie, who balanced an enormous plate of cookies in her hands. They were still warm, and the smell of the chocolate chips made her mouth water. She walked to the front desk and let the woman at the computer sneak a couple before she buzzed them through to the back. Dr. Underwood was waiting.

"A double batch?" Underwood's walrus mustache twitched, and his eyes narrowed. "What's the occasion?"

Cassie handed him the plate and hooked a thumb over her shoulder. "My sister's in town. I know you don't like civilians in the back, but I was hoping you'd make an exception. She's a psychologist, and I'm hoping she might lend her opinion on this one."

Cassie could feel Laura's inquisitive gaze on her, but she ignored it. Whether Laura wanted to weigh in with her thoughts was up to her. For now, it was just a way to get her in the room.

"Humph." Underwood eyed Laura and then eyed the cookies. They must've made a convincing argument because he turned around and led them down the hallway. "I didn't know you had a sister."

"I'm full of secrets. She lives in California. I don't get to see her much." Cassie glanced at Laura. "I hope that's gonna change."

"My brother lives in Washington." Underwood snuck a cookie off the plate and put the whole thing in his mouth. "Every year, we ride to Beresford, South Dakota. We eat at Bertz's Sports Bar and Grill, grab some sleep, and then turn around and go back home."

"That's an awful long trip just for a burger and wings," Laura said.

Underwood shrugged. "My baby needs to stretch her legs once in a while or she gets cranky."

Laura quirked an eyebrow at Cassie.

"His Harley."

The three of them descended the stairs, and Cassie felt the humor drain from her body. As usual, the chill in the air was indicative of more than just the cooling system that kept the bodies cold. No, supernatural activity persisted down here. She couldn't always see it but did always feel it.

Underwood popped another cookie in his mouth and set the batch on a stool near the door. He then brushed the crumbs out of his mustache and snapped on a pair of gloves. "Robert Shapiro. Sixty-three. Strangled."

"That's our guy."

Underwood nodded and made his way over to one of the cooling units and pulled it open. He slid the tray out, and the three of them stared down at the sheet-covered body. Without ceremony, Underwood pulled the sheet back to reveal Shapiro's head and chest. Laura let out a little gasp.

Cassie had seen far too many dead bodies in her lifetime, but it never got easier. The pale skin. The blank eyes. The unnerving stillness of the body. There was something unnatural about staring death in the face.

"What do you want to know?"

"Can you walk us through the injuries?"

Underwood used his pinky to point at the strangulation marks. "This is the actual cause of death. Windpipe was crushed. There was a fair amount of strength put into this. It did some damage."

"Does that mean the perpetrator was a man?" Cassie asked.

"No way to tell for sure. A grown adult has the strength to cause this kind of injury, regardless of gender or biology. People can do incredible things when they have adrenaline pumping through their veins. There've been countless stories of people lifting cars off the ground to help those pinned underneath. Mothers tapping into superhuman strength to save their children."

"Was it with a rope?"

"No." Underwood leaned in closer to the body. "It'd leave fibers behind. The pattern of the bruise would reflect the weave of the rope. No, it was something smooth."

"Smooth? Like what?"

"I'm fairly certain it was a tourniquet. It matches the ligature marks on his neck. His collar contained trace elements common in various popular tourniquet brands.

"What about the legs?" Cassie asked.

Underwood whipped off the rest of the sheet to expose Shapiro's body in full. Laura looked away, but Cassie couldn't take her eyes off his injuries. He'd been cleaned and taken care of as much as possible, but he was still a mess. Bones stuck up through his skin from his knees to his ankles.

The happiness in Underwood's voice indicated—not for the first time—how much he loved his job. "Did you know our bodies replenish our cells every seven to ten years? Some of them faster than others. Our bones take about a decade to be completely replaced."

"I did not know that." Cassie finally met his eyes. "So, we have a new skeleton every ten years or so?"

Underwood shrugged. "Guess you could say that."

"Weird."

"Yeah." Underwood's eyes lit up for a moment, and then he returned his gaze to the body between them. "Someone took a sledgehammer to his legs."

That caught Cassie's attention. "Really?"

"The points of impact show as much. It was something heavy and swung with force. I'm fairly certain based on the shape of the bruising and the way the bone shattered."

"You keep saying fairly certain." Laura's voice sounded small in the large room. "How certain is fairly certain?"

"Ninety-nine percent."

Cassie didn't miss the defensiveness of his tone. "He's not supposed to say he knows for a fact, but Dr. Underwood is a brilliant medical examiner. When he says *fairly certain*, you can basically take it as gospel."

Laura nodded but said nothing else. She was looking a little green.

"And there was heroin in his bloodstream?" Cassie asked.

"I'd say more than adequate to kill him twice over. But the strangulation did him in."

"You're aware this mirrors a case from over twenty years ago?"

Underwood nodded and grabbed a folder off a nearby table. "The detective sent what he had of the original autopsies on the seven bodies found. Three pulled in from the ocean, four dug up in the woods."

"How would you compare their wounds to Shapiro's wounds?"

"Nearly identical."

"And when you say nearly—" Laura began.

"I mean identical." Underwood's voice was gruff. "There's only so much we can tell from the four victims buried in the woods because their bodies weren't found for some time. But, since their broken bones match the broken bones of the first three victims, we can assume the same method of murder."

"Plus, the four victims from the woods were also addicts recently released from prison, so they're definitely from the same victim pool."

"Correct." Underwood's mustache twitched as he calmed down. "We now have eight victims in total. All found with complex fractures of the tibia and fibula. Each patella was shattered, but the femurs were intact."

"Do you know why that would be?" Cassie asked.

"The femur is the strongest bone in the body. It's not impossible to break, but it's much easier to take out someone's knees and shatter the bones in their lower legs. Once you do that, the objective is complete."

"Objective?" Laura asked.

"Immobilize the victims. It'd be extremely painful to walk on injuries such as these."

Cassie started pacing to help keep all this information straight in her head. The movement also helped combat the chilly air. "Eight victims total, each with nearly identical leg injuries. The three that washed up on shore were also strangled. I'm guessing those marks were—"

"Nearly identical." Underwood flipped a page in the folder he was holding. "My predecessor also assumed the weapon of choice was a tourniquet."

"I don't think it takes a genius to put two and two together here." Laura blushed under the gaze of Cassie and Underwood. "All the victims were recently released addicts. They'd been pumped full of heroin and killed with a tourniquet. The murderer had a vendetta."

"He did." Cassie pointed to Shapiro. "This is the original serial killer."

"Fascinating." Underwood stared at the body in awe. "I'd love to study his brain."

"That's above my pay grade." Cassie shook her head. "We finally solved a twenty-year-old murder, but only because the original killer wound up being killed in the exact same way."

"So, now we have to figure out who murdered the murderer."

"Considering how many victims this man had, there are plenty of people with motive." Cassie ran a hand through her hair. "But who'd be able to solve a cold case that the Savannah PD couldn't even close?"

18

DAVID STOOD WITH HIS BACK AGAINST THE FAR WALL AND SURVEYED THE mess he'd made of the room. About twenty minutes prior, he'd rolled up his sleeves and gotten to work. He'd cleared all the boxes and bags of old evidence from the table and laid out each letter from Robert Shapiro's house, almost 200 in total. Now, his brow was beaded with sweat.

He'd grouped them by name and was unsurprised to find Shapiro had corresponded with more than seven people. David and his colleagues figured there were more victims, but they never could get an estimate on how many more were out there. David remembered trying to collate a list of names of recently released addicts who'd gone missing, but that was comparable to keeping tabs on a hundred birds without the use of trackers. Most of these guys didn't have families or homes to go back to. They lived on the streets or under bridges, and if they didn't want to be found—which they often didn't —then they stayed out of arm's reach of the law.

"Twelve victims," David mumbled to himself. "Five bodies missing."

With the cold case solved, David had to turn his attention to who killed Shapiro. The families of the victims were all prime suspects, but tracking all of them down was going to take some time. He now had the names of the final five victims thanks to the letters, but no clue where to find their bodies. There was likely some evidence hidden within the correspondence but combing through them one by one would be a tedious task.

A sharp knock at the door stole his attention, and as it opened, Harris popped her head through.

"Ah, perfect timing. I need a distraction."

"Looks like you've got your hands full." She closed the door behind her and surveyed the table full of letters. "You need help?"

"You offering?"

"Oh, no. But Paulson has been following me around like a lost puppy. He needs a menial task to keep him out of my hair."

"I think he's taken a liking to you."

"Unfortunately for him, he's not my type. Want me to send him in?"

"I don't like people touching my things. They mess it all up."

Harris rolled her eyes. "You're worse than a four-year-old. Has anyone ever told you that you have control issues?"

"My wife."

"You should listen to her."

"That's what she keeps saying." David huffed. "If you're not here to help, then what? To annoy?"

"Something like that." Harris plopped down a chair, then kicked her feet up on the table, careful to avoid the letters. "I needed a break. Figured you could use one, too."

"I'll take any excuse."

"How's Cassie?"

"Good, I think. Her sister's in town. It's weighing on her. Doesn't want to get her involved, but I have a feeling that's not going to last long."

"Is her sister anything like her? You know." Harris widened her eyes and wiggled her fingers around.

"What the hell was that supposed to be?"

"You know, does she see things?"

"No, I don't think she sees things." He gestured toward her hands. "Or does terrible impressions of Jack Sparrow."

"Poor Cassie. She must feel so alone sometimes."

The thought had occurred to David more than once. "She's tougher than she looks. She can handle it. Besides, she's got me."

"I'm not discounting that, but I think she needs more than just you. More than just us. She needs friends. She seemed so lost during the Baker case. It can't be easy seeing what she sees."

"I don't think it is. But I've known Cassie a long time. She's always struggled with her gift. It takes a toll on her sometimes. But this is the first time I've seen her embrace it like this. Before, she'd treat it like a job. A necessary evil. Now she's treating it like a calling."

"Good for her." Harris let the silence carry on for a moment or two. "Okay, I've got a moral dilemma for you."

"Go for it."

"This guy, Shapiro. You're pretty sure he killed how many people?"

"Twelve. At least."

"Right. Twelve people. Someone comes along and kills *him*. Is that person good or bad?"

"Is this a trick question?"

Harris laughed. "Not really. It's the Dexter dilemma, isn't it?"

"That TV show where the serial killer killed other serial killers?"

"Exactly. What Dexter did was wrong within the confines of the law, but he likely saved countless lives while doing it. I mean, the FBI tells us there's what, fifty to a hundred active serial killers at any time in our country alone? Following that train, Dexter stopped dozens of murderers from taking more victims. Shapiro was a prolific serial killer. If we'd have caught him twenty years ago, he would've been arrested, tried in front of a jury of his peers, convicted, and likely sentenced to death. The person who killed Shapiro carried out that same sentence, only he saved taxpayers a cool hundred grand a year."

"But you're talking about a person taking matters into their own hands. We have laws against that. Part of our job is to make sure that doesn't happen."

"True." Harris let her feet drop to the ground as she leaned forward in her chair. "But our system isn't perfect. Humans are flawed, and so the system is flawed. How many criminals have you seen walk over the years? Hell, you can even look at this case. You said yourself your Captain didn't put as many resources into it as he should have, and because of that, Shapiro got away with his crimes for two decades."

David thought of Stockton's easy dismissal of the case. He thought the victims weren't important. Weren't worth his time. And so he let the bodies pile up. "That's a big jump from 'we could've done better' to 'we should be applauding the guy who killed him.'"

"I'm not applauding anyone." Harris held up her hands in surrender. "You know me. I'm as by-the-book as they come. I'm not asking whether Shapiro's killer committed a crime. He did. I'm asking whether he did anything *wrong*."

"It depends on who you ask. Christianity tells us *Thou shalt not kill*. But an atheist might have a different opinion. We give leeway to cops and members of the military, provided there's a valid enough reason to kill someone. But does it really make a difference whether the person who killed Shapiro was a soldier or a civilian?"

"These are all good questions, but I think you're avoiding the answer. I'm not asking just any Christian or any atheist or any cop or any soldier. I'm asking you."

David's mouth twisted to the side. "I'm not sad Shapiro is dead. But whoever killed him still ended another person's life. We have a process to go through before we can enact capital punishment. They skipped those steps. That's wrong, no matter how you look at it. I'd still arrest them. I'd still want them to be punished for their crime."

"Let me ask you this, then." Harris leaned back in her chair. "What if it was Novak instead of Shapiro? What if someone had killed him before he ever laid his hands on Cassie? Would you still arrest the killer, or would you thank him for a job well-done?"

David didn't know what to say. He wanted to believe his opinion wouldn't change, that he'd be tried-and-true no matter the circumstances. But when it came to Cassie, all bets were off. If he could've shielded her from all the pain she'd experienced, he would've stopped at nothing. If someone had hunted Novak down and killed him in his sleep, he would've shaken the person's hand and sent them on their way.

Harris seemed satisfied with his stunned silence. She stood and opened the door with a smirk on her face. "Just something to think about. I'll send Paulson in to help you."

19

"So, we never really talked about last night," Laura said.

Cassie looked up from a table covered in antique dinnerware and found Laura avoiding her gaze and inspecting a stoneware flowerpot with a yellow daisy design. They were at the Paris Market on West Broughton to see if they could find any cute houseware items to take home to their mom in a few days. It smelled like musty books and furniture polish.

"Is there stuff to talk about?" Cassie asked.

Laura finally looked up, her face full of concern. She lowered her voice to a whisper. "We saw a dead body."

Cassie laughed. "You say that like we found one on the side of a road. We were in a morgue. We were there because of a murder investigation—for which your sister is a consultant, not a suspect, I might add."

"I know, I know." She looked back down at the pot and then returned it to its place on the shelf. "It was just strange."

"I know." Cassie moved on from the dinnerware and went to inspect a lavish set of teacups decorated with tiny peacocks. "I guess I'm just used to it these days."

"Does it ever bother you? Seeing dead people?"

Cassie understood she meant dead bodies and not ghosts, but her answer wouldn't have been different. "Sometimes. It's never easy to stare into the face of your own mortality. But it becomes less shocking. It becomes more about figuring out what happened to the person than trying to digest what you're seeing."

"I think I'm still digesting."

Cassie put the peacock teacup down and walked over to her sister. "You don't have to be comfortable with it. I don't think you're supposed to be. I know I'm not. Resigned, maybe. But not comfortable."

"But you do like it."

Cassie blinked. "Sure?"

"I saw the way your face lit up. Saw how interested you were in trying to solve the mystery. You live for this stuff."

"I don't think I live for it, but I find it... intriguing."

Laura shot her a look and moved on to a large collection of vintage Savannah postcards. She flipped through them so quickly, Cassie doubted she saw any of them. "I'm just worried about you."

"You're always worried about me." Cassie crossed her arms. "What is it this time?"

Laura pretended to be engrossed by the postcards. "You've surrounded yourself with death. You've chosen to explore it. To get closer to it. After what's happened to you, I don't think that's a good idea. I'm worried that you're not allowing yourself to move on from *him*."

"You mean Novak?"

"Yeah, *him*."

"Why am I the only one who will say his name? I want to remember who he was. I want to remember what he did to me. I can never forget it, Laura. Never. I'm not holding onto it because I can't move away from it. I'm holding onto it because it's part of who I am. It's shaped me. The more I try to push that away, the harder it is for me to accept it. You're a psychologist, you should know this."

Laura's head snapped up. "There's a difference between accepting what happened to you and going out and looking for trouble."

"You think that's what this is? Looking for trouble? You think I *want* history to repeat itself?"

"No, of course not."

Cassie didn't have any words. She shook her head and walked down the next aisle, fuming, not seeing any of the antiques in front of her. She stopped at a display of vintage typewriters, but she had no interest in figuring out what made them so special.

Laura rounded the corner and stopped at Cassie's shoulder. "I'm sorry. That's not what I meant."

Cassie turned to face her. "Then what did you mean?"

"I guess I meant I don't understand why you do this. It can't be easy for you. You're either the bravest person I know or the stupidest."

"Can't I be both?"

That made Laura laugh. "Yeah, I guess you can."

"You could just ask, you know."

"Ask what?"

"Ask why I do this."

"Oh, it's that easy? You'll actually tell me? You do have a habit of keeping secrets from me."

Cassie hated that Laura had a point. "Ha, ha, ha. You're freakin' hilarious."

"Thank you." Laura curtsied. After her smile faded, she went back to avoiding Cassie's gaze. "Why do you work as a consultant for the police? Why do you feel such a strong need to stare death in the face every day?"

Cassie opened her mouth and then closed it. She thought it'd be an easy answer, but like most things in life, it was far from it. This would be the perfect opportunity to tell Laura everything. The floor was hers, and if she wanted to, she could confide in Laura about her abilities and the ghosts, about Novak and Sarah Lennox, and about the ghost of Robert Shapiro and the man he'd killed.

But she couldn't do it.

An invisible fist closed around her throat, and suddenly her mouth went dry. She was scared—truly frightened to the core—that her sister would reject her. Would she believe Cassie could see ghosts? If she didn't, would she recommend she spend some time in a psych ward? Even if she believed her, would Laura understand she couldn't ignore the people reaching out for help?

"I guess I do it because it makes me feel in control." A half-truth was still a truth, right? "I've helped a lot of people over the years. Saved countless victims from untimely deaths. Helped families move on after a tragedy. And brought justice to people who think they can play God. It makes me feel good."

"But does that goodness outweigh the danger? Is it worth it?"

"Yes." Cassie's voice was firm. Definitive. "Every time. I know it sounds cheesy, but this is my calling. This makes me feel like I can change the world around me. I can save people's lives. I can help people move on. I'm not hanging onto a past that frightens me. I'm trying to make a future where everyone can feel safe."

A slow smile crept across Laura's face, and her eyes looked watery. "That was beautiful."

Cassie blushed. "It's just the truth."

"You were always my hero, Cassie. I always wanted to be like you. I'm glad that hasn't changed."

Cassie's blush deepened. Emotion clogged her throat. "That means a lot coming from you."

Someone tapped Cassie on the shoulder.

"Excuse me?" The sisters turned to find a middle-aged gentleman with large, round glasses staring at them. "I can see you're having a moment, but I was wondering if I could get a peek at that Remington behind you?"

Cassie turned and realized they were still standing in front of the typewriters. "Sorry. We'll, uh, have our moment somewhere else."

"Thank you."

Cassie and Laura scurried off, giggling. For the first time since they were teenagers, it felt like they were best friends again. No matter what was between them, they would always be sisters, but she hadn't felt this close to Laura in a long, long time. And she wanted to hold on to that feeling for as long as possible.

But the shrill sound of her ringtone broke the moment when it sang out from the bottom of her purse.

"Turn it off! Turn it off!" Laura was still laughing. "Oh God, it's so loud."

Cassie dug around in her purse until she felt her cell and immediately answered it without even looking at who was calling. She couldn't keep the laughter out of her voice. "Hello?"

David's voice felt warm and welcoming on the other end. "Are you *giggling*?"

"Maybe I am."

"Are you drunk? High? In extreme duress?"

"I'm happy, David. I know it's a shocking concept, but it happens from time to time."

Laura mouthed the name *David* and waggled her eyebrows. Cassie laughed again.

"It sounds good on you." He hesitated, and Cassie could tell he was weighing his next words carefully. "Am I interrupting?"

"Not really. Laura and I were just at the Paris Market trying to find a gift for our mom. We'll head out soon. Maybe grab something to eat. Why, what's up?"

"How do you think your sister would feel about putting her degree to the test?"

Cassie looked up at Laura, who still had a smile on her face. She looked years younger with the glow of happiness around her. "As long as she doesn't have to look at another dead body, I'd say she'd be down for anything."

"Another dead body?" David sounded alarmed. "Did something happen? Are you okay? Why didn't you call—"

"Relax, dad."

Laura mouthed the word, "Dad?" with her face scrunched up.

Cassie waved her off. "I took her to the morgue. Dr. Underwood explained Shapiro's injuries to us and compared them to the original victims. Let's just say it wasn't quite the sister bonding time she was hoping for."

Laura pouted. "I thought the cookies were going to be for us."

"In that case," David continued, "I can guarantee there will be no dead bodies. Just a bunch of letters. I'd like to see if you get anything off them. And I'd like her professional opinion about Shapiro's mental state. Think she'd be up for it?"

Cassie pulled the phone away from her face. "How do you feel about reading a bunch of letters written by a serial killer?"

Laura tried to hide the way her eyes lit up, but Cassie saw right through it. "That could be of professional interest."

Cassie placed the phone back against her ear. "We're in."

20

"DAVID, THIS IS MY SISTER, LAURA. LAURA, THIS IS DAVID."

David leaned forward and extended a hand. "It's a pleasure to meet you. I've heard a lot about you."

"Good things, I hope?" Laura replied.

"All good things. Cassie says you're a psychologist. I was hoping to pick your brain."

"I'll see what I can do."

"Have a seat."

David pulled out a chair for Laura and then one for Cassie. The latter grated across the floor like nails down a chalkboard. They were inside the same room Cassie had visited earlier, but now David had replaced the boxes of reports and evidence with the letters they'd found in Shapiro's house. The room looked just as disorganized as before, but the dim lighting made it easy to gloss over the clutter.

"Have you made any progress?" Cassie gestured to the letters on the table.

"Yes, and no. There's a lot to go through." He turned back to Laura. "How much do you know about the case?"

Laura exchanged a look with Cassie. "Um."

"You're not in trouble." He chuckled. "If Cassie trusts you, I trust you. Even if you weren't her sister. But I'm assuming good genes run in the family."

"I don't know much, I guess. We saw Robert Shapiro's body last night. He killed all those people twenty years ago, right?"

"That's right."

"And I know you're looking for the person who killed him."

"Correct again."

She looked down at the table. "And he wrote these letters to the victims?"

"Yes." David sounded both excited and exhausted at the same time. "We've got two goals right now. One, we're trying to locate all known family members of each victim. We have twelve sets of letters here, all addressed to former inmates at the Coastal State Prison. Now that we have the name of everyone he killed, we can locate all their living relatives."

"Is that just to tell them what happened?"

"Not exactly. The family of the victims are our prime suspects. They would have enough motive to want Shapiro dead. Someone figured out he was the serial killer, considering he was murdered in the same manner as his victims, so it's a logical first step."

"Twelve sets of letters?" Cassie leaned closer to one of the piles in front of her. She avoided touching it in case it affected her. She hadn't decided how she'd play that off in front of her sister. "Are we sure these are all of his victims?"

"No, not entirely." David leaned against the table and surveyed their evidence. "The first letter is dated a few months before the first victim washed ashore. It lends credence to the idea that it was Shapiro's first kill."

"But?"

"But there's no way to know without asking him." David glanced at Cassie with a smirk on his face that she hoped Laura didn't catch. "It's possible he killed prior to that first victim and just didn't keep the letter. Maybe he killed someone else as practice. Someone not in his typical victim pool."

"Someone who wasn't an addict?" Cassie asked.

"It's possible, but unlikely. He has an obvious motive. Several years passed between his wife's death and that first letter. He could've been doing anything in that time. Maybe he was killing, or maybe he was just preparing."

"Preparing?" Laura looked a little green again. "What do you mean?"

"He had to find victims who would satisfy his urge to kill. In this case, addicts recently released from prison. He had to figure out how to get close to them. How to build rapport. Then you're talking about logistics—where would he kill them and how? He needed weapons. He needed heroin to inject them with. That all costs money. It takes time."

"If he tried to kill someone else, is that something you'd be able to find out? Without a letter, I mean."

"Maybe. I've got Officer Paulson on the case. He's looking into police reports from Shapiro's assumed active years and trying to see if anything matches up. He'll pull all records of dead bodies with similar injuries, even if they're not identical, plus anyone who reported an assault that might match our case."

"That sounds like it could take a while," Cassie said.

"That's why we've got a second goal," David said.

"Which is?" Cassie asked.

"Since it's going to take some time to track down the family members and figure out which ones are the more likely suspects, the second goal is to find the five remaining bodies." He turned to Laura. "We found three when they washed in from the ocean. Once that got public attention, the bodies stopped dropping—or so we thought. He just changed tactics. He started burying them in the woods south of Pembroke. We found them two years later while we were looking for some missing kids. Then the trail went cold again."

"Until now. Twenty years later."

"Better late than never," David said. "We know for a fact there's at least five more victims. I'm hoping the letters will point us in the right direction."

"Not that I'm complaining—because this is far more interesting than a night in front of the television—but how can we help? Why do you need a psychologist?"

"I've been through the letters once myself, but I need another couple sets of eyes. There's a lot of information here."

"And before you ask." Cassie held up a hand to Laura. "David is very particular about who he lets in the circle. This is a privilege, Laura. Don't abuse it."

David rolled his eyes. "I've got plenty of guys who will do the work if I tell them to, but not everyone is cut out for this kind of stuff. Cassie's a natural, and given your education and experience, I'm hoping you can lend a hand, too."

"I'm happy to help, but I've never dealt with anything like this before. I counsel people after a trauma. I don't try to make sense of a serial killer's ramblings."

"That's the thing, these are not the ramblings of a serial killer. Or, at least, what Hollywood has convinced us a serial killer should sound like. They're thoughtful, empathetic letters written between what appears to be two friends."

A shiver went down Cassie's spine. "In reality, they're between a murderer and his future victims."

"Where I'm having trouble is differentiating between fact and fiction." David picked up a letter and skimmed it. "There's information in all of these that is contradictory. He tells one inmate he's unemployed and another that he's a veterinarian. In one, his wife is still alive, and in another, she died of cancer a few months prior. We need to figure out which are obvious lies and which are the truth."

"How will that help?" Cassie asked.

"He mentions several locations throughout his letters. Some of them might be real, which means—"

"They're potential burial spots," Laura finished.

"You got it." David winked at her. "See? You're a quick learner. Just like Cassie."

Laura beamed.

"Anything else we should look out for?" Cassie asked.

David set the letter down and shrugged. "Anything. I want to get into this guy's head. I want to know what he was thinking. There's still one big question we haven't answered yet."

Cassie looked around at the table and took in the dozens and dozens of letters. Twelve victims were twelve too many, but was that number significant? "Why did he stop?"

"Bingo."

"That might not be a question we can answer." Laura gestured to the letters. "Like you said, the first victim might not have been his first kill. The last victim might not have been his last kill. Does he have another set of letters hidden somewhere?"

"Not that we know of, but it was difficult to find this set," David said. "Who knows what else he'd gotten up to over the years."

Cassie's stomach dropped. She didn't want to run into Shapiro's ghost a second time, but if there were more victims out there, they deserved to have their souls laid to rest along with the rest of them.

David must've noticed the look on Cassie's face because he offered her a reassuring smile. "But as much as I'd love to answer that question for the sake of my sanity, it's not at the top of our list. For now, we need to figure out where he buried those final five bodies. Meanwhile, my team is doing their damnedest to get us a list of potential suspects."

Laura clapped her hands together. She had a gigantic smile on her face. "Then I guess it's time to get to work."

21

THREE HOURS LATER, THEY WERE HALFWAY DONE ANALYZING THE letters. There were nearly two hundred of them to go through with a fine-tooth comb. Cassie's eyes burned and her throat was dry. She had a harder time than she anticipated parsing out real and relevant information amongst what Shapiro had made up to cover his tracks.

But what Cassie found most frustrating was the lack of psychic vision off the letters. Not even the hint of a vibe that could tell her which victim might be important to investigate. She felt some relief because she didn't have to explain her gut feeling to her sister now, but she also felt angry. Why couldn't she control her abilities? Why couldn't she decide when they worked and when they didn't? Did God have a sense of humor? Or maybe the Devil enjoyed singling her out occasionally to make her life miserable.

David must've seen her eyes glossing over because he tossed his pen down and then stretched his neck to one side and then the other. "Let's take a break. Go over what we've noticed so far. I need a change of pace."

Cassie tossed her pen down as well. "Me too."

"Me three." Laura agreed.

"A consensus. Perfect." David got out of his chair with a groan and started pacing the length of the room. "Okay, Laura. I'm curious to pick your mind first. What've you got?"

Laura looked down at the yellow legal pad she'd been scribbling on and skimmed her notes. "Shapiro is a smart guy. He uses a lot of the same techniques as therapists who want to ingratiate themselves with their clients."

Cassie stifled a yawn. "What do you mean?"

"It's clear he's done his research on the victims. It isn't overtly obvious, but a few times he's brought up specific subjects first—certain familial relationships, events, locations. This sparks a response in the recipient. He's guiding the conversation. He's laying a foundation of trust that he can then later use. Or, rather, abuse."

Cassie looked over at David. "How would he get this information? Maybe he talked to them in person? Talked to their family members?"

"I doubt he talked to them in person," David said. "There'd be a record of him at the prison, and he'd want to avoid detection at any cost. He might've talked to a family member or two, but again, he'd want to keep a low profile. We know he was smart, methodical, and patient. He wouldn't want to do anything to give himself away."

"It was the mid-nineties." Laura tapped her chin with her pen. "The internet was around, but not as widely used as it is these days."

"He could've picked up information in the newspaper when they were arrested. Maybe he went to some proceedings. If you hang around in the right places, you can learn a lot. Let's remember he was also a postal worker, so he worked for the government."

Cassie nodded. "Maybe he knew someone who could get him information."

"Exactly." David tipped his head back at Laura. "What else you got?"

"He was an active listener. Empathetic. Understanding. Non-judgmental. He took the information they told him and used it to his advantage. He'd be more open and vulnerable with them first, so they either felt comfortable or compelled to return the favor. Most of the information seems to be fake—or, at least, only a partial truth—but it still worked. Just about every time."

"Some of what they'd opened up about in these letters were deeply personal." Cassie flipped through a few of the pages in front of her. "Loss of a child. Being closeted. Experiencing abuse."

"He would become their genuine friends," Laura explained. "They had nothing better to do in prison but write letters and wait for a response. He became their sole confidant."

"And the final letters always end the same." David chose one at random and held it close to his face. "Congratulations on your release. Let's celebrate. Dinner's on me."

"The response was always enthusiastic." Laura looked down at her notes. "It's sad, really. They thought they had made it out. They thought they'd found a friend or a sponsor or a partner in crime. Instead, he betrayed them. Murdered them."

The room was silent. Cassie felt the pain of Laura's words. It *was* tragic. Whether any of the victims had planned to sober up didn't matter. They were human beings. They'd deserved to live. They'd deserved a chance.

Cassie was the first one to break the silence. "What about the final victim?"

David walked over to the pile of letters written between Shapiro and victim number twelve. "These letters feel more sinister to me. More pointed."

"Sinister how?"

David shook his head. "I can't put my finger on it. The way Shapiro writes in this one is less empathetic, less consoling."

"Less like a friend? That could be significant."

"Still like a friend, but less like a confidant. More like a... conspirator." David looked down at the letter with a furrowed brow. "At one point the victim seems remorseful. He wants to get clean. But Shapiro steers him in the opposite direction. Encourages him to be bitter. It's subtle, but it's there."

"That is interesting." Laura held out her hand and David handed the stack of letters to her. "There are more letters here than the others."

"Like I said, it's subtle. He spent a lot longer communicating with this one. And from what I can tell, most of the other letters overlapped in one way or another. He was writing to a few at a time. Not this one. Victim twelve was a solo act. Shapiro's entire focus was on him."

"That's significant." Cassie eyed the stack of papers. She hadn't looked through them yet. Would they reveal anything to her? "Do we know who the victim is?"

"Still waiting on more information." There was a light knock at the door. "Speak of the devil."

Officer Paulson stuck his head through the door. He was young, with big brown eyes and short-cropped hair. He was tall and scrawny, and Cassie wondered how he ever expected to be a cop with more skin and bones than muscle on his body. But he was quiet and polite and looked up to David. Cassie liked him.

"Sorry to interrupt, sir, but we got a hit on the search you had me do of reports potentially connected to the original searches."

David gestured for Paulson to enter the room. "What'd you find?"

"In 1992, we have a record of a man named Carl Graham, filed a report after being assaulted. His knee was shattered, but he attracted the attention of a bicyclist who chased off the assailant."

"I assume they never caught the guy?"

Paulson shook his head. "It was dark, and neither of them saw who had attacked Graham." Paulson licked his lips as his gaze skittered around the room. "There's something else, too."

"Well, spit it out. We don't have all day."

"At the time, Carl Graham had just gotten out of prison."

"What was he in for?"

"Breaking and entering." Paulson let the silence build for a few seconds. "And possession."

David slapped him on the back, and the force almost sent the young officer tumbling to his knees. "Excellent work, Paulson. Let me know if you find anything else."

"Yes, sir."

After the door closed, David turned back to the sisters. "He has a slight flair for the dramatic, but he's a good kid."

"Kind of cute, too," Laura added.

Cassie rolled her eyes. "Focus." She turned back to David. "So, what's this mean?"

"This means Laura needs to hold down the fort for a couple hours." When she nodded, David smiled and turned to Cassie. "It also means you and I are going on a field trip. Carl Graham just became our prime suspect in the murder of Robert Shapiro."

22

David pulled up to a small warehouse off West Gwinnet Street. They'd stopped at Carl Graham's house first, but no one was home. His workplace was their next choice: Malcolm Manufacturing, a distribution center for industrial supplies. He'd been working there for the last five years. He had a colorful record, but it seemed he'd cleaned up his act over the last decade.

"We have a plan?" Cassie had one finger already hooked around the car's doorhandle. "Or are we just winging it?"

"We're playing it cool." David stepped out of the car and walked around to meet her at the hood. "I just want to talk to him. Get a sense of who he is. Maybe he'll make this easy and run for it."

"How's that easy?" Cassie looked down at her footwear. She was still wearing her Chucks, but they weren't exactly sprinting shoes. The driveway was loose gravel, and she could already feel the way her ankle would roll if she attempted to chase down a perp. "I'm not built for speed."

David hoisted up his pants, which were a tight fit around his midsection these days. "Me neither, but at least we'd know he's guilty."

"Guilty of something, at least. Remember, not everyone loves the cops like I do. Some people run because they're scared."

David grumbled something under his breath but didn't make any further comment. Instead, he headed for the front door. A small office was situated inside, and a woman sat behind a plexiglass window. She looked straight out of the 1950s with cat-eye glasses, a small beehive hairdo, and a string of pearls around her neck. She didn't look up when they entered.

"Help you?"

"Hi there. Do you have a Mr. Carl Graham working for you today?"

"And who's inquirin'?" She looked up now, but her hands never stopped typing on her keyboard.

David flashed his badge. "Detective David Klein. Savannah PD."

She paused. "Is he in some sort of trouble?"

"Would that be a surprise to you, ma'am?"

The woman shrugged and resumed her typing. "Carl's a good worker. Here every day. Never causes trouble. He's got a record, but I try not to judge. Everyone's got a past. Some people just need a chance at a future."

"Wise words, ma'am." David laid it on thick, but the woman behind the plexiglass didn't seem to mind. "Is he in?"

"I'll call him to the front, just give me a minute."

"Ah, if you could not tell him—"

"Not tell him you're cops. I know the drill, honey. You can sit over there."

Cassie looked over her shoulder to a small waiting area. It comprised two chairs, a tiny table, and a single magazine. When she sat down next to David and picked up the magazine, she realized it was a catalog of the company's products.

"Thrilling literature," David said.

Cassie opened it anyway. "Good enough for me."

But she didn't have to wait long for Graham to show up. Before she knew it, a man stood in front of them with a weary look on his face. His features were gaunt and haggard, like he'd lived a life twice as long as his age indicated. He had a scruffy beard, dark eyes, and his clothes appeared to be a size too big.

"You lookin' for me?"

"Mr. Graham?"

"Yeah. What's this about?"

"Mind if we step outside?"

Whatever suspicions Graham had of them must've been confirmed because he looked like he'd do anything just to get back to work. But instead of putting up a fight, he nodded curtly and turned to the woman at the front desk.

"If Harry comes lookin' for me—"

"I got you covered, sweetie, don't worry. I'll send Lawrence over to your station. He's not doin' much of anything today, anyway."

"Thanks, Miss Mary."

"Anytime, hon."

Graham pushed through the open doors. As Cassie followed behind him, she noticed a slight limp in his right leg. Paulson had said the assailant had shattered his knee. Did he still suffer from those injuries all these years later, or could it be unrelated? Maybe he'd sustained injuries when he'd murdered Shapiro.

Graham led them around the side of the building where they wouldn't be disturbed, then leaned back against the wall and lit a cigarette. "You the police?"

"Detective David Klein. This is my associate, Cassie Quinn."

Graham took a few seconds to study each of them and then nodded as if he'd verified their identities on some internal server in his head. "Am I in trouble?"

"Have you done anything wrong?"

Graham blew out a cloud of wide smoke and shrugged. "Depends on who you're askin'. Lotta people think they're doin' the right thing when they ain't. And vice versa."

David pointed at his right leg. "What happened there?"

"Old injury from years ago." He lifted his pant leg to reveal a prosthetic limb. "Still bothers me from time to time. 'Specially when a rainstorm's comin'."

"Is that from the incident back in '92? Where someone attacked you and shattered your knee?"

Graham's eyebrows disappeared into his hairline. "Yeah. I was stupid back then. Didn't take care of it. Got mixed up in a lot of bad situations. They ended up amputating it." He looked down and spat between his shoes.

"Sorry to hear that."

Graham shrugged. "My own damn fault. 'Sides, I get disability. Helps pay the bills."

"Did you ever figure out who attacked you?"

"Not a clue. Was dark that night. I know it was a man. About my height. Bigger than me, but not by much." He pulled at his shirt and let it fall back into place. "I used to be bigger. Can't build muscle like I used to."

"Anything else you remember?"

"He was older than me. White. Happened so fast. I was in a lot of pain. That's mostly what I remember." Graham looked between David and Cassie. "Why you askin' me about something that happened twenty years ago?"

David pulled out a picture of Shapiro. "Do you recognize this man?"

Graham took the picture and held it close to his face. He studied it for a minute and then shook his head. "Can't say that I do. Why?"

"His name is Robert Shapiro. We believe he might be the man who attacked you."

"Really? Is he gonna get in trouble for what he did to me?" Graham pushed himself off the wall. He looked a little more animated now. "Can I sue him? Not gonna lie, I could use the money."

"Unfortunately, he's dead."

Graham deflated. "Figures. How'd he die?"

"A horrific incident."

Graham made a non-committal noise. He seemed lost in thought for a moment before he looked back up at David. "You think I had something to do with it?"

"The thought crossed our minds."

Graham held up his hands. His cigarette was nearly down to the butt now. "Look, man, I didn't do it. I swear. That was a long time ago. Yeah, I get mad about it sometimes, but sometimes I'm grateful it happened to me."

"Grateful?"

Graham flicked his cigarette butt to the ground and stamped on it. "I was in and out of jail a lot back then. My life was a mess. I was always hurting people. Not physically. Just lettin' 'em down, you know? My mother. My girl. Even got a kid somewhere in the world. Don't know who she is because her mom took her and ran. I don't blame her. I couldn't have raised a kid back then. Couldn't raise one now."

"What changed?"

Graham pointed to his leg. "This. Changed my whole life. Not right away. Got hooked on prescription drugs after that. Messed up a few times. Almost died. But I finally woke up. Realized I didn't want to do it anymore. Didn't want to be angry. Didn't want to be disappointed in myself."

"That's good," Cassie offered. "You should be proud of that."

Graham shoved a hand in his pocket and pulled something out. He handed it to Cassie. "Been sober seven years. Shoulda been ten, but I fucked up—oops, sorry, ma'am. I messed up a little in the middle there."

Cassie smiled and handed the chip back. "You did a good job, Carl. That's really amazing."

He beamed as he took the chip back. He looked years younger. "Thanks. I take it pretty serious. Have to. Malcolm, the owner, he's been sober goin' on twenty-five years. Gave me a job. Helped me turn my life around. It's not perfect, you know? It's still shitty most days.

Pretty crappy, I mean. But it's better than it was. I don't ever want to go back to the way it was."

After a beat of silence, Graham looked at David. "Am I in trouble?"

"No, you're not in trouble, Carl. We may have some follow-up questions for you in the future, but you have nothing to worry about."

Graham nodded. "I'm home most nights after six. Don't really have anywhere to go."

David walked Graham back into the building and then met Cassie at the car.

"What now?" she asked.

David sighed and shook his head. "Back to square one."

23

"When you said back to square one, I didn't think you meant here."

David put the car in park, and Cassie leaned forward to look at Shapiro's ranch-style home once again. A shiver ran down her spine, but goosebumps didn't erupt on her skin as they had when she'd been there before.

"We're just parking in the driveway." David pointed to a similar house next door. "I want to talk to the neighbors."

"Hi there, Mr. and Mrs. Smith," Cassie said. "Were you aware your neighbor was a serial killer?"

"I'm hoping they might know of his comings and goings over the years. Did he stay home a lot, or did he leave every weekend? If he left every weekend, where would he go? That might give us an idea of where he buried the last set of bodies."

"Think he'd divulge that kind of information to them?"

"Don't know until we ask." David pushed open his door and stretched his legs. "Shapiro got away with murder for decades. He likely let some information slip over the years. It may have been innocuous then, but it could help us now."

"Good enough for me." Cassie hopped out of the car and pointed at Shapiro's house. "As long as I don't have to go back inside there."

"We'll try to avoid it at all costs, but I make no promises."

Cassie didn't argue. If David asked her to, she'd do just about anything to help her friend solve the case. Her relationship with David was unconventional, but she liked it that way. They had a professional respect for each other, but Cassie could rely on him for the personal stuff, too. Like dealing with her sister.

"Thanks, by the way." Cassie looked over at him. "I forgot to say that earlier."

"For what?"

"Asking for Laura's help. I don't know how she feels about all this, but I know she's trying to understand it. And I think you got her hooked on trying to figure out how Shapiro ticks."

"It can be addictive," David said. "That need to solve the mystery. To complete the puzzle. Sometimes you get closer than others. She has a good mind for this sort of thing. I think she's going to be a big help."

"Me too. Gotta say, it feels nice to confide in her. I was having these recurring dreams, but the more I open up to her, the more in control I feel of them. Isn't that weird?"

"Your dreams are always weird, Cassie. That's the least weird dream you've ever told me."

Cassie laughed but smothered it with her hand. They were standing on the doorstep of the neighbors who lived to the right of Robert Shapiro. She knew nothing about them, least of all if they'd be willing to talk about the man who lived next door, but she was sure they'd be more hesitant to share information if she stood cackling on the other side of their front door.

David knocked and a sweet older woman greeted them. She must've been in her eighties, but her track suit gave her an air of athleticism, and she seemed to have more energy than Cassie did most days.

"Hello there." There was a touch of confusion in her smile. "Can I help you?"

"Ma'am, my name is Detective David Klein. This is my associate, Cassie Quinn. I was wondering if you might have a few minutes to answer a couple of questions about your late neighbor, Mr. Robert Shapiro?"

"Yes, of course. Come in."

The woman led them into the kitchen and ushered them into a pair of chairs. She poured them each a glass of lemonade and set a plate of chocolate chip cookies down in the center of the table. The sweet smell of sugar and chocolate saturated the air.

"Straight from the oven. Please, help yourselves." She walked over to the staircase and called upstairs. "Henry? Dear? Could you come down here, please?"

"Something the matter, Margery?"

"The police are here to ask us some questions about Robert."

Shuffling sounded from overhead, and then the stairs creaked beneath the weight of an older gentleman who looked to be as healthy and fit as his wife. They were the idyllic image of an older married couple—white hair, lots of wrinkles, and gentle eyes that put Cassie at ease.

David stood to shake the gentleman's hand. "Detective David Klein. And my associate, Cassie Quinn."

"I saw Robert just last weekend. He looked healthy."

"I don't think the police would be here if he had a heart attack, Henry." She turned back to David. "We saw something happened, of course. There were police cars all over the place. But they couldn't tell us how he died."

"You're right, uh, Mrs.—"

"Call me Margery, dear."

"You're right, Margery. Robert Shapiro was murdered a few days ago, and we're still trying to put the puzzle pieces together."

"Murdered?" Margery put a hand to her mouth. "Who would do something like that?"

"We have a few working theories, but for now, we're wondering how well you knew Mr. Shapiro?"

"My goodness, we've known him for forty years. We were never close—he was a private person—but you say hello enough times over the years, and you feel a certain kinship."

"What can you tell us about the type of person he was?"

"Quiet. Private, like I said." She looked at her husband with a sad smile on her face. "When his wife was alive, he was a little more jovial. A little friendlier."

"He changed after that?"

"A bit," Henry said. "I talked to him a few more times than Marge, here. Mostly superficial topics, you know. Best way to remodel the bathroom. How to grill a steak. Manly things." He winked at Cassie, and she couldn't help but giggle.

"You went fishing with him a few times," Margery offered.

"I did. Us men don't talk as much as the ladies. It was just a peaceful sort of getaway."

"I understand." David shifted in his seat, and Cassie could tell he was trying to ask the right questions without giving away who Shapiro was. "How did he change after his wife died?"

"He didn't leave his house much at first." Margery frowned. "Always looked more disheveled. Didn't say hi when we'd see him. Don't think he was being rude. I think he was in his head. Didn't hear us, you know?"

"For a few years there, we thought he was getting better. Seemed more sociable. He left the house a bit more often, anyway. Then it petered off again. The last few years, he was especially quiet. He'd go to work. Come back. His car was always in the driveway."

"Were you aware of any land Mr. Shapiro might've owned? Even the fishing spot—somewhere he'd go to get away from the world?"

"The fishing spot was mine," Henry said. "Told him he could go up there any time, but I don't think he did. Fishing was more my thing than his. Had to sell it back in '99 when things were tight. They ended up leveling it out and building an apartment complex. Such a waste."

"Anything else you could think of? Any amount of land might be what we're looking for."

Margery looked at David, and then at Cassie. "I have a feeling there's more to this story than you're letting on."

David sighed. "It doesn't paint a pretty picture, ma'am."

She waved him off. "I've lived a long time, Detective Klein. I've seen plenty of ugliness. Don't mince words for my sake."

David looked to Cassie, and she gave him a reassuring smile. When he turned back to the older couple, his face was stoic. "We have powerful evidence supporting the idea that Robert Shapiro killed at least twelve people over the course of several years back in the nineties."

Margery gasped but quickly recovered. "You're right, that sure isn't a pretty picture." She hesitated. "Are you sure?"

"Quite sure, ma'am. We've found an abundance of evidence, and while trying to solve his murder, we'd like to put together the final pieces of what happened twenty years ago. We have yet to discover the bodies of several of his victims, and we think he could've buried them on some plot of land kept away from the public eye."

"I don't know of any land he might've owned," Henry started, "but his sister-in-law might?"

"Sister-in-law?"

Margery nodded. "Her name is Tamara Partridge. She came around a lot in the beginning, right after her sister died. I think maybe she thought Robert would be a comfort. Or that she could be a comfort to him. But he quickly put an end to that. Didn't want to see her. She and Susanna looked similar, you know."

"No, I didn't know that." David tapped his pen against his notebook. "Do you know where she lives?"

"Yes, I can give you her address." Margery walked across the room and pulled open a drawer full of notebooks. "I send her flowers every year on her birthday. We talk every so often. She and her husband have always been kind to us, and I think they like talking about Susanna. We knew her, briefly, and it seems to help when we share what we remember."

"That would be a big help, ma'am, thank you."

Margery scribbled the address down on a piece of paper and handed it to David. She had a faraway look on her face. "You think you know someone."

David placed a gentle hand on her shoulder. "People have a way of surprising us, even from beyond the grave."

Cassie couldn't help the smirk that found its way to her lips. Story of her life.

24

DAVID AND CASSIE FOUND THEIR WAY TO THE FRONT DOOR OF MRS. Tamara Partridge's townhouse. It was a modest home in a pleasant neighborhood right outside Savannah. Close enough to downtown that it wasn't an awful trip, but far enough away to enjoy suburban life. The smell of seared steak and apple pie snuck through a cracked window and enveloped the porch. David's stomach audibly growled.

"I hate to call on people around suppertime." He patted his belly.

Cassie patted David's arm. "I love that you're more concerned about when we're dropping by than *why* we're dropping by."

"I just don't want to be rude."

She glanced at his midsection. "Just ask for a bite. You know you want to."

"That's not what I mean."

Cassie giggled. "I know."

When David knocked, a woman in her early sixties answered the door. She had long gray hair pulled back in a half ponytail, and she wore dark slacks and a cream-colored blouse. She looked like she'd just returned home from work.

"Hello, Mrs. Partridge?" David said.

"Yes, that's me."

"My name is Detective David Klein." He gestured to Cassie. "My associate, Cassie Quinn."

"Detective?" She looked past them as though searching for a crime scene. "Is something wrong?"

"That depends on how you look at it, ma'am. May we come inside?"

"Sure, but I'm right in the middle of making dinner, if you don't mind?"

"No, no, of course not. I'm sorry we didn't stop by sooner." He shot Cassie a look that screamed *told you so*. "We'll try to be out of your hair quickly."

The woman led them into the kitchen, where Mr. Partridge chopped vegetables with a large butcher knife. His hair was salt-and-pepper, and he had a thick chevron mustache to match. With glasses and a pencil stuck behind his ear, he looked like a professor in an apron.

"Dear, these are detectives, came to ask us some questions."

"Oh?" Mr. Partridge stopped mid-chop and looked David and Cassie over. "Has something happened?"

"I'm afraid so. Your brother-in-law, Robert Shapiro, has died."

"Oh." Mrs. Partridge leaned against the counter. Her face was neutral, but her eyes were sharp. "If it were as simple as that, I don't think the Savannah PD would send out a couple of detectives, would they?"

"One detective," Cassie corrected. "One, uh, associate."

"No, ma'am. Not as easy as that." David shifted his weight to his other foot. "No easy way to say this."

Mr. Partridge resumed chopping. As Cassie took a few steps closer, the pungent smell of onions caused her eyes to weep. She looked to David to see if he noticed, but he said nothing.

"Best to just get it out," Mrs. Partridge said. She went over to a pot on the stove and started stirring. "I'm a rip-the-Band-Aid-off kind of person."

"Well, okay then. We have evidence to believe your late brother-in-law was a serial killer."

It felt as though someone hit the pause button on the entire room. Cassie could only hear the bubbling of the liquid on the stove, the searing of steak in the cast iron pan, and smell a sour scent emanating from somewhere in the kitchen. It turned her stomach, and she wondered if it'd be rude to excuse herself from the room.

Mr. Partridge was the first to break the silence. "Robert? Are you sure?"

"Quite sure." David looked to Mrs. Partridge. "After your sister's death, it seems he found an outlet for his anger."

"He wasn't the same after Susanna died." Mrs. Partridge grabbed a towel and wrung it between her hands. "I tried to help for a while. Did the best I could, but he pushed me away. Told me I shouldn't come around anymore."

"He threw you out of the house." Mr. Shapiro chopped his vegetables more roughly. "Dirty bastard."

"So, there's no love lost between you three?"

Mrs. Partridge looked away. "I wouldn't say that."

"I would." Mr. Partridge put down the knife. He took off his glasses, cleaned them, and returned them to his face with a huff. "Robert was always good to Susanna. But I never liked him. I always thought—"

"You never thought anything." Mrs. Partridge threw the towel down on the counter, and Cassie got the distinct impression this was a fight they'd had more than once. "You loved Robert like a brother. For ten years."

Mr. Partridge glanced at David and Cassie and decided not to press the subject. "He was strange after her death. He'd always been quiet, but not like that. He was practically a recluse. Tamara used to take casseroles over to his house twice a week for a year. He never ate them, but she did it anyway. She was mourning her sister, too. Thought they might console each other. He was only interested in being angry. In blaming someone."

"Your sister was killed in a car accident, isn't that right?" David asked.

"Yes. The man behind the wheel was very sick," Mrs. Partridge said.

"He was a heroin addict." Mr. Partridge didn't mince words. "He died instantly. Robert always hated that. He wanted him to die a slow death. Wanted to be the one to put him out of his misery."

"We think that's why he started killing other addicts. He was trying to find closure, in his own way."

"That's horrific." Mrs. Partridge clutched her stomach, and for a second, Cassie wondered if she smelled the sourness of the onions, too. "I never would've known. Never would've guessed he was capable of that."

Mr. Partridge kept his mouth shut but it seemed like he didn't agree with her.

"We have reason to believe he murdered at least twelve victims—"

Mrs. Partridge sucked in air through her teeth. "Twelve!"

"—but we can't locate the last five. We were hoping you might know of some property Robert might've owned? We haven't been able to locate anything ourselves."

Before Mrs. Partridge could answer, Cassie felt bile building in her throat. She took a step backwards and knocked into a kitchen chair. All eyes turned to her. She blushed. "I'm sorry. Do you have a bathroom I could use?"

"Sure." Mrs. Partridge pointed past her. "Down the hall. Last door on your right."

"Thank you."

Cassie fled the room. As soon as she made it to the bathroom and shut the door behind her, her stomach erupted and she found herself puking into a stranger's toilet. As terrible as she felt, all she could hope for was that no one heard her.

After she'd emptied her stomach of the day's contents, she flushed the toilet and washed out her mouth with water from the faucet. The sour smell had dissipated, and now she only smelled the onions, along with the pleasant aroma of sauce.

Cassie closed her eyes and shook her head. The pungent odor had come and gone just as quick, but it had been enough to send her running to the bathroom. Was something wrong with her, or with the house?

She looked to the mirror, hoping she didn't appear as sweaty and pale as she felt.

She wasn't alone.

Cassie whipped around and met empty air. When she turned back to the mirror, the figure stood just over her shoulder. She was a slender woman with dark hair and vibrant eyes. She did look just like Tamara.

"Susanna?" Cassie whispered.

The woman smiled.

Cassie looked over her shoulder again, but there was still no one behind her. She turned back to the mirror. "Why are you in there?"

Susanna shrugged.

Fair enough, Cassie thought. The ways of the spirit world were still unknown to her. Ghosts could show up in a myriad of ways. They could communicate in the strangest of fashions. It was hard on some days, but she'd learned to accept what came.

"You want me to tell your sister something?"

Susanna nodded.

"Can you speak?"

Susanna opened her mouth and moved her lips, but Cassie couldn't hear a single word. The mirror, for whatever reason, was a barrier between them. The woman on the other side frowned.

"I don't suppose you know sign language?" Cassie shook her head. "Not that it matters. *I* don't know sign language."

Susanna paused for a moment, and then she slowly and deliberately held her stomach and looked like she was in pain. Cassie felt the echo of her upset stomach before it vanished again just as quickly.

"Is she sick?" Cassie's eyes widened. "Oh my God, is she pregnant?"

Susanna leveled her with a glare.

"Right, right. Too old for that. So, she's sick?"

Susanna nodded.

"Something to do with her stomach?"

Susanna nodded again, but this time looked annoyed.

"Just want to be clear." Cassie wracked her brain. "Ulcer?"

A shake of the head.

"Cancer?"

Susanna froze. Then she slowly nodded her head.

"Stomach cancer." Cassie said it more like an evil utterance than a question. "Is it bad?"

Susanna leaned toward the mirror and put her hand against the glass like it was a window. Her eyes were enormous. Pleading. Cassie placed her hand against the mirror, too, and she could feel fear radiating off the woman. She felt her stomach bubble again. The sour scent of the onions assaulted her nose. She had to take a step back to clear her head.

"Okay, okay. I get it." She pushed the bile rising in her throat back down. "But how am I going to—"

A sharp knock at the door scared her. Her head whipped in that direction. She could see the shadow of a pair of feet on the other side.

"Who is it?"

"Me." David's muffled voice came through the door. "You okay?"

"Yeah. Hang on."

Cassie turned back to the mirror, but Susanna had gone. The only evidence of her presence was the barest outline of a handprint on the mirror, and even that faded.

A few seconds later, Cassie emerged from the bathroom having made sure she didn't look a complete mess. David waited for her by the door. The Partridges stood there with sad smiles on their faces.

"Are you sure you don't want to stay for dinner? I don't eat much these days."

Cassie winced. "No appetite?"

"Not really. I always feel sick after I eat, so I don't see the point. Old age, I guess."

"Could it be a sign of something else?" Cassie inquired.

Mrs. Partridge waved her off. "I'm healthy as a horse, I promise. Don't worry about me."

"Thank you again for the tips," David said, holding up a piece of paper. "We appreciate your time."

"Of course. I hope you find what you're looking for. Those poor souls."

Cassie didn't know what to do. Social etiquette told her it was time to go, but how could she leave and say nothing? She dragged her feet as she backed out of the door, trying to find the words that would make Mrs. Partridge understand what was causing her symptoms.

Without the proper words, Cassie allowed them to usher her over the threshold. The Partridges said their goodbyes and began closing the door. But Cassie glimpsed Susanna in the windowpane, and that's all it took.

She stuck her foot out and winced as the door crushed her toes. The couple both looked alarmed.

David took a step toward her. "Cassie—"

She ignored him and grabbed Mrs. Partridge's hand. The woman gasped and tried to pull away, but Cassie held on tighter. She looked her square in the eyes with the most beseeching look she could muster.

"Ma'am, I know you don't know me. I know you have no reason to trust me and definitely no reason to not think I'm a crazy person." Cassie swallowed audibly. "But please go to the doctor. Tell your doctor about your symptoms. Make sure they check your stomach."

Mr. Partridge looked at David. "What's going on?"

"Cassie is, uh, very intuitive, sir. I think you should listen to her."

Mrs. Partridge never broke eye contact with Cassie. The look on her face went from one of shock to one of fear, but Cassie didn't think it was just because she'd spooked Mrs. Partridge. The woman nodded. This time, when she tried to pull away, Cassie let her.

"I didn't mean to frighten you." Cassie tried to get the last of her words out as Mr. Partridge swung the door shut in her face. "I'm sorry."

The force of the door slamming blew Cassie's hair back from her face and erased the sour smell. The lock clicking into place sounded like a gunshot. When she turned to David, he had a bemused look on his face.

"You gotta figure out a better way to tell people they're dying."

Cassie stepped away from the door and headed back toward David's sedan.

"You try finding a way to say *your dead sister told me you have stomach cancer* without sounding nuts. Then we can talk."

"Oh no, that's your job." He had a shit-eating grin on his face now. "And you couldn't pay me a million bucks to take it from you."

25

David had driven down the road and parked on the curb to put distance between Cassie and the Partridges, who regretted inviting the pair for dinner and were relieved David and Cassie had turned down the invitation. She sensed David regretted not getting at least a couple forkfuls of steak if the way he patted his belly was any indication. It didn't help that his air freshener smelled like a vanilla milkshake.

He pulled out the slip of paper the Partridges had given him and handed it to Cassie. "Three options. First one was a getaway the Shapiros used to take advantage of back in the late eighties. But it's about two hours away, so an unlikely candidate."

"Option two?" Cassie asked.

"A plot of land they'd been interested in buying and building a house on. Mrs. Partridge doesn't think Shapiro got around to buying it, and we didn't find any record of it in his name, but who says he didn't purchase it under a fake name or an LLC or under the table altogether?"

"Valid point. Option three?"

"An old apple orchard just north of Rincon. That one's a bit of a stretch. It's in Mr. Partridge's name. The land hasn't been taken care of in quite some time. She said Shapiro had always talked about cleaning it up, planting new trees, and starting a business their kids could take over."

"It's got a personal touch. That sounds like a pretty good lead to me."

"Is that a feeling or an observation?"

"An observation." Cassie's phone vibrated in her pocket. She put it on speaker. "Hey, Laura. Please tell me you've got something for us."

"There's a lot here, you guys. I don't even know where to start."

"Let's start with the stuff you know for sure," David said.

Laura exhaled and it crackled into the phone. "He talks a lot about the coast. The ocean."

David leaned forward so he could talk into the phone better. "Unlikely. We know he already tried dumping bodies in the ocean. Didn't work out for him."

"He could've found a better way," Cassie suggested.

"Maybe, but that wouldn't be the first place I looked," David said. "What else you got?"

"He talks a lot about trips up north. But, like, *north*. Montana. Canada."

"Also unlikely." David looked dejected.

"Anything about building his own house? Or planting fruit?" Cassie asked.

"Did you say fruit?" Shuffling sounded on Laura's end. "He talked a lot about fruit, actually. About picking apples and peaches. Wanting to start his own business. He offered jobs to a few of the guys. I figure that might be how he met up with some of them. Promise them a job, get them excited to check out the orchard, and take 'em out."

David and Cassie's gazes locked. "Bingo."

"Think that's our place?" Laura asked.

"Best lead we've got so far." David put the car in gear. "We're going to check it out."

"All right. Good luck. I'll be here."

"Take a break if you need to, Laura," Cassie said. "You don't have to stay there all night."

"Nah, it's fine. Paulson's been feeding me coffee every hour. No way in hell I'm going to sleep any time soon."

Cassie hung up and looked expectantly at David. "You really think this could be it?"

"Only one way to find out."

The trip to Rincon took about thirty minutes. Cassie navigated them right up to a gated entrance made of more rust than metal. The orchard had sat for who knows how long as a useless piece of land. It would've cost more than the Partridges could afford to get it back in working condition. Robert Shapiro had had a plan, but all that went down the drain when his wife died.

"I guess this is the right place." David leaned into the steering wheel to get a better look out the window. "Hard to tell out here what's what. Don't want to be walking on someone else's land, making a fool of ourselves."

"It's the right place." Cassie had hardly noticed the trees beyond the fence. She only had eyes for the figure in front of her. Her chest tight, she continued, "I see him."

"Who?"

"The man from the other day. The one we thought might've been Robert Shapiro but turned out to be one of his victims."

"Think that means his bones are here?"

Cassie shrugged. "There could be a million reasons he's right here, right now. But yeah, I'd put money on this being his final resting place."

"Shall we see if he leads us to the jackpot?"

Cassie shot David a look but followed him out of the car anyway. "Can we not call the pile of dead bodies we're looking for *the jackpot*?"

"I suppose I shouldn't say that in front of your friend."

If the gate had been closed with a padlock at some point, it was long gone now. David pushed it open and waited until Cassie passed through before closing it behind them. There were a few paths forward, but they looked more like deer trails than anything else. A few beer cans and a pack of empty cigarettes told them local kids had also found the abandoned piece of land and used it as a party spot.

"Which way?" David held his hands out to either side.

Both paths looked identical to Cassie. Grass and weeds had long taken over. It was past the time for harvesting apples, but since there had been no one to pick them, they'd fallen to the ground and rotted. A sickening, sweet scent filled the air and threatened to upset Cassie's still-queasy stomach.

But more than that, she felt the touch of that red-hot anger she'd been desperate to avoid.

"Shapiro's spirit is here, too." She swallowed the lump in her throat. "It's faint. Distant. But he's pissed."

"Well, is he pissed to the left, or the right?"

Cassie closed her eyes. In the inky blackness behind her eyelids, she could see the faintest hint of scarlet. It was pulsing, but not in rhythm with her own heartbeat. No, it lived and breathed because of another. Shapiro was more than a ghost now. He was made of emotion. And that made him so much stronger.

Cassie squared up the blotch of red in her vision and then opened her eyes. "He's pissed to the left, apparently."

David gestured for Cassie to lead the way, and after a moment's hesitation to consider what bugs they were about to collect on their person, she pushed aside the weeds and started walking.

"I'm not sure what we're getting into." Cassie threw a look over her shoulder. "This is something different."

"I don't like different." David grunted as he pushed past a low-hanging tree branch. "What you've already got going on is different enough. We don't need to add more different to it."

"That was an appalling use of the English language."

"But you still knew what I meant."

"Barely," Cassie said under her breath. "I know. And I'm worried about it. Shapiro is stronger than most ghosts I've encountered. He found a way inside me. He manipulated my feelings. Amplified them."

"Why?"

Cassie shrugged. "To feed off them? Might give him power. When he was in my house, it was uncomfortable, but tolerable. When I was in his house—whole different story."

"Yes, I remember the part where you passed out."

"His house is one of his seats of power. He has more control over that domain than other places."

"And what about this domain?" David asked. "Out here in the middle of God knows where."

"He buried his victims here." Cassie was just spit-balling. There were no hard and fast rules for these things, but she had built up an arsenal of likely truths over the years. "I'd say he's got a reason to be attached to this place."

"And that's bad for us?"

"Well, it's bad for me."

David grunted. "What's bad for you is bad for me. I'll have to carry your ass back to the car."

"You're hilarious." Cassie couldn't keep the smile out of her voice, no matter how hard she tried. "A true paragon of comedic genius."

David chuckled and soaked in the compliment for a minute or two before breaking the silence. "Can you describe him to me? Describe how he feels different?"

Cassie slowed to a stop and closed her eyes again. Shapiro was still there. The red-hot pulse of his anger was larger now. Closer. She could taste it. Like ash in her mouth. She couldn't tell precisely what he was angry about, but his fury was enough that even death couldn't tame it.

"He's mad." *Understatement of the year*, Cassie thought after the words left her lips. "Really mad."

Oh, yeah, much better.

"Mad about what?" David asked.

"I don't know. Just feels like an assault on my senses. The closer we get to him, the stronger it is. Maybe I'll be able to tell you if I don't pass out again."

"What about our mystery victim? He still around?"

Cassie kept walking forward, letting the pull of Shapiro's spirit guide her way. They passed dozens of apple trees, either laden with heavy fruit or surrounded by a rotten carpet. The heat of the day thickened the air. She could hear David huffing behind her.

When they reached a fork in the path, she didn't need to close her eyes and recenter herself to Shapiro's presence. The figure of his victim stood to the left, looking just as remorseful as he had before. But hope shined in his eyes. Cassie and David were getting closer.

"He's still here," she said.

"We have a list of names of the remaining five victims, along with their criminal records. The problem we have is getting the prison to work with us. The warden isn't making it easy."

"Is that strange?"

"Not really. His name's Wickham, and he's a bit of a dick, if I'm being honest."

"Does he not like you or do you not like him?"

"Little of both. He's always rubbed me the wrong way. He gets more than he earns if you know what I'm saying. He lives a pretty lavish life."

"Anything you can do about it?"

"Me? No. Not my job. Not my taskforce. Savannah PD? Yeah, absolutely. But he's friendly with those guys. They'd never turn him in. He's part of the crew, even if he isn't on the streets with the rest of us."

"That's reassuring." Cassie kept walking down the left path. Every step seemed to bring with it a barrage against her senses. Hot air that seemed to envelop her. Putrid fruit. A rush of anger. She felt sick to her stomach that Wickham—a man she didn't even know—could get away with a crime while punishing those who had done less than he had. "We're getting close."

"How can you tell?"

"I have the urge to rip someone's head off."

"Ah." David chuckled. "Considering I'm the only other living person here, I'll ask you to refrain."

"I'll do my best."

Cassie followed the path in front of her until she wound up under a large willow tree. She heard the faintest whisper of bones calling out to her. Begging her to release them. Their voices were a chorus of pain just beneath the surface of the earth.

"Here." Cassie confirmed.

"You sure?"

She shot David a look that would destroy most men.

"Right. Got it. Don't question the psychic."

Cassie circled the tree once and knelt at its base. She put her hand to the dirt and felt it pulsing under her fingertips. The pain of Shapiro's victims radiated through her hand, then her arm, and right into the base of her skull. The strength of it nearly sent her sprawling backwards.

David crouched beside her. "Are you okay? What's going on?"

"I can feel them. His other victims. They're all here, right beneath the surface."

If David said anything else, Cassie didn't hear it. Two things happened simultaneously—the mystery victim who'd visited her appeared at the base of the tree, and Shapiro himself materialized only a few feet away.

Shapiro's aura was still that deep, pulsing red. The anger radiating off him made Cassie's legs shake. The pain in her head intensified to where she could barely keep her eyes open. It was like the worst migraine she'd ever experienced, multiplied by a thousand. She couldn't stop herself from crying out. But instead of being afraid, she felt only anger. It flowed through her veins like molten lava until it had her jumping up and backing away from the tree.

"No, no, no."

"What's wrong? Cassie, what's going on?" David grabbed her

shoulders and shook her until she looked him in the eye. "Talk to me. What's happening?"

She had to use every ounce of her strength to keep from passing out. Her knees were weak. All she wanted to do was close her eyes and disappear forever. "The victims are in so much pain. They're so afraid. He's feeding off it. It's giving him power. Every second he's around them, he gets stronger."

"Can he hurt them? Can he hurt you?"

"I don't know." Cassie grabbed her head between her hands and squeezed. She wanted to pull out her hair. "But it's not fair. It's not fair."

"What's not fair?"

Cassie squeezed her eyes shut as she dropped to a knee. She couldn't fight it anymore. Couldn't think. Could only feel. The words came unbidden. "It's not fair what he did to them. What gave him the right? He was mourning his wife, he understood how horrific it is to lose someone you love, and yet he did that to a dozen other people. What gave him the right?"

"He didn't think of it that way. He didn't think of them as people."

Cassie exploded with anger. "Don't defend him. They were people. They were living, breathing people."

"I know—"

"They had lives. They had hopes and dreams and families. They had futures." There was a growl in her voice that scared her. "He took all of that away. He stole it. What gave him the right?"

"Cassie, you have to resist him. You can't give him any more power."

Cassie stood so fast she knocked David back a couple feet. She pointed to where Shapiro had buried his victims. Their whispers were louder now. She wasn't sure if she was hearing them in her head or if they existed outside. Ignoring them was useless. It would only do more damage.

"That could've been me. I was there, in their shoes, but I survived."

She stalked toward Shapiro. The aura surrounding him deepened and turned black. "Do you hear that? I survived. And you may have killed them, but they're not gone. You failed. You tried to erase them, but it didn't work. And you know what else? What you did to those people was unforgivable. You can't stay here forever. You'll burn in hell for what you did."

A wicked grin formed on Shapiro's face. One second, he was still a few arm lengths away, and the next, he was standing right in front of Cassie. Her throat closed. Her skin burned as if she were on fire. Sweat poured from her temples, and her vision blurred.

But then her ghostly visitor appeared and acted as a cool salve against her skin. He formed a barrier between her and Shapiro, and for a moment she felt the reprieve of the killer's effects. She could breathe again. Shapiro looked surprised his victim had the audacity to challenge him, and when he moved to push him out of the way, the other man stood firm.

The whispers beneath her swelled. She dropped to her knees. Her head was clear enough to realize she looked insane, but there wasn't any time to think about what David thought of her in that moment.

"You can stop him," she said. "He's feeding off your fear. Your despair. Show him you're not afraid. Stand up to him. He can't fight all of you at once. We're here. David and I. We know where you are now. We'll get your bodies to your families. You'll be put to rest. But first you have to show Robert Shapiro he didn't win."

Cassie held her breath as the air shimmered around her. Shapiro's last victims appeared one at a time until all five of them stood against him. Gnashed teeth replaced his wicked grin. He charged at Cassie but met resistance.

His victims kept her safe.

As her body cooled and her mind stilled, Cassie felt peace settle over her that came as much from herself as it did those around her. She smiled at David, who stared at her with wide eyes and a slack jaw.

"It's going to be okay," she reassured him.

He nodded, though he looked anything but convinced. Cassie turned back to the scene in front of her. Shapiro backed away now. Terror rested in his eyes. As his victims advanced on him, they pulsed with a white light. She couldn't see their faces, but she could feel their strength. They were united. The pulsing of Shapiro's blackened aura slowed. The glow faded as his victims grew brighter.

A few more seconds, and he'd be left pale and weak.

He turned to flee, but the man closest to him reached out and took hold of his wrist. Shapiro cried out, but another of the men latched onto him. Soon, all five had a part of him. They dragged him to his knees. They moved in until Cassie couldn't see him anymore. His screams faded. Soon, she couldn't feel him at all.

One by one, the victims dissipated, leaving only her visitor. He gifted her with a soft smile before fading away himself. The whispers ceased. She turned to David.

"It's over."

26

THE NEXT DAY, CASSIE STILL FELT EXHAUSTED FROM THE ENCOUNTER IN the orchard. Her muscles ached, and she was tired down to her bones, but the satisfaction of having found the five missing bodies was enough to get her out of bed and dressed to go to her therapy appointment.

Cassie felt her phone buzz and dug around inside her purse until she found it. "David says he has some information on the bodies we found yesterday. He was wondering if we can stop by after the appointment?" She conveyed the message to Laura.

"Fine with me." Laura's yawn was so big, Cassie could count her molars. "But I want lunch and about three iced coffees first."

Cassie sent a reply to David and then tossed her phone back in her purse. The floor that where her therapist's office was located had ceased making her nervous years ago, but it all looked different and more imposing now that her sister was sitting next to her.

Cassie still had a lot of opening up to do with Laura, but she was more concerned about how she would open up to her parents. Laura was doing the best she could, but it was hard for her to be objective.

When Cassie asked if she'd like to meet her therapist, Laura was all for it.

At the time, Cassie was, too. But now? She wasn't so sure.

The waiting room was empty except for the two of them. Cassie could hear the old building creak and pop, and her nerves were on edge thanks to the ghost of the little boy who wouldn't take his eyes off Laura for more than a second or two at a time. That mystery continued to gnaw at Cassie until she wanted to pull her hair out.

But approaching footsteps saved her from any dramatics. Her therapist rounded the corner with an enormous smile on her face and held out her hand to Laura.

"So, you must be the sister." Dr. Greene began.

"What was your first clue?" Laura asked.

"You know, just an educated guess. You two really look nothing alike."

Cassie laughed at the joke, though her heart wasn't in it. As Dr. Greene led them back to her office, she threw one more glance over her shoulder to check on the little boy, but he had disappeared.

"Have a seat, please. I'm so glad you're joining us today, Laura."

"Thank you for inviting me." She glanced at Cassie with a smile. "We've had a bit of a turbo-charged reunion, but I'm really glad I made the trip."

"Cassie, you were pretty worried prior to Laura's visit. How are you feeling now?"

"Better." Cassie nodded her head a few times as she tried to find the words. "Still worried. I don't want to mess it up."

"Why are you afraid you're going to mess it up?"

Cassie shrugged. She couldn't say her worry stemmed from her fear of her sister—and her parents—finding out about her abilities. "I guess I'm just afraid there's something about me now that didn't exist when I was younger and they might not accept me."

"Do your parents dislike people who are different?"

Cassie blanched. "No, not at all. They raised us to be tolerant and open and loving to everyone. They taught us the world was full of people who were different, and that we'd have to work every day to make sure we learned about other cultures."

"That's fantastic." Dr. Greene smiled. "What makes you think you're the exception to that rule?"

Cassie opened her mouth and then snapped it shut. She glared at Dr. Greene. "I hate when you do that."

"Do what? Prove that your anxious thoughts are unrealistic and illogical?"

"Yes. You should just let me suffer in peace."

Laura snickered.

"I assume that, because your sister is here today, she already accepts you as you are?" When Laura nodded, Dr. Greene continued. "Does that make you feel better about reuniting with your parents?"

"Yes, but I'm still nervous."

"It would shock me if you weren't." Dr. Greene crossed her legs at the ankles and leaned forward. "Remember, the goal here is not to convince anyone that you're worthy of love and acceptance. That's a fact. The goal is to be your authentic self and see how your parents react."

Cassie felt tears forming in her eyes. She couldn't look at Laura. "And if they reject me?"

"Then it'll simply be another obstacle to overcome. It won't be easy, and I can't promise it'll be painless, but it is possible." She held up a finger. "And remember, expending energy on the unknown will not change the outcome, no matter how much you wish it would. For now, it's important to put your best foot forward. After that, we can work through the outcome together."

Cassie nodded and blinked away her tears. When she looked over at Laura, she saw her sister had started crying somewhere along the way.

"Have you still been having nightmares about your family?" Dr. Greene asked.

"Yeah. They're getting a little better, though. I can control the car more now than I used to."

"Oh, the dream where I'm a little girl?" Laura looked between Dr. Greene and Cassie. "The one tied to Sarah Lennox?"

Dr. Greene looked to Cassie. "Sarah Lennox?"

"Yeah, that's something else I wanted to talk about. I brought up the dream while Laura and I were out to lunch with our friend Michael." The memory still made Cassie blush. "Turns out, I don't remember as much about that time as Laura does."

"Oh?" Dr. Greene looked interested now. She adjusted her glasses to hide her excitement; but Cassie had known her long enough. "What sort of memories are missing?"

Cassie hesitated. How could she possibly talk about Sarah Lennox's disappearance without crossing into forbidden territory? Which would be worse, saying *I used to talk to ghosts*, or *I still talk to ghosts*?

"I brought up the fact that Cassie used to talk about Sarah like she was still there, even after she'd disappeared." Laura's voice was measured, as if she were trying to avoid upsetting Cassie a second time. "It's the reason we stopped talking to the Lennoxes."

Cassie startled. "Wait. What? You never said that."

Laura gave her a sad smile. "You did kind of run off on me."

Cassie's blush deepened. "Not my finest moment."

"Why did you run away?" Dr. Greene asked.

"Embarrassment." Cassie looked up at the ceiling. She wouldn't lie about her feelings, but she didn't have to look her therapist in the eye while she talked about them, either. "It scared me I didn't remember something I should've."

"It's completely normal for people to remove difficult or traumatic memories. You know that," Dr. Greene said.

"I do," Cassie replied.

"But it still bothered you?" Dr. Greene asked.

"One of those easier-said-than-done moments." Cassie turned to Laura. "Am I really the reason we stopped talking to them?"

"I wouldn't say it was your fault." Laura's voice was gentle, but Cassie could read between the lines. "I think you just upset them during a tough time. Mom didn't like how Mrs. Lennox talked to you. I think the falling out was between the parents more than anything. Then they moved away about a year later. There wasn't any time for reconciliation."

"What happened? What did I say?" Cassie asked.

"I only remember bits and pieces. After Sarah left, we went over to their house. I was excited because we didn't get to go over that often, but I also knew Sarah was gone. Mom had tried to explain it to me. That she was missing, and her mom and dad didn't know where she was. She told me not to talk about Sarah unless Mrs. Lennox talked about her first."

"I'm guessing I didn't get the same memo?"

Laura shrugged. "If you did, you ignored it. Mom took us over there to eat with Mr. and Mrs. Lennox, and Sarah's sister, Jessica. I think that was her name. We had mom's lasagna."

"How do you remember that?" Cassie asked.

"Mom never made lasagna. We had it, like, once every couple years at most. It was my favorite. I was excited to eat it. But then I remember being disappointed because I only got to have a couple of bites before we had to leave."

"God, what did I say?"

"You started talking about Sarah right away. It upset me because Mom told me I couldn't talk about her, but apparently you could. I missed her, too, and I wanted to know what happened to her. You know, it wasn't until later that I realized what had happened to her. That she went missing. Michael and I looked it up after you left the other day. They arrested someone for kidnapping one of the kids who'd gone missing. They found evidence he'd been in contact with other kids, including Sarah, but they couldn't prove he was the one who took them. And they didn't know what he'd done with them."

"So he got away with it?"

"They gave him fifty years for the case they could prove, but their hands were tied for the rest without stronger evidence. I guess their line of thinking was that at least he was off the streets. They always thought he had a partner, but they never found out who. The guy refused to talk, and none of the other families got justice."

"That's horrible."

"What happened at the dinner, Laura?" Dr. Greene asked. "Do you remember?"

"Mrs. Lennox must've said something about missing her or not seeing her for so long because Cassie kept saying she saw her the day before in our backyard." Laura turned to Cassie. "You kept saying, 'Tell them, Laura. Tell them she was in our backyard yesterday.'"

"But you never saw her." Dr. Greene confirmed.

Laura shook her head. "Mrs. Lennox got so upset. She kept asking Mom if she knew where Sarah was, and Mom kept insisting that she didn't. Mrs. Lennox kicked us out, and then I remember the cops coming by later that night to talk to you."

"So, Mrs. Lennox sent them over," Dr. Greene said.

"That's my guess," Laura replied.

"Do you remember anything else from that night?" Dr. Greene asked.

"Not really. I was only five years old. Some parts stick out more than others."

"Do you plan on talking to your parents about this?" Dr. Greene asked. "About your missing memories?"

Cassie would rather bury the memories as deep as they could go, but that would be a disservice to Sarah. Not to mention the little boy who was somehow connected to the case. He'd waited so long to reach out to her. She couldn't turn back now.

"Yeah." Cassie's voice wasn't as confident as she would've liked. "Yeah, I think I will."

27

After the sisters got back into Cassie's car, Laura was the first to break a beat of silence.

"Well, that was kind of intense."

"Yeah." Cassie's voice sounded muffled even to her own ears, and her head was still light from the appointment. She focused first on her toes, then her legs, then her arms, and finally her head. She felt clear again.

"You okay?" Laura stretched her seat belt across her chest.

"I'll be better with some pizza in my stomach."

"Sold." Laura fist-pumped. "Want to go to Vinnie Van GoGo's?"

"If you're asking me if I want to eat several slices of pizza the size of my face, the answer is yes."

Cassie drove to the restaurant. Laura grabbed a table on the patio while Cassie ordered at the counter. Her mouth was already watering. Seeing slices so big they hung off the serving platter did not help tame her hunger.

A petite teenager with her hair in pigtails picked up a notepad. "What can I get ya?"

"Half pepperoni and spicy Italian sausage. Half mushroom and olive. Two Cokes."

"Got it. You out on the patio?"

"Yes, ma'am."

"I'll have it out for you in about ten minutes.

"Excellent."

Cassie felt someone walk up behind her but did not hear them. "That's quite the combination."

A pleasant shiver ran down Cassie's spine. Just his voice was enough to affect her. That, along with the hint of his cologne. She turned and confirmed her fear. Jason stood there with a smile on his face. Her pulse quickened. "Yeah, my sister and I couldn't decide what would be best."

"Oh, is your sister in town? That's nice." He kept smiling, but he looked sad. "I'm hoping that's the only reason you didn't text back." An awkward silence ensued. He quickly followed up with, "And the pizza here is so good, it stands on its own with just cheese. Anything else is just a bonus."

It took Cassie a few seconds to realize what he was talking about, and then the late-night text came flooding back. She gasped and slapped a hand over her mouth. "Oh my God, I'm so sorry. I completely forgot. I've had a lot going on."

"It's okay." He rubbed the back of his neck. "Honestly, I regretted it as soon as I sent it."

"No, no, it was really sweet."

"Sweet..." His hand caught at the crown of his head.

The woman at the counter interrupted them. "Can I get you something, sir?"

"Ah, large pepperoni, please. To go."

Cassie stepped off to the side. She waited until he finished ordering before she put a hand on his arm. "I'm really, really sorry I didn't respond. This isn't at all how I wanted it to go."

"And how did you want it to go?" Jason's voice was gentle, but an apprehension in it made her heart ache. "Because I have to be honest, I'm getting mixed signals from you."

"I know. You are. And that's completely my fault." Of course, as soon as she talked candidly with Jason, she couldn't find the words. "I really like you. A lot."

There, that was a start, right?

"But?"

"But I have a lot going on at the moment." Cassie's stomach twisted. That didn't sound right either. "I'm having a little trouble balancing everything. I have some things I need to figure out with my family and another case I'm working on the with the Savannah PD."

"Another case?" Was he annoyed? Surprised?

"Yeah, this guy was murdered, and it turned out that he was a serial killer from, like, twenty years ago. And now we have to figure out who killed *him.* David and I just found the last of his victims yesterday." Cassie saw a train of thought take seed in Jason's mind and rushed on. "My older, very married, totally platonic friend David. By the way. In case you were wondering." She smacked her forehead with the base of her palm.

Jason smiled and looked away. "I was wondering."

Cassie shook the embarrassment away. "The point is, there's a million things going on in my mind at once these days. I'm working through a lot of stuff. And I don't want to burden you with that."

"It wouldn't be a burden, Cassie." He took a step closer. "I like you too, but I feel like there's this whole other part of you I don't know yet. And I want to. I really do. But you gotta let me in. A little, at least."

It was a few seconds before Cassie remembered to breathe again. "I'd like that, too."

Jason took a step back, and the spell was broken. "I understand if you don't trust me yet—"

"I do trust you." She rushed to answer and regretted it. "Kind of. I mean, it's not that I don't trust you. It's just... it's a lot. There's a lot going on." She rambled now. "A lot going on at all times. I'm a hot mess. In case you didn't notice."

"Oh, I noticed." He laughed, and the deep baritone of his voice made several women and a couple men turn to stare. "But it doesn't bother me."

"It bothers me." That was maybe the most honest thing she'd said to him so far. "I just want to get it under control before I start seeing someone. Before I bring someone into my orbit. My life can get crazy sometimes."

Jason stared at her for a moment, and she couldn't read his expression. After what felt like an eternity, he shrugged. "It won't work."

"What?"

"It won't work."

"No, I heard what you said. And I'm afraid of what you might mean."

"I mean—does anyone have their life under control? I know I don't. If I waited to be in control of everything, I'd never go on another date again. Hell, I'd never leave my house. You can't anticipate what life is going to throw at you. You have to work with what you've got."

Cassie bit her lip. He wasn't wrong, but her life was a little crazier than most.

Jason took her hand in his. "All I'm saying is that I really like you, Cassie, and I'd like to get to know you better. I think you feel the same way, but something is holding you back." The look in his eyes told her she wouldn't like this next part. "But I can't wait forever. That wouldn't be fair to myself."

"No, it wouldn't." She tried to swallow, but the lump in her throat stopped it. "I wouldn't want to do that to you anyway."

Cassie glimpsed red curls out of the corner of her eye. When Laura walked up to Cassie, Jason dropped her hand.

"I was wondering what was holding you up." Laura said with a curious tone. Her smile beamed.

"Oh, Laura, this is Jason from work. Jason, this is my sister Laura."

The heat from his hand lingered for a few seconds, but then it was gone. "We ran into each other."

"Oh, *the* Jason? The hottie from work?" Laura's smile showed all her teeth. "My sister is chaos walking, but I guarantee you'll never be bored with her around."

Jason laughed. "It's not me you have to convince, it's her."

Laura looked surprised, but Cassie pushed her back toward their table outside. "It was really, really great seeing you, Jason. I promise I'll text you back. And I'll see you at work next week, okay?"

"Okay." His smile was sad as he waved goodbye.

"But our pizza." Laura tried to dig her heels in.

Cassie gritted her teeth and pushed harder. "They're bringing it out to us."

Once they sat down, Laura put her chin in her hands and stared at Cassie. "You undersold him in the looks department. That smile? What I wouldn't do—"

"Hands off." Cassie snatched her Coke off the table and took a sip. It must've been delivered while she was talking to Jason.

"My hands are *so* off." Laura crossed her arms. "But yours seem to be, too. What gives? He's obviously into you."

"I've got a lot going on—"

Laura waved her off. "No excuses. Only real answers."

Cassie huffed and set her drink down. After she made sure Jason wasn't within earshot, she leaned in. "He knows nothing about me. Nothing about the attack. Very little about how I help the police. Then again, I guess I spilled the beans on that one. I was kind of nervous."

"What? You think he won't like you because something out of your control happened to you?" Laura leaned in until they were nose to nose. "Is he secretly a terrible person?"

"No. Of course not. He's sweet and gentle and understanding, and one time he helped me through a panic attack."

"So, what you're telling me is that he's wonderful and there's no reason he would reject you or make you feel bad for your experiences."

"Are you and Dr. Greene in cahoots?"

"No, we're observant. And honest." Laura scrunched up her face. "Do people even say cahoots anymore?"

"Lots of people say cahoots, Laura."

"No, only you, Cass." She held up her hands. "Okay. Okay. I think you're *hangry*. This pizza needs to get here ASAP."

Cassie didn't argue. She remained lost in thought until their giant pie arrived. As the server promised to get them a couple of refills, Cassie noticed Jason leaving with his own pizza in hand. She couldn't help but wonder if it was just for him or not. He'd been clear about how much he liked her, but he'd also been clear he wouldn't wait forever.

She took a bite of her mushroom and olive pizza but found it didn't solve any of her problems.

28

As soon as Cassie and Laura walked through the door and into David's chilly meeting room, he threw his arms out wide and shouted, "Congratulations!"

Cassie hesitated before letting the door shut behind them. "For what?"

"Shapiro's case has officially been closed. Well, unofficially officially. There's still a lot of paperwork and wrapping up of loose ends, but we have everything we need, including his last victims."

Cassie was glad, but her heart wasn't in it. "That's great."

"Where's the enthusiasm? We just solved a twenty-plus-year-old cold case on a serial killer."

"Big lunch." Cassie caught the way Laura glanced at her and hoped David didn't notice. "I don't have room for enthusiasm."

"What about you, Laura? Will you be excited with me? It's a damn good day."

"I could make room for some enthusiasm, yeah." Laura held up her hand and David high-fived it. "Not to rain on our own parade here, but explain to me again how we're sure there are no more missing victims?"

David made a face. "You guys are a load of fun today. To be honest, we don't know that for sure. Paulson is still searching our records for any bodies that may have turned up with similar injuries that might not have been previously connected to the cold case, but he hasn't found anything yet. We're going to do another thorough search of Shapiro's house and related properties, but I doubt we'll find anything."

"Why's that?" Laura asked.

David glanced at Cassie, and now she was hoping Laura didn't catch the exchange between them. "You know, just a hunch. I assume he'd keep all his tokens—the letters—together in one place, but there's no way to tell for sure unless we find more or come up with another body. For now, however, this case has been laid to rest."

"Good riddance," Laura said.

David clapped his hands together. "Which means we can finally focus on the problem at hand. Solving Shapiro's murder."

"Do we have to?" Cassie was joking—mostly. Going home and taking a nap sounded better by the second. "He was a terrible person."

"According to the law, yes, we have to," David responded.

"Fine."

David gestured to the table in front of them, which had once again been transformed. "Please meet Shapiro's twelve victims. They're in no particular order. I've collated all the information we have on every single one of them, including a photograph, their records, and other miscellaneous information."

"Including family members?" Cassie asked.

"Especially family members."

Cassie and Laura circled the table until they stood next to David. Laura leaned in closer. "How sure are we that the most likely person to have killed Shapiro is a family member of one of his victims?"

"Not sure at all." David shrugged after Laura shot him a confused look. "Right now, a family member is our best first guess. They have proper motivation, so now it's just about finding those who would have had knowledge, skill, and opportunity."

"So, we start here. And if this doesn't work out?"

"We keep looking." David sighed. "I hope it doesn't come to that because I hate starting back at square one, but we have some options. Maybe he tried to take an apprentice under his wing and that person got pissed. Or he took a new lover who found out about his past and killed him. Could be an amateur sleuth stumbled upon the case, and instead of making a podcast out of it, they took matters into their own hands. Perhaps—"

Laura held up her hands. "I get it. I get it. There are lots of possibilities. Let's just start with this one."

David smiled over at Cassie. "She really is a quick learner."

Cassie was only half paying attention to the banter. Either her eyes were going bad, or her Spidey senses were tingling. She took a step closer to the table and leaned over the pictures of the twelve victims but couldn't even read the name of the first because it looked like someone had blurred it out. She tried blinking her eyes to clear it, but nothing worked. And when she looked at the victim's face, it looked as though someone had scratched it away with the tip of a knife.

As Cassie made her way down the line, she found most of the victims appeared this way. So against her better judgement, she gathered those files together and set them to the side before her vision cleared and she couldn't remember which had appeared normal and which had been blurred out.

"What are you doing?" Laura asked.

Cassie pointed to the four remaining files. "I think we should look into these first."

David pulled those four close and started flipping through the first one. "Sounds good to me."

"What do you mean that sounds good?" Laura looked from Cassie to David and then back again. "You just decided that at random."

"Not random. Just our own kind of system."

Laura looked like she didn't want to be rude, but Cassie could tell she wouldn't drop the subject. "How does this system work, exactly? You close your eyes and point?"

"No, my eyes were open."

"This is just sort of how we operate." David was trying to sound nonchalant, but he clearly wasn't reading through the papers in front of him. "Cassie has a trained eye for these things. She gives us a starting point, and we narrow it down from there. Usually works."

"But she didn't even look through the files." Laura walked over to the pile Cassie had dismissed and grabbed the first one. "Look, this guy has two brothers who were both in jail for aggravated assault. They were each released within the last year. That's someone we should look into."

David glanced at Cassie but didn't offer a defense.

Cassie turned away, hoping Laura would take a hint and end the conversation. "We can look into them after we look into those four."

Laura's face reddened. "You know that makes no conceivable sense."

Cassie ignored her and looked over David's shoulder. She was at war with trying to be inconspicuous in front of her sister and trying to just solve this case already. Still exhausted from yesterday, her encounter with Jason had upset her more than she'd realized. All she wanted to do was go home, curl up with Apollo, and sleep for the next twenty-four hours.

But any chance at not being obvious went out the window when she noticed the next file David flipped through.

"That's him."

David glanced up at her, then back down at the photo in his hands. "The guy from yesterday?"

"Definitely." Cassie leaned in closer. He looked younger in the photograph, but she recognized his sad eyes from when he'd first visited her in her dining room. "We should look into him first."

Laura walked over. "What guy from yesterday?"

"One of the bodies we found."

David had messed up the second the words left his mouth.

Laura crossed her arms and did another excellent impression of their mother. "You mean one of the twenty-year-old dead bodies from yesterday? The completely decayed bodies? The bodies you couldn't possibly visually identify?"

"Yes?" David looked to Cassie for help, but all she could do was rub her temples.

Laura's anger turned to hurt. "If there's something you don't want to tell me or something I'm not supposed to know, I can leave. I just thought you wanted my help. I can—"

"No, no, we do want your help." Cassie sighed. "I know it's weird, but trust me, okay? I have a feeling about this."

"A feeling?" Her voice sounded even more skeptical than the look on her face. "Really? These are people's lives. If your feeling tells you to go after the wrong person, who knows what kind of damage you could do. If you decide to ignore a literal pile of potential suspects, the killer could end up getting away. I thought you were joking, but did you really mean you don't care about solving this case?"

"I care. I—"

"You're not acting like it." Anger resurfaced. "What you're doing is extremely irresponsible."

"Laura, please—"

"Cassie." David's voice was dead serious, and both sisters looked over at him in concern. "This guy has no living relatives."

Cassie forgot about the fight with her sister. "That's not right. I saw him. He was there from the beginning."

"I know, but you can check for yourself. He never married. Never had kids. Spent most of his life in and out of jail, to be honest."

"Could there be someone we don't have a record of? Anyone?"

"I suppose it's possible. Biologically, he could've had kids and not been part of their lives. But then that leaves you wondering—"

"Why one of his kids would avenge his death by killing Shapiro."

"Exactly."

Laura threw her hands in the air. "Will someone, for the love of everything good and holy in this universe, tell me what's going on? What do you mean you saw him? We're talking about the same guy, right? The dead one?"

Before Cassie could respond, Laura jabbed a finger in her direction.

"The next words out of your mouth better be a direct and truthful answer to my question, Cassie, or so help me God."

29

THE AIR IN THE MEETING ROOM WAS HEAVY AND SUFFOCATING. THE chill they had encountered upon entering was now uncomfortable, humid, and hot.

Cassie and David exchanged a look.

Laura's voice had a growl to it. "Don't do that."

David looked away first. "Don't do what?"

"That." She waved her hand at the two of them. "Whatever that is."

Cassie was sure laughing would be the wrong response in this moment, but she was having a hard time holding it back. She mimicked her sister's gestures. "I have no idea what that means."

"You guys talk to each other. Silently. I'm not stupid, you know. I'm a psychologist. I'm trained to watch body language. I can tell when someone is lying. I can tell when someone is keeping something from me. I wasn't going to say anything because you're my sister, and I want you to trust me on your own terms and not mine, but I'm really confused. Screw that. I'm beyond confused." There were tears in her eyes now, and Cassie could tell she was seconds away from a meltdown. "This trip has been really weird. And you've been really weird. And I'm trying to do the best I can to be a good sister, but I feel like nothing I do is enough. Nothing I do will get you to open up to me."

Cassie's eyes started to water now. "What? No. Come on. You're the best sister I could ask for."

"Then why won't you tell me what you're hiding from me? Is it bad? Are you afraid I won't be okay with it?"

Cassie felt a lump rise in her throat, and she had to work to keep her voice even. "Yeah. That's exactly it. I don't want you to think of me any differently."

"Why would I think of you any differently? You're my sister." She sniffled. "I just don't get it. You're always on edge. And, like, I get it, you've been through a lot of shit. But you talk about it like that's not a big deal. Like it doesn't affect you that much anymore. And when it does, you tell me. So, it must not be that."

"Laura—"

"You freaked out at breakfast the other day. During therapy, it sounded like you were holding something back. And now, with this? How could you just know those things? You're smarter than that. You're not that cavalier, so there's something else going on." Laura was pacing now. "Then again, you've always been that way. Always known when something was off. Always known things you shouldn't have known. I just thought you were a nosy older sister when we were growing up. But this? This is weird. This is—"

She froze.

"Laura?" Cassie took a step forward. "Are you okay?"

"You said you saw him." She pointed to the file that David was still holding in his hands. "You said you saw him from the beginning. What did you mean by that?"

Cassie's voice faltered, and she looked to David, who just shrugged.

"You might as well tell her. She's three-quarters of the way there already anyway."

Cassie scowled at him. When she turned back to Laura, her sister had the strangest mixture of expressions on her face. It was anger and hurt and expectancy and incredulity all rolled into one. "When I said I saw him," Cassie said, swallowing audibly, "I meant I *saw* him. In my dining room. That day that I dropped the coffee mug. That's why I dropped it."

"You saw him in your dining room?" Laura looked at David, who nodded, and then returned her gaze to Cassie. "You saw the *dead* man in your dining room."

"Yes."

"Was he hanging out eating toast? A bowl of cheerios? Smoking a joint?"

"Not exactly." Cassie pulled out a chair and sat down. She waited for Laura to do the same before she continued. "He was just standing there. I saw his injuries, and that's why I called David right before we left to go to The Pirates' House. I know you heard me on the phone."

"I couldn't hear what you were saying, though." Laura flushed. "It was muffled through the door."

"I told David what I saw, and he told me they'd just found a body that matched the man's injuries. But it turns out that the body was Robert Shapiro, and the guy I saw was—"

"Timothy Jennings," finished David.

Laura stared at Cassie for a full minute. Anger gave way to misty eyes. "You're not joking, are you?"

"I'm not."

Laura looked to David.

"She's not."

"You're not." Laura got up and started pacing again. "Okay. So, what are you trying to tell me?"

For all the worry Cassie had indulged in over the last few days regarding her sister accidentally finding out about her abilities, she had spent little time planning what she'd say to Laura if it ended up happening.

"What I'm trying to tell you is that I...have I guess you'd say psychic tendencies."

"Tendencies?" Laura questioned.

"She's being modest." David interjected.

Cassie glared at him. "Comments from the peanut gallery are unacceptable at this time."

"Noted." He leaned back against the wall and crossed his arms, content to observe once again.

Cassie turned back to Laura. "I can see dead people." She held up a hand. "And I swear to God if anyone makes a *Sixth Sense* reference, I'm going to blow a gasket."

David snickered. "As long as you know I'm thinking it, that's good enough for me."

Laura rolled her eyes. "And you know about this, David?"

He sobered slightly. "I do."

"For how long?"

"Ten years? Yeah, ten years sounds right."

"Ten years?" Laura blanched, and then Cassie saw the gears turning. "You mean—"

"Yes. Well, kind of." Cassie sighed. "Look, can you sit down? You're making me nervous."

"*You're* nervous?" Laura laughed, but she sat down anyway. "What does this even mean?"

"It means that I can see ghosts. Not all the time. Not all ghosts. I don't know how it works, just that it does. I also get feelings. See visions. Have dreams."

"Dreams?" Laura perked up. "You mean like the nightmare you've been having?"

"Yeah, like that. Which brings me back to your other questions. And David? Strap in for this one. I used to think that whatever happened to me with Novak, almost dying on that night, gave me this ability to see through the veil, or whatever you want to call it. But now I'm not so sure."

"Oh?" David paid closer attention now. "Did some new information come to light?"

Cassie rolled her eyes. "David has a lot of theories about how this works and why it happens."

David rolled his eyes. "She hates my theories."

"I don't see a point in your theories. There's a difference." Cassie waved him off. "But what I'm getting at is, Laura remembers me being weird when we were kids. Talking to people who weren't there. Having feelings. Being intuitive. That makes me think this didn't originate on that night with Novak."

"So, what does it mean?" Laura asked.

"I have no freaking clue. Maybe this is just who I am. And who I've always been." She turned to David. "There was this little girl I was friends with when I was a kid. Sarah Lennox. She went missing. I think I used to talk to her ghost."

"You think?" David asked.

"That's the thing. I don't remember." She gestured to Laura. "She does. Those memories are gone for me."

"Any idea why?"

Laura shrugged. "Could be trauma. If she saw something she wanted to forget, she could've repressed the memories."

"What about her abilities?"

When Cassie turned to Laura, too, she laughed. "Why are you looking at me? I'm a psychologist. Not an expert on psychics."

"No, but do you think psychic abilities could work the same way?" Cassie asked. "Repress memories long enough, and they're completely forgotten. Repress psychic abilities long enough, and they lay dormant?"

"I mean, I guess. It sounds logical. But I have no idea if that's how it works. I doubt anyone does with any kind of certainty."

Cassie let the room fill with silence. "So, you believe me, then?"

"That's a hard question to answer."

Cassie's face flushed. This is what she worried about. Being rejected. Laughed at. Being institutionalized. Being—

"Do I believe you? Yes." Laura smiled when Cassie looked surprised. "You're my sister. I know you. You're not crazy, and you have no reason to lie to me. Do I believe in psychics and mediums and all that? No. Or at least I didn't. But I believe in you, so that kind of changes things, doesn't it?"

"If it helps," David chimed in, "I've been working with Cassie for a long time. I didn't believe in psychics either. I still don't. At least most of the ones who claim to be. But Cassie, whatever she is, she's the real deal. She's solved more cases than I can even remember off the top of my head. She's got an excellent reputation around here."

"Really?" Laura looked proud now. "That's awesome."

Cassie blushed. "I couldn't ignore it if I tried. And trust me. I've tried."

"So, this was the thing? The thing you were hiding from me?"

"Yeah, this was it. What, you want more? I'm not sure there's something bigger than *my sister, the ghost magnet.*"

"That's a good title for a television show."

"Let's not go there."

Laura leaned over and hugged Cassie, who returned the gesture with as much love as she could muster. "I'm sorry you felt like you couldn't tell me."

"You're a psychologist. You'd be entitled to think I was a little crazy."

Laura sat back in her chair with wide eyes. "Oh God, are you going to tell Mom and Dad?"

The thought had occurred to her. "Can we jump that hurdle when we get to it? For now, I just want to bask in the glow of finally getting that off my chest. I feel a hundred pounds lighter."

And she did. Cassie knew, without a doubt, that her troubles were far from over. Maybe they were just beginning. But just like Laura knew Cassie, Cassie knew Laura, too. Her sister would tell her if she was worried about her. It would be a learning curve for the sisters, and a million questions were bound to come.

Cassie caught the smile on David's face. Not for the first time, she was grateful to have him in her life. She was thankful he'd been there when she'd had the discussion with Laura. He was a good cop, but an even better friend.

30

LAURA'S SMILE WAS TOO WIDE. TOO BRIGHT. "SO, HOW ACCURATE ARE these feelings of yours?"

Cassie felt so relieved at being able to talk openly with her sister that she couldn't help the laugh that bubbled out of her. Her entire body felt lighter. "They're not just feelings, you know. I see people."

"Okay, I get that. And that's both creepy and cool, but it's a valid question, right?" She looked to David and then back at Cassie. "Have any of your visions been wrong before?"

"None of them have been wrong, per se. But I have misinterpreted them."

"So, the answer is yes?"

"The answer is kind of."

Laura rolled her eyes and gestured to the four folders David was still holding. "I'm asking how sure you are that our killer is related to one of these four victims."

"Well, that's the trouble. Sometimes I get answers before I get the questions themselves." Cassie sat down, now suddenly sober. They still had a lot of work ahead of them. "When I looked at the pictures, eight of them had their names blurred out and their faces scratched away. I don't think we're meant to look into them further."

David held up the other four. "And these appeared normal?"

"Right. Our mystery ghost seems significant, but I don't know why. What did you say his name was?"

"Timothy Jennings."

"Timothy Jennings." The name seemed foreign in Cassie's mouth, despite her feeling like she knew the man. At least in his life after death. "What do we know about him?"

"He has no living relatives."

"He was one of the final five victims," Laura suggested.

"There you go." Cassie felt a thrill run through her. "We wanted to know why Shapiro stopped killing, right? Maybe Jennings was his last victim. That could have given him more power to come to me."

"That would make sense," David said.

"Does it?" Laura asked. "Does anything make sense when it comes to all of this?"

"Not really," David offered. "I've learned to just go with it. But it seems plausible, which is a step in the right direction. Jennings is significant in some way. Maybe he was simply our key to finding the final bodies, or maybe he was Shapiro's last kill. It says here he'd been arrested quite a few times for possession with an intent to distribute. That means he was a dealer."

"Definitely someone Shapiro would want to take off the streets," Cassie said.

"Oh, what if he was the original addict's dealer?" When they met Laura's idea with blank stares, she hurried on. "I mean, what if he was the dealer who sold the heroin to the guy who killed Shapiro's wife? And Shapiro tracked him down? He couldn't kill the guy who killed Mrs. Shapiro, but Jennings would've only been one degree separated, right? Maybe he even supplied the guy with his heroin that night."

"It's a good theory." David scribbled some information on a notepad. "I doubt we'll find any evidence, but theories are good. Theories are where we get our start."

"What's our theory for these other three, then?" Cassie asked. Her frustration mounted. "They must be significant. One of them must be the answer to our question."

David gave both Laura and Cassie a folder to look through. "Only one way to find out."

Cassie looked down at the picture in her hands and traced the contours of his face with her fingertip. She vaguely remembered the face from the second group of victims—the ones discovered in the woods. His name was Joseph Warren. He'd done a stint in Coastal State Prison right around 1992 for possession. He'd gotten out early on good behavior.

She skipped to the information on his family. He didn't have any children of his own, but he had a nephew who'd done time for aggravated assault. He also had a deceased sister, which meant Warren might've been the one to raise his nephew. If that were the case, the nephew would've had motivation enough to avenge his uncle. And he certainly had the disposition.

"I've got a contender," Cassie said.

David looked up. "Yeah? Good. Because I've got bupkis."

Laura closed her folder and dropped it on the table, sending a nearby photo skittering to the other side. "And I honestly don't know what I'm looking for, but it doesn't seem to be here."

Cassie handed David the folder. "He's got a living nephew, Marcus Valencia, who he might've raised and who has done time for aggravated assault."

"That sounds promising." David flipped open the folder and started perusing it.

"Promising, but enough for a warrant?" Laura asked.

David didn't look up. "We don't need a warrant to talk to him. It'll be up to him whether he wants to do it at his place or ours."

There was a gentle knock on the door. When it opened, Harris stuck her head through the opening. "Hey, I heard my favorite ghost herder was in today, so I just wanted to drop by. See if I could get my fortune told."

"You're hilarious. Really, you and David should open a comedy club. You could name it Tom, Dick, and Harris. You've gotta know someone named Tom, right?"

"Oh, yeah, Tom in accounting." Harris snapped her fingers. "But he died. Think you could talk him into joining us, anyway?"

Laura threw up her hands. "Did everyone know but me?"

Cassie threw her head back and laughed. "Detective Harris, this is my sister Laura. She just found out my deepest, darkest secret about —" Cassie checked her imaginary watch "—ten minutes ago."

"Jesus. Good thing I took a bathroom break on my way here then. How'd she take it?"

"Better than you," Cassie said. "But it was a very brief overview."

David checked his real watch. "How busy are you?"

Harris waved him off. "It's just paperwork. Who needs to do paperwork? What can I do for you?"

"How do you feel about babysitting?"

"Do I have to take them both?" Harris eyed the sisters, and then pointed at Laura. "I'll take her, but I don't want the troublemaker."

Cassie scowled. "Who are you calling a troublemaker?"

"You. Clearly. That was a distinct jab at you, Cassie. I couldn't have been any more obvious." Harris turned to Laura. "This one got me into a shootout a month or two ago."

"A what?" Laura turned white and began wrenching her index finger with her opposite hand. "Are you serious?"

Cassie slapped a hand against her forehead. "Ten minutes ago, Harris. Ten minutes. We have to ease her into this."

"Cassie, you mentioned ghosts. You didn't mention bullets."

David held up his hands. "Cassie and I are gonna go pay a visit to our new suspect. I'd love it if you made the less troublesome Ms. Quinn comfortable. She's a psychologist, so maybe pick her brain."

Cassie scowled at him, too. "Do I have a target on my back or something?" She turned to Harris. "Will you put in a good word for me? Tell her I'm brave and heroic."

"Buy me dinner, and it's a deal." She turned serious. "Wait, does she have superpowers, too? Can she levitate? Freeze time? Throw people across the room with just her mind?"

Laura scoffed. "I wish." She looked at everyone in turn. "But seriously, was I the only one not in the loop? If I didn't know better, I'd say it was a conspiracy."

"Please, don't say the c-word around here." David stood. "It makes people nervous."

"He's not wrong." Harris opened the door and let Laura walk through first. "C'mon, Quinn. We'll swap stories about Cassie. I want to know all the embarrassing ones."

"Not funny." Cassie shouted, but the door was already swinging shut.

31

"You know the drill." David leaned back in his seat, eyes squinted, scanning the area.

Cassie followed his gaze. They were looking in the same direction, but for vastly different things. "Let you do the talking. If I see anything spooky, make sure I tell you about it."

David paused as he unbuckled his seatbelt. "I never said the word spooky."

Cassie licked her lips and tried to shake some of the nerves out of her arms. "Well, that's the general idea, right?"

"I guess." He grunted as he opened the door and got out of the sedan. "But I think we can come up with something better than *spooky*."

"Ominous? Macabre? Lurid?"

"Exsanguinous?" David looked proud of himself.

"You've been doing your crosswords. Ghosts do sometimes have blood, though."

"Let's stick with macabre, then."

"You got it, boss."

Cassie followed him up the front steps of a tiny beige house with no more than four or five rooms. It had a small backyard cordoned off with a wooden fence. Some pickets were made of different types of wood, like they'd been broken and replaced over the years without too much care. She dragged her fingertips across the brick façade surrounding a support post for the patio roof. It was rough, like sandpaper, but crumbled under her delicate touch.

David knocked on the door, and there was a shout from the back. About thirty seconds later, a man Cassie's age answered. He wore a black Slipknot t-shirt. Their music was too hard for her, but she once found their costumes entertaining. No longer. Too close to the things she saw. The guy had one earbud in and a scowl on his face. She could hear the music pumping out of the earbud.

"Who are you?" he asked.

"Detective David Klein. I'm with the—"

Before David could finish, Marcus Valencia took off running through his living room and out the backdoor. David didn't hesitate, and neither did Cassie. She was right on David's heels as he sprinted through the house and across the backyard. Marcus tried to launch himself over the picket fence, but David was too close. He grabbed the man's ankles and yanked him to the ground.

Barking erupted from the other end of the yard, and a massive German Shepherd emerged from a doghouse a size too small. He wore a chain around his neck, but Cassie couldn't tell how long a leash it was. She heard Marcus yelling, and the dog ran straight for them.

Cassie didn't think. She just moved. She was close enough that when she jumped in between the Shepherd and David, the dog had no choice but to either crash into her or come to a complete stop. Luckily for her, he chose the latter.

She stood as tall as she could and squared up her shoulders. She stared deep into his eyes until she had his absolute attention. The barest tingle of connection tickled the back of her neck. "Sit."

The dog looked confused, like he wasn't sure why this crazy lady was telling him what to do. He looked to Marcus, but Cassie drew his attention back to her.

"I said sit." The dog bent his legs, but his butt still hovered above the ground. Cassie lowered her voice. "All the way. Sit."

The Shepherd obeyed. Then he cocked his head to one side.

Cassie changed the pitch of her voice. "Good boy! You're such a good boy." She moved forward and stuck her hand out so he could smell it. When he gave a tentative lick, she used that as her cue to give him all her love. "You're so good. What's your name?"

She looked over at Marcus and David, who had identical expressions of shock on to their faces. She made eye contact with their suspect.

"Uh, Bear?" Marcus said.

"Bear." She turned her attention back to the dog and scratched behind his ears. "You're such a big fluffy teddy bear, aren't you?"

"What the hell?" Marcus said. "You broke my dog!"

"Gave him some discipline." She let Bear lick her face. "Then let him feel some love."

"Cassie, what were you thinking?" David sounded scared and astonished at the same time. "He could've torn you to shreds."

"No way. Dogs love me. Never been bit. Not even once. It's like we have a connection."

"You still shouldn't have done that." David turned back to Marcus. "And you're under arrest."

"For what? I didn't do nothin'."

"You know, they always say that." David handcuffed him and sat him up against the fence. "If you didn't do anything, then why'd you run?"

"I ain't like no pigs."

"Clever. No matter, we seem to like you. We kept you real close after that aggravated assault charge."

"I did my time for that. You can't come here harassin' me. I'll sue you."

"I'd like to see you try. Funny thing about aggravated assault is that it's not a big jump to murder. So, do you want to make this easy on me and confess?"

Marcus had been paying more attention to Cassie and his dog than David, but when he heard the word *murder*, his head snapped up. "What the hell you talkin' about? I didn't kill anyone."

"Then why'd you run?"

"I got weed on me, man. Check my pockets. But I swear to God I didn't kill anyone."

"Okay, okay. Calm down." David searched one pocket, then the other. He pulled out a couple of joints. "Well, that part's true at least."

"All of it's true." Marcus hung his head. "I don't want to go back to jail. Please. I'm sorry. You can keep it. I won't tell anyone, I swear. I'll get clean. I promise. This is my last day of smoking."

Cassie patted Bear's head one last time and stood up. "Oh, yeah, he sounds like a hardened criminal, doesn't he?"

"Some people are good liars," David said.

Marcus had tears in his eyes now. "Who do you think I killed? I swear, I don't know them."

"All right, all right, relax." David wiped the back of his neck. "Answer some questions, and if I'm satisfied, I'll take the cuffs off, okay? I'll even let you keep the weed."

Marcus blinked away his tears. "Really?"

"I'm not here for the weed." David hoisted him to his feet. "Do you know a man named Robert Shapiro?"

"No. Never heard of him. Is he the dead guy?"

"Yeah, he's the dead guy. We found him under a bridge last week, and we think you had something to do with it."

"Why?" Marcus shook his head. "Wait, did you say last week? Man, I wasn't even here last week. Been in Arizona for the last ten days. Just got home yesterday. You can check my bags. I ain't even unpacked yet."

"They inside?" David asked.

"Yeah."

"Show us."

Marcus led the way while David kept a hand on his elbow. Cassie unhooked the chain from around Bear's neck, and the dog bounced up and down, wanting to play.

"Come on, Bear. You get to come inside. We'll see if mean old Marcus has any treats."

The word *treats* sent the dog bounding forward, almost knocking Marcus over. The man yelled out something about not letting dogs in the house, but neither Bear nor Cassie cared what he had to say. David sat Marcus down on the couch and turned to Cassie.

"Keep an eye on him for a second?"

"Not a problem."

She told Bear to sit, and he didn't hesitate this time. She smiled at the incredulous look on Marcus' face and then started searching for treats. Meanwhile, David made his way to the back of the house, undoubtedly searching for Marcus' bedroom and his unopened luggage.

When he emerged a minute or two later, he had a mid-sized suitcase in his hands. "This it?"

"Check the tags, dude. You can see my return date."

"Return dates don't tell me what day you left, genius. You still could've killed him."

"Come on, man. I don't even know who this Schafer guy is. Swear it."

"Shapiro."

Cassie found a small bag of dog biscuits on the counter. Right next to it laid an email receipt for Marcus' trip to Arizona. She handed the paper to David and a biscuit to Bear, who took it gently and walked over to the corner of the room to eat it.

"The dates work." David shook his head. "Damn it."

Cassie could feel his frustration. "Back to square one?"

David tossed the piece of paper on the couch next to Marcus. "You've really never heard of a man named Robert Shapiro?"

"Yo, I swear to God. Never. Who is he?"

David and Cassie exchanged a look. She decided to rip the Band-Aid off. "He's the man who killed your uncle, Joseph Warren."

"Uncle Joe?" Marcus' eyebrows knit together. "He died when I was a kid."

"So, you weren't close to him?" Cassie asked.

Marcus shrugged. "Not really. He tried to take care of me after Mom died, but then he disappeared. I kept a low profile till I turned eighteen so they wouldn't throw me into foster care."

David looked back at Cassie. "Yeah, square one."

"I haven't thought about him in years. And you're the second person asking me about him. Is there something I don't know about?" Marcus leaned forward. His eyes widened. "Yo, did Uncle Joe leave me money?"

David froze. "What do you mean, the second person?"

"What?" Marcus said. "The right hand doesn't know what the left hand is doing? You're the second cop to ask me about him."

"Your right hand and your left hand are going to be permanently cuffed behind your back if you don't start being real clear, real fast. I'm tired of this shit."

David's outburst caught Cassie off guard and she took a step back.

Marcus sat up straight. "There was a cop or, I don't know, maybe a security guard. A couple months ago. He was asking me all sorts of questions about Uncle Joe. Where he used to hang out? How many times he'd been in prison? If he had any friends who were still alive. Like I said, I was just a kid. I didn't know any of that stuff. I tried running from him, too. He didn't cuff me though. Gave me a hundred bucks to answer his questions."

"What did you tell him?" David asked.

"All I remember was he got out of prison, and he was excited about something. Said he had a big windfall coming. He was always saying stuff like that. Never worked out for him, but he never gave up. Stupid dick."

"Do you remember what he was excited about?"

"Said he was gonna go into business with some guy selling apples or something. Can you believe that? Uncle Joe made decent money on the side. He didn't need to sell freaking apples."

Cassie looked to David. "Sounds like Shapiro."

"Yeah, question is, who's this other cop?"

"Maybe he wasn't a cop. A security guard or something. I don't know. He was arrogant like a cop, but without the balls to match." When David and Cassie both looked confused, Marcus rolled his eyes. "Cops will push you around. Cuff you. Threaten to arrest you. He didn't do that. He was built like a cop, but he handed me a wad of cash. Means he had the swagger but not the authority, you feel me?"

"Yeah, we feel you." David stared at Marcus for a few seconds, but Cassie couldn't tell what was on his mind. Finally, after Marcus started squirming, David smiled. "Correctional officer."

"Yeah, like that. Security guard."

"What did he look like?"

"White. Younger than you, but older than her."

"Hair color? Eye color? Facial hair? Tattoos?"

"He wore a hat, so I didn't see his hair. I don't remember the color of his eyes, man. I wasn't paying that close attention." He swallowed audibly. "No facial hair. And I don't remember no tattoos."

David uncuffed Marcus then turned to Cassie. "I know where we have to go next. You ready? Say goodbye to your new friend. You can't keep him."

Marcus glared at the dog and grabbed his collar, yanking him closer and eliciting a soft whine from the animal. David stopped dead in his tracks.

"You know what? I changed my mind. He's coming with us."

Marcus' head snapped up. "You're not takin' my dog, man. Fuck that."

David dangled the handcuffs from a single finger. "It's either the dog, or I start tallying the number of convictions I can get you for, and you found out quickly how high I can count."

Marcus glanced at Cassie, who crossed her arms and did her best to look as confident as David. She didn't know if they could get in trouble for taking the man's dog, but even if it wasn't exactly legal, she doubted Marcus would press his luck. He cared more about his own skin than his dog's.

Marcus released Bear's collar and threw up his hands. "You want anything else while you're here? My car? My TV?"

David ignored him. He pushed open the front door and held it for Cassie, who patted her thigh and watched with delight as Bear stuck close to her heel. He kept his eyes trained on Cassie and didn't even hesitate when she opened the door to David's sedan and let him jump inside.

Cassie and David both slid into the front and cast a glance back at the dog. He was already curled up on the back seat, the tip of his tail wagging in delight. Cassie couldn't help the smile that formed on her lips. She looked up at David.

"Now what?"

32

CASSIE HAD DECIDED BEAR NEEDED A BATH AND A GOOD MEAL BEFORE she could even think about what to do with him next. They dropped him off at David's house, much to his wife's surprise. David promised it would only be for a day or two. Maybe they'd be able to find him a nice permanent home on their own, rather than taking him to a shelter.

Cassie's brain was whirring. Could she take him? Apollo had never been around a dog before, and she had no idea how Bear would react to a cat. Besides, would she even be able to take care of a German Shepherd with everything going on with her life?

Her day dreaming was interrupted when David kissed his wife goodbye and ushered Cassie back into the sedan. He knew exactly where they needed to go next: Coastal State Prison.

It was not a spectacular facility. They'd last renovated in the late nineties, and while most prisons weren't known for their artistic value, Cassie thought the medium-security facility could use a facelift.

The stark lights, imposing walls, and stern security guards left something to be desired, but it was the oppressive atmosphere that made her want to turn around as soon as they crossed the threshold. More than the presence of a few wandering ghosts, Cassie felt depression wrap an arm around her shoulders and squeeze tightly. The facility was full of bad memories that hung in the air, just waiting to attach themselves to someone like her.

Marcus Valencia's reveal that a correctional officer had visited him had the gears turning in David's brain, and he made a beeline for Warden Preston Wickham, who Cassie learned was David's least favorite person in the world.

When they arrived at the prison entrance and announced their intent to see the Warden, a few of the security guards looked nervous. Wickham and David's relationship must've been common knowledge because none of them wanted to break the news to their boss.

A rather rotund officer looked Cassie up and down as she and David made it through the metal detectors, and without taking his eyes off her, he called for one of the other officers to come forward. "Santiago. Take our esteemed visitors to the Warden."

"Yes, sir." Santiago was tall, thin, and very green. He seemed to know what he was getting himself into but realized he didn't have a choice. He offered David and Cassie a meek smile, then led them toward the Warden's office.

The prison was quieter than Cassie had expected. Too many movies had her believing there'd be shouting and catcalling and a general ruckus to contend with. But Santiago didn't take them anywhere near the prisoners. Instead, he led them down a short hallway and into a small office with a couple of waiting chairs. A secretary looked up from her computer and eyed both Santiago and his guests. She must've had some idea of what was going on because she looked back down at her computer, forcing Santiago to knock on Wickham's door himself.

Santiago emerged thirty seconds later with his head hanging. He didn't make eye contact when he gestured for the two of them to make their way inside. Cassie had the impression that while

Wickham had allowed them through the door, they weren't in for a welcoming party.

"Preston." David's voice was booming. Over the top. "It's great to see you again."

Wickham stood up from behind his desk. He wore a beige suit with a navy tie. His hair was thick and white, and his mustache must have been the envy of every man he encountered. He was undoubtedly handsome, but Cassie couldn't dismiss the icy darkness in his eyes. She sensed he was a very shrewd man.

"David. Hope you've been well." Wickham's voice sounded tight. "Who's your friend?"

"This is Cassie Quinn. She's helping me out with our murder investigation. You remember the one."

"I do." He gestured to the chairs in front of him. "Close the door, won't ya, darlin'?"

Cassie didn't like the assumption in his voice, but she decided that if David was playing bad cop, she'd play good cop. She let the door shut behind her, then sat down in an upholstered chair next to David. It looked like Wickham had hired a fancy interior designer to decorate his office.

His desk was a dark cherry wood. The chair he chose for himself was even more lavish than the ones he provided his guests, and beautiful framed landscapes covered the walls. In the corner sat a small bar. He held up a decanter full of amber liquid, but both Cassie and David declined.

"I wasn't expecting you today, David. I keep a tight schedule, and I prefer when visitors book an appointment through my secretary. You understand."

"I've been trying, Preston. It seems there's never an opening."

"Like I said. I keep a tight schedule."

"Unfortunately, death waits for no one. You're aware of the details of our investigation?"

"I've skimmed your messages, yes." Wickham returned to his seat, drink in hand. "I'm sure my secretary—"

"I've moved beyond the need to look into the victims." David's voice was calm and friendly. Cassie had never seen him so openly disingenuous with his hospitality. "Now I need information about one of your employees."

That caught Wickham's attention. "My employees? If you want information on them, I'll need to see a warrant."

"I'm speaking to you from one man of the law to another. We need a list of your employees, both former and current. We'll start with the last thirty years, and then go from there."

Wickham threw back his head, grabbed his stomach, and laughed. If it weren't for the ice that had remained steadfast in his eyes, Cassie could've mistaken him for Santa Claus in a three-piece suit.

"There is no way on God's green earth I'm letting you into our records for the past *thirty years*. You're out of your mind, man. Truly out of your mind. My men have done nothing wrong. I won't have you targeting good people and getting everyone riled up because you want to swing your dick around in front of a pretty lady."

Cassie groaned theatrically. "Can we leave everyone's dick out of this? 'Cause I guarantee I'll put you to shame? I have a job to do, Warden. Just like you. The snide remarks and unveiled sexism are hardly attractive. They make you a smaller man than you already are, and I don't think you can afford to take that risk." Cassie smiled to cover her anger. So much for being the good cop. "We believe the killer is a correctional officer who worked at this facility, likely in the early to mid-nineties. I assume he would have had close contact with prisoners suffering from addiction. He would've formed a bond with the ones murdered. It's the most likely reason he sought out their killer."

Wickham looked from David to Cassie and back again. "Who's in charge, you or her?"

"You might be the densest man I know, Wickham. And in case it wasn't clear, that is not a compliment." David shook his head. "We're trying to catch a killer here. Why are you so intent on wasting everyone's time, most of all yours?"

"Because I don't like you, Klein." Wickham stood up, and from Cassie's vantage point in the chair in front of Wickham, she felt every inch of his full height. "It's as simple as that. You're looking for a correctional officer who murdered a serial killer? I'd sooner shake his hand than turn him over to you."

David stood, and though he didn't match the Warden's physique, David possessed an inherent self-assuredness. Wickham could posture all he wanted, but he'd never be the type of man David Klein was every single day of his life.

"I don't much like you either, Wickham, but I'm not letting that get in the way of justice."

"I'd like you to leave now, David. You've outworn your welcome."

"That implies there was a welcome to wear out." Cassie didn't bother being quiet about it.

David cracked a smile. "She's right. I'm not going to leave, Wickham. You're going to help us, and you're going to do it with a smile on your face. Do you want to know why?"

Wickham was silent.

"I bet you do." David kicked his feet up on Wickham's desk and linked his hands behind his head. "You're going to help us, or I'm going to go back downtown and file a report on you. It's going to include all the information I know. Do you want to know what sort of information I know, Wickham?"

Silence again. But this time, Wickham looked the tiniest bit uncomfortable.

"You've been embezzling money from the prison and putting it in your pocket. The routine searches of your prison cells have turned up fewer drugs in the past few years. You couldn't afford your house, your car, or your mistress on the wages you're meant to be earning. And I know you're in real tight with a few of the boys in blue who would be real mad if they found out you confessed everything to me in exchange for a deal where you get to walk off into the sunset scot-free."

"You have no proof."

"If I didn't have proof, I wouldn't be sitting here as cool as a cucumber while you've got sweat drippin' down the side of your face."

Wickham pulled out a handkerchief and dabbed at his forehead. "What do you want?"

"I've already been clear on what I want, as has my associate." David dropped his feet back to the ground and stood up. Cassie mirrored him. "I want a list of every officer who was regularly in charge of any, some, or all of our twelve victims."

Wickham stood frozen for a few seconds before turning on his heel and walking to his door. He opened it with such precision he looked like a robot. And when he spoke to his secretary, his voice was void of any emotion.

"Lorraine, please make sure Detective Klein and his associate have everything they need."

"Sir?"

"Just do it." His voice held a twinge of annoyance now. "Any records they need to see, make sure they see them. And then make sure someone sees them out."

"Yes, sir."

Wickham brushed by David without so much as looking him in the eye. As he turned to shut the door, Cassie couldn't help herself.

"And don't forget to smile, darlin'."

Wickham slammed the door shut with such ferocity his secretary jumped.

A few seconds later, Cassie heard him talking to someone on the phone, and she wondered whether he was getting his affairs in order in case David didn't stay true to his word.

33

LORRAINE WAS A THIN YOUNG WOMAN IN A DRESS AND CARDIGAN. SHE wore large, round glasses and had her hair twisted up into a tight knot. She had trouble looking both David and Cassie in the eye, and whenever either of them talked to her, she'd blush so deeply, her ears would turn pink. A light scent of vanilla hung in the air around her.

But what Lorraine lacked in social adeptness, she made up for in her talents on the computer. As soon as David started describing the parameters for their search of the prison's records, her fingers flew over the keyboard. The cadence of her typing soothed Cassie.

"There are over fifty employees who fit that description." Lorraine's voice was quiet, but clear. She had a thick southern accent that told Cassie she enjoyed horseback riding, over-sweetened lemonade, and helping her mama bake pies on Sundays. "Male. Worked between the years 1990 and 2000. Regularly oversaw prisoners recovering from an addiction."

Cassie looked over at David. "That is a pretty wide search parameter. And we can't even guarantee those aspects apply to our guy."

"We walk in one direction and we either hit a gold mine or a dead end. We'll figure out which it is eventually, and we'll adjust course when it happens." David pointed to the open space next to Lorraine. "Do you mind if we—?"

"Not at all." She moved over, and David and Cassie grabbed the two waiting room chairs and scooted in next to her. It was tight, but once Lorraine turned her computer monitor, Cassie could see exactly what they were looking at. And it was a lot of names.

"What else can we do to narrow this down?" Lorraine asked.

David scratched his chin. "Can you search for incident reports?"

Lorraine nodded. "Keywords?"

"Excessive force." David stopped her before she could start typing. "But not against him. Filed against one of the other guards."

Lorraine hesitated for only a fraction of a second before she followed David's instructions. The list narrowed to thirteen.

"Okay, now we're getting somewhere." David leaned closer. "Our guy killed Shapiro in the same way Shapiro killed his victims, so he cared enough about the victims to avenge their deaths. This was personal. There's got to be a reason."

"We know he wasn't related to any of the victims," Cassie offered. "Otherwise, he would've come up in our searches. Maybe he had a personal relationship with one of them, either as a friend or something deeper?"

David snapped his fingers. "How many of these guys got in trouble for having relations with inmates?"

Lorraine made a few keystrokes, but the computer only produced an error message. "Nothing."

David cursed and watched as she brought the previous thirteen names back to the screen. "What else could make it so personal for him?"

"Former addict?" Cassie suggested. "Or someone in his family is an addict?"

Lorraine hit a button, but the same error message popped up. "I can search for incidents where an officer was reported for substance abuse, like drinking on the job or getting caught taking illegal substances, but I can't search for their family members."

David sat up straight. "You guys have a psychologist, don't you? For just the inmates or the officers, too?"

"Both. Dr. Yang. She's mostly for the inmates, but all the officers are encouraged to talk to her, too."

"Can you print us that list?"

Lorraine hit a couple buttons, and the huge, boxy printer behind her started chugging away. It must've been ancient. Cassie half-expected there to be a crank on the side that you'd have to turn to make it work. Lorraine pulled out the pieces of paper and handed them to David.

"Thank you for your help. If this doesn't work out, we may be back." He produced his card. "You seem like a capable young woman, Lorraine. I hate to see you working for a man like Wickham. If you ever find yourself in need of a job putting your computer skills to better use than secretarial work, call me. I might be able to find an opening for you at the station."

Lorraine's eyes were huge as she took his card and held it in her open palms as if it were a baby bunny. "Thank you."

"You're quite welcome. Now, if you'll be so kind as to direct us to Dr. Yang's office?"

Dr. Yang's office was at the end of a drab hallway. Her door was cracked a few inches, and Cassie glimpsed her filling out paperwork before David knocked and startled her. She had long black hair tied back into a ponytail and wore a navy-blue pants suit.

"Sorry to disturb you," he said, "but could we have a moment of your time, Dr. Yang?"

"Of course." She stood and shook David's hand, then Cassie's. "And you are?"

"Detective David Klein and Ms. Cassie Quinn."

"Detectives?" Dr. Yang's eyes flickered to the door and back. "What seems to be the issue?"

David smirked. "You've given yourself away already, Dr. Yang. Are you worried about yourself or someone else?"

Dr. Yang smiled, and her eyes danced with laughter. "Neither.

Curious who you're here for and whether I'll have a job in the morning."

"I'm not here for the Warden. Not yet at least. And I'm sure you'll still have your position come tomorrow." David handed her the stack of papers Lorraine had printed for them. "I'm wondering if you recognize any of these names?"

Dr. Yang shifted through the papers. "A few of them. About half were before my time. I've at least said hello to the rest of them once or twice."

"Any names stand out for any reason?"

"What is this about?"

David pointed to the chair in front of her desk, and when Dr. Yang nodded, all three of them sat down. "We're conducting a murder investigation. We believe the suspect has worked here at one point or another. We've narrowed down the list to those names, and we're hoping you could help point us in the right direction."

Yang's smile was tight. "You know I can't do that. It would be an enormous breach of confidentiality."

"I was afraid you were going to say that." David shifted in his seat, and Cassie could tell he was getting desperate. "Look, the last thing I want to do is get you in trouble. I strong-armed Wickham into helping us, but he's a dick. I don't like him."

Dr. Yang laughed. "You'd be in the minority if you did."

"But you seem like a reasonable, accomplished woman. I won't jeopardize that. If you tell us to leave, then we'll leave. But I'm hoping you'll hear me out before you do that."

"I'm listening."

"Over twenty years ago, a single man killed twelve people. They were all addicts, and all former inmates of this prison." He stubbed his finger on the desktop. "A few days ago, that man wound up dead. Killed in the same manner as his victims. We've been chasing our tails since then, and I'd be lying if I said I wasn't tired. I'm at the end of my rope here."

"Metaphorically speaking, I hope?"

David smiled. "Metaphorically speaking. We've chased a lot of leads, and they've all wound up as dead ends. I think this one is different. We know a correctional officer visited the nephew of one of the victims asking a lot of questions. Our suspect is a white male in his late forties or early fifties. We have reason to believe he'd feel a close personal connection to the original victims, whether it was because he was an addict himself or knew someone who was. And by the look on your face, I have reason to believe a particular person came to mind as soon as I mentioned those details."

Dr. Yang looked from David to Cassie and then back down at the list in her hands. When she looked up again, her eyes were determined. "I'm sorry, but I couldn't possibly share that information with you. If you can get a warrant, I'd be happy to help. But until then, my hands are tied."

"Dr. Yang, please—"

"I'm sorry." Dr. Yang stood and held out the papers. "I can't help."

"I understand."

Cassie wanted to say something—anything—to get the psychologist to change her mind. She didn't want her to break any rules, but she also knew that following the rules meant delaying justice—even if it was justice for a serial killer.

David reached for the papers, but Dr. Yang didn't immediately let them go. She waited until she had David's full attention. "There are seven days in a week, Detective. I'm sure you'll figure it out."

David smiled. "I'm sure I will."

Cassie followed David through the door and down the hallway. When they reached the end of the corridor, he brought the papers close to his face and counted down the page. "Number seven. Noah McLaughlin."

"You think that's our guy?"

David looked downright giddy now. "Only one way to find out."

34

As soon as Cassie saw her sister pull onto Noah McLaughlin's road, she waved Laura down and directed her to park on the side of the road a few houses away. McLaughlin's house was crawling with cops, and the neighbors who were home at this time of day were either peeking through their blinds or standing on the sidewalk, pointing and whispering to each other.

Laura put the car in park and hopped out. "Well, this looks like a party."

"They got the warrant for McLaughlin's house, but they had to do an initial walkthrough before we could get in there. Once that's done, David's going to set aside some time for us to help him go through the war room."

"War room?"

Cassie led her sister over to where a couple of people had gathered on the other side of a barrier the police had erected on the sidewalk right outside the house. She leaned in closer to Laura so the others couldn't hear.

"That's what they've been calling it. Apparently, McLaughlin has a whole setup. Hundreds of pages of information and printouts and notes. He kept journals. Had a ton of pictures. Detailed maps. He figured out what Shapiro had done well before the police did."

"So, he's definitely our guy."

Cassie nodded. "Now we just have to find him."

Laura turned as a news van pulled up. "Well, he's gonna know not to come back here."

Cassie watched as her favorite blonde reporter hopped out of the van and directed her camera guy to face the house while she checked her makeup and got ready to go live. It was Annette Campbell, the woman who'd made Harris' life a living hell a few months ago. Cassie hadn't seen much of her on the news lately, but she still had a job, so Harris had kept her word about not getting her in trouble if she played by the rules.

"This might get messy," Cassie said.

"You know her?" Laura asked.

"I know *of* her. We weren't formally introduced." Cassie watched as Campbell fluffed her curly blonde hair. "She's ambitious."

"That doesn't sound like a compliment."

"It is. I think she's going to be a great reporter. But she still needs to learn not to step on people along the way. Or maybe she has learned that. We'll see, I guess."

A police officer on the other side of the barrier caught Cassie's attention. "Boss wants to see you two."

Cassie nodded and squeezed past the onlookers. She ignored their confused and curious looks and made her way up to the front of the house with Laura on her heels. They each had to put on protective shoe coverings and latex gloves before they were allowed inside. David was waiting for them.

Cassie hooked a thumb over her shoulder. "Our favorite reporter is outside."

"I know. I invited her."

Cassie stopped in her tracks. "Oh?"

"Better to have her working with us than against us. One of the neighbors would've called the media sooner or later. I gave Ms.

Campbell a head start, as long as she promised not to go live before anyone else arrived."

"Smart man."

"I have my moments." He waved the two of them along. "Come on, I'll show you what we're working with."

Cassie followed David through the living room, up a set of stairs, and to a door that led to the attic. Cassie could feel a shift in atmosphere. It wasn't as strong as Shapiro's entity, but a heaviness indicated McLaughlin had spent hours in the attic pouring over this case and stewing in his own anger and hurt. The subtle smell of cigarette smoke emanated from the room.

"Wow."

David looked her over. "You feel something?"

"A lot of pain. This was personal for him."

David nodded and led them up the last set of stairs and into the attic. Cassie was momentarily taken aback by the overwhelming influx of sensations. Not only was the back of her head tingling with the pain and strife McLaughlin had left behind in this room, but her eyes couldn't focus for the sheer amount of sensory input in front of her.

Every wall had papers and photographs. There were two plastic folding tables fitted end-to-end that took up the entire length of the room, and stacks of papers and books were strewn across the floor. A singular chair sat in the middle of everything, like the eye of the storm.

"Jesus." Laura's jaw was hanging open. "How long did it take for him to do all this?"

David walked over to the table and picked up a notebook. There was nothing special about it. You could buy one at the store for less than a dollar. Most college students had at least a half dozen of them. But instead of writing equations or historical facts on the pages, McLaughlin had kept a journal of all his findings about the case.

"It's going to take a while to go through everything, but this isn't the only one." David gestured to three more notebooks like the one in his hands. "He kept extremely detailed notes. From what I gather, he just liked to journal. He'd start off with an overview of what happened at work, then he'd jump into some personal thoughts, and then he'd write about his latest findings in the case. There's at least a couple years' worth of notebooks here."

Laura walked across the room and picked up one of the other notebooks. "This will tell us everything we need to know. Motive. Process. Execution."

"Why wouldn't he just burn all of this?" Cassie still couldn't process just how much information was in the room. "I mean, Shapiro's dead. He carried out his mission. He might've gotten away with it. But now we have all this evidence. Why didn't he try to hide it?"

Laura shrugged. "He spent a long time putting this together. And you said it had to be personal, right? Maybe burning or getting rid of the evidence was never an option. Or maybe he meant to and just never got around to it."

"A killer who procrastinates," Cassie quipped. "What's next?"

Laura ignored her. "Or he didn't care if we found it."

"Why wouldn't he care?" Cassie asked.

"He could be states away at this point." David's shoulders dropped. "He could be dead. Maybe he had a plan to disappear. It wouldn't matter if we found this if we could never find *him*."

"What I really want to know," Cassie said, taking a step closer to one of the walls covered in photographs, "is how he figured out it was Shapiro."

David joined her. "I haven't had much time to go through his materials, but from what I can tell, it took a lot of research, leg work, and determination."

"Well, we've already established he knew the victims, right?" Laura asked. "And he was friendly with them."

"Exactly." David pointed to the notebook in her hands. "There are a couple entries in that one that talk about how he'd check up on the guys who had been released. McLaughlin did a lot of volunteer work for homeless shelters and food kitchens. He'd see a lot of these guys after they got out. But not always. And sometimes they'd disappear."

Cassie turned. "Shapiro?"

"No. McLaughlin wasn't just looking into what Shapiro was doing. In fact, that wasn't even where this started. In one of the earlier notebooks, he talked about having a hard time keeping tabs on the inmates who left the prison. A lot of them went back to the streets, and then he couldn't find them again."

"There's a huge link between homelessness and mental illness, as well as addiction," Laura said. "Being homeless is incredibly stressful —never knowing where you're going to sleep or where your next meal is coming from—and that can increase anxiety and depression. Stress can lead to psychosis, and there's evidence that it can increase the likelihood of developing disorders like schizophrenia."

Cassie gestured to the surrounding chaos. "What made him figure out there was something else going on here? How did he realize these deaths related to the disappearances?"

David shook his head. "I still don't have an answer for that, but a lot of the homeless people on the streets run in similar circles. They all have their own groups where they feel safe, but there's a huge us-versus-them mentality."

"As in the homeless people against people who aren't homeless?"

He nodded. "And against the police. I'm thinking that's how Shapiro got away with this for so long. He tricked these former inmates into meeting up with him, pretending to be their friend or pretending to have an opportunity for them, and then killed them. They'd disappear, and their friends on the streets had to know something. They would've noticed the disappearances, would've realized something was wrong. They would've been able to identify Shapiro if they'd gone to the police. But the police are the bad guys. They wouldn't reach out to the police for help."

"Especially since the police were doing such a good job of ignoring the case anyway." Cassie blew hair out of her face. The heat of the attic was oppressive. "If any witnesses came forward, they would've thrown their statement in the back of a drawer somewhere. Just like they did with Carl Graham."

Laura closed the notebook in her hands and picked up another one. "What I want to know is what happened to McLaughlin."

David chuckled. "Don't we all."

"No, I mean, I want to know what happened to him that made him kill Shapiro," Laura said. "He worked at Coastal State Prison for a couple decades, right? Knew all these guys. He volunteered and worked soup kitchens. You see, he did his best to watch over the people of Savannah who didn't have anywhere else to go. He knew something was wrong, and by the looks of it, he started to gather information on Shapiro over a year ago. So, what made him decide to kill Shapiro instead of turn him in?"

"Maybe he didn't trust the police either," Cassie offered.

"Maybe, but I keep going back to how personal this is for him." Laura tipped her head back and searched the ceiling for answers. "He knew about Shapiro, and instead of gathering evidence and turning it in, he killed him. He knew about Shapiro for a while, but he chose last week to kill him. Why? What changed?"

Cassie shrugged. She didn't even know where to begin to answer that question. She looked around the war room like it would give her answers. There was so much information here, so much time and energy put into solving this case, there had to be a picture or a page or even a single paragraph that could point them in the right direction.

A map along the far wall drew Cassie's attention. She walked over and stared at it for a few minutes before comprehending what was in front of her. It was Savannah and the outlying towns. Different colored dots littered the map. They were centered around the city, but a few reached farther than that.

David stood beside her. "Look at that. He was marking where the victims disappeared. Where they were found. Where they traveled to and from in between. This is where he started figuring out something else was going on and that there was a serial killer on the loose."

Cassie was only half listening. As her eyes roamed over the map, that feeling of desperation and anger and sadness increased. Cigarette smoke filled her nostrils. Her stomach churned. She felt dizzy.

And when her gaze landed on the town of Keller, she nearly lost her lunch.

Cassie pressed her finger to the map. The faintest ringing of church bells sounded far off in the distance. She knew without asking that no one else could hear them. She turned to David.

"He's there."

35

DAVID HESITATED ONLY FOR A MOMENT BEFORE HE TURNED AND descended the stairs from the attic. Laura and Cassie followed him a few seconds later and found him already engaged in conversation with Paulson. The dusty smell of the attic hung around them like a shroud.

"Tell the Chief we've got a location on McLaughlin. We have no reason to believe he's armed or dangerous, so we don't need the entire department on our ass, okay? I'm going to drive ahead and get a lock on him. Make sure he doesn't disappear. Keep me updated every step of the way, okay?"

Paulson nodded and scurried off. David turned back to the sisters.

"Laura, I'm afraid I'm gonna have to leave you behind again. Cassie's got more experience with this."

"Does she have to go with you?"

"Have to? No." He smiled. "But if McLaughlin has already moved on to the next location, having her by my side might be helpful."

"I'll be fine." Cassie placed a reassuring hand on her sister's shoulder. "Promise."

Laura looked doubtful, but she didn't argue. "Anything I can do?"

"Keep your phone on you. Keep looking through McLaughlin's notes upstairs. I don't think he's dangerous, but we still have a couple missing pieces of the story. I'd like to know them before we meet McLaughlin for the first time."

"The media's out front. What are we going to do about that?" Cassie asked.

"We go out the back."

Before Cassie could follow David back downstairs, Laura pulled her into a hug. "Just be careful, okay? And keep me updated? Don't take any risks. And listen to David."

"Yes, Mother." Cassie smiled. "I'll text you."

Cassie caught up with David, who went through the backdoor, around the block, and down the street to where he'd parked his sedan. As he slid into the front seat, he turned to Cassie. "Any idea where precisely, or are we just gonna go knocking oh every door?"

She already had her phone out and was searching a map of the area. She pinched the screen to zoom in and tapped on a spot. "I'm guessing it's the Presbyterian Church on Belfast."

David put the car in drive and pulled away from the curb. He circled the block once, where they saw more people had gathered in front of McLaughlin's house. There was another news van out front now, which meant Campbell had likely shared select details of the investigation with her viewers.

"What'd you tell her?" Cassie watched as the second news crew scrambled to set up.

"The basics. Murder investigation tied to a cold case. Didn't want to give away too much yet, in case McLaughlin slipped through our fingers, but I promised her another exclusive later down the line."

"Think she'll hold up her end of the bargain?"

"What, to stop being a pain in our asses? Probably not." He chuckled. "But she's doing a little better at toeing the line now. She's a quick learner. And I think she wants to be a good reporter. She just needed to learn a hard lesson first."

David spoke again after a few beats of silence.

"How are you holding up? How's it been having your sister in the know?"

"Oh, you know. Weird and incredible all at once." A bubble of laughter rose in her chest. "I feel like I can be myself around her now. But I also feel vulnerable. She took it well, all things considered, but I can tell she still has a lot of questions. A lot of reservations."

"I still have a lot of questions, and I've known about your abilities for a decade. I think it'll turn out just the way you want it. She's a good person. A good sister. You guys will figure everything out."

"I hope you're right." She turned to him now. "What about you? How are you doing?"

David smiled, but it didn't quite meet his eyes. "I'm doing okay. Job doesn't get any easier, but that sorta comes with the territory, you know?"

"Doesn't seem fair."

"Lisa's been saying the same thing for years. She keeps bringing up my retirement right as I'm falling asleep, like maybe she can trick me into leaving the force early."

"How's that working out?"

"Not in her favor." His smile was sad. "I keep telling her I have too many problems to solve. Can't hang it up just yet."

"The world needs you." Cassie patted his arm. "I don't know what I'd do without you."

"Eh, you'll figure it out. You'll have to, sooner or later."

"Preferably later."

David cleared his throat, and Cassie got the sense this was something he thought about often. "All of our days are numbered. I think you remember that better than most. God knows I never forget it. Sometimes I feel like I've got one foot in the grave."

"Don't be ridiculous. You're not that old, David."

"Age has nothing to do with it. Not in my line of work."

"You know something I don't know?"

"All I'm saying is—if anything happens to me, I hope you don't have to look at my ugly mug after I'm gone."

Cassie shifted her whole body in the passenger seat to face him. "Should I be worried? I thought you said McLaughlin wasn't dangerous."

He waved her off. "This isn't about McLaughlin. I just mean in general." He took a deep breath and kept his eyes focused on the road. "I've seen enough of what you do. How it takes a toll on you. I'll never think of your abilities as anything other than a gift, but I hope that after I'm dead and gone, I stay that way. Wherever I end up, heaven or hell, I hope it's a direct ticket, one way."

"Well, lucky for you, you're gonna live to the ripe old age of one hundred and two. By then, I might even be long-gone."

David chuckled, but he didn't seem like his usual self. Something was on his mind, but before Cassie could dig any deeper, her phone buzzed in her hand. It was Laura. She put it on speaker.

"Did you find anything?" Cassie asked.

"Did you know McLaughlin had a sister?" Laura responded.

Cassie and David exchanged looks. She brought the phone closer. "Negative."

"Her name was Ashlynn. I think she was his little sister. She's been in and out of trouble her whole life. Jail. Addiction. Abusive relationships. But he never stopped caring about her. Never stopped trying to get her into rehab and to turn her life around."

"What happened to her?" Cassie asked.

"She was murdered."

"Jesus." Cassie cocked her head to the side. "But Shapiro—"

"No, Shapiro didn't do it. They caught her killer. It was an ex. He's in jail. He'll never get out. He had quite a record, too."

David flicked on his turn signal and guided the car to the right. "Guess that explains why he was always volunteering. Why he cared so much about the inmates."

"I think that also explains why he killed Shapiro." Laura paused, and Cassie could hear her flipping through pages on the other end of the phone. "Even though the guy who killed his sister got what was coming to him, he felt powerless. It didn't bring his sister back. He couldn't hurt the person who hurt him, and then he stumbled upon these other people, these other addicts, who'd been murdered. And the police ignored their cases. He felt like he had to do something about it."

"Kind of ironic, don't you think?" Cassie shook her head. "Shapiro kills all these people because he couldn't kill the person who murdered his wife. McLaughlin killed him because he couldn't avenge his sister in any other way."

David's laugh was dark. "I believe we call that poetic justice."

Laura sighed. "But that still doesn't tell us why *now*. Why all these years later? There's got to be something that pushed him over the edge."

David directed the car into a parking lot, and when Cassie looked up, she realized they were sitting outside the Presbyterian Church in Keller, Georgia. It was a modest building that looked more like a house than a place of worship.

The smell of cigarette smoke filled the inside of the car, and it took all of Cassie's willpower to stop herself from gagging. "He's here."

David put the car in park and switched off the engine. "Then how about we introduce ourselves."

36

DAVID HOOKED HIS FINGERS AROUND THE DOORHANDLE. "STAY HERE."

Cassie unbuckled her seatbelt in defiance. "No way."

"Just wait here, Cassie. We don't know if he's armed. We don't know how he's going to react to being found."

"Which is why you shouldn't go in there alone." Cassie didn't wait for his permission to open her door and get out of the car. She waited until he stepped out of the sedan and locked eyes with her. Her heart was pounding, but she felt strong and calm, despite the situation. "I promise I'll stay back. I promise I won't escalate the situation. Blah, blah, blah. I know the drill."

David rolled his eyes. "She says *blah, blah, blah.*"

But David didn't argue. There was no point. They both knew that when he asked her to come along, there'd be no way she'd stay behind in the car if they caught up with McLaughlin. But they both knew he had to say it, regardless.

Cassie hung back for a few seconds before following in David's wake. She'd sounded cavalier when she talked about being part of this final showdown, but she was nervous. She knew a few things about getting out of a sticky situation, but she'd be useless if he had a weapon.

In other words, she was a liability.

But she was determined not to put David in a situation like that. She didn't have an ego, so she felt comfortable hanging back if that's what the confrontation called for. David was the lead, the one with the badge and the gun. He was in charge, and she had no interest in raising a mutiny.

David retrieved his gun from his holster, but he kept it pointed square at the ground. There was no service today, but that didn't mean the church was empty. If McLaughlin were inside, other people would be as well. If the situation went south, a long-distance chat with God could turn into a face-to-face meeting.

David pushed the church door open, and Cassie cringed as the hinges squeaked. Stale air rushed out of the opening and hit her in the face. Something about churches always made her nervous. Maybe the formality of the institution. Or the expectation. Or the fact that she had psychic abilities.

Magic powers were kind of frowned upon in most religious communities.

The pair moved forward as quietly as possible. David didn't creep along but stepped lightly. They had to look inconspicuous enough to not be noticeable, but they also had to be on guard. Cassie's palms started to sweat, so she rubbed them on her jeans. It didn't do much good, but it made her feel a little better.

David looked over his shoulder at Cassie and held up a hand. She didn't dare disobey. If McLaughlin was armed, they'd both be better off if she had one foot out the door.

David pushed forward with his gun hidden by his frame. Cassie craned her neck to see past him. The inside of the church stood in stark contrast to the exterior. It was beautiful, with rich wooden pews, an imposing organ, and several stained-glass windows.

An elderly couple sat in the front row on the righthand side. A pastor stood next to them with a sad smile, nodding his head in understanding. On the left, a few rows back, sat a lone man with his head bowed. He wore a large jacket and a hat. From this vantage point, Cassie couldn't see if he was armed.

David walked a few feet closer and then stopped. He must've made a positive ID because he raised his gun and took a ready stance. No one else in the church had noticed him yet. Against her better judgment, Cassie took a few steps closer.

"Savannah PD." David's voice bounced around the cavernous interior of the church. "Noah McLaughlin, you're under arrest for the murder of Robert Shapiro. Put your hands where I can see them."

The entire room froze. Then, the old woman let out a little gasp. Her husband put his arm around her shoulder and drew her in close while the pastor stepped in front of them. All three looked anxious and confused.

McLaughlin's head rose inch by inch until he looked over his shoulder and straight at David. His gaze darted to Cassie and then back again, and she felt herself shrink back a few inches. He didn't look scared or even worried. In fact, he looked at peace.

"My name is Detective David Klein. Put your hands on top of your head and link your fingers."

McLaughlin did as he was told, but Cassie felt like he moved at a snail's pace. The potent smell of stale cigarette smoke rushed back to her, and she wrinkled her nose against it. She hoped her stomach would cooperate.

The pastor stepped forward. "Detective, is this really necessary? You're in a house of God. I'm sure this man will cooperate. Won't you, son?"

McLaughlin didn't move. He just kept his eyes forward and his hands on his head.

"Sir, I need you to take the others outside. Backup is on the way. We'll be out of your hair shortly."

The pastor looked like he wanted to argue, but he nodded toward the elderly couple and helped the man steady his wife on her feet. They took the long way around the pews, choosing to walk along the far wall, and then shuffled out past Cassie. She nodded encouragingly and waited until they crossed the parking lot before turning back to the situation at hand.

David circled McLaughlin. "Are you armed?"

"Yes, sir." McLaughlin's voice was steady. "I've got my pistol on me."

"Where is it?"

"In the bag at my feet."

David nodded and then started forward, taking his time and assessing McLaughlin along the way. Cassie felt herself creep closer and closer, but every time she did, she'd get another whiff of cigarette smoke and her head would swim.

"How'd you find me?" McLaughlin asked.

"That's a bit of a story."

"Tried pretty hard to stay off the radar. Rental car. Picked a direction at random. Hell, I'm not even Presbyterian."

"We had a secret weapon you couldn't have anticipated."

"I see." McLaughlin cast another look over his shoulder. "Is she the secret weapon?"

"You could say that."

David was within arm's reach of the other man. He kicked the bag at McLaughlin's feet to the other end of the pew. The man made no movement. David gave McLaughlin a last look and then, satisfied, David took two large steps back. "Keep your hands where they are. Stand up slowly. Then lay down on your stomach and put your hands behind your back. Do you understand?"

"I understand. I'm going to start moving now."

McLaughlin's hands stayed clasped above his head as he stood up and shuffled out from the pew and into the center aisle of the church. He got down on one knee, then the other. Then he hesitated and looked up at David.

"Unhook your hands, get down, and then clasp them behind your back."

McLaughlin did as he was told. He leaned forward and pressed himself against the floor. He brought his hands up behind his back and waited for his next instruction.

Cassie couldn't see McLaughlin's face from her vantage point, and she wondered what kind of expression his face held. Was he as unhinged as the person he'd killed, or was he resigned to his fate?

David's voice echoed around the church. "Cassie, I need you to come over here."

"What? Why?"

"I don't trust him. I need you to grab my cuffs and put them on his wrists. Do you understand?"

"Yes."

"Come over here."

Cassie didn't move.

"Now."

The command forced Cassie's feet to move forward. One second, she was standing near the door to the outside world, and the next, her hands were closing over the cold metal of the cuffs hanging off David's belt. She looked up at him, but he never took his eyes off McLaughlin.

"I don't know what I'm doing."

"I'll walk you through it."

"I don't know if I can—"

"I don't trust him, so you get to decide between cuffing him yourself or watching me hold him at gunpoint until backup gets here. We don't really have another choice. I'm not taking my gun off him."

Cassie swallowed the lump in her throat and looked down at the cuffs. She'd been around enough officers in her time that she knew the basics. She pinched the metal arm of one cuff until it ratcheted open and then did the same with the other side.

"Start with his right. Pinch it tight. Then move on to the left."

Cassie shuffled forward. She only hesitated for a moment before she knelt down beside him. Her hands were slick with sweat and shaking. The smell of cigarette smoke made her gag and cough. But as she turned her head to the side, McLaughlin exploded with power.

It happened too fast for Cassie to process. One minute, he was on his stomach, and the next, he'd rolled onto his side and swung his leg up. He planted his foot on Cassie's hip and shoved with all his strength. It didn't hurt, but it sent her sprawling into David. She heard the gun skitter across the floor as the two of them collided.

WHEN SHE NEXT LOOKED UP, McLaughlin was standing over them with his own gun pointed at their heads. He used it to point to the pew behind them. "Sit there, please."

DAVID HELPED CASSIE to her feet. She caught sight of his gun, but it had slid across the polished wooden floor and landed at the base of the pulpit. She hesitated for only a moment before sliding into the pew McLaughlin had pointed to. David slid in after her, placing his body between her and the man aiming a pistol at her head.

McLaughlin took two steps back, sat down on the opposite side of the aisle, and then took the gun off them, laying it across his lap and pointing the muzzle toward the front of the church. Cassie, however, noticed he hadn't lifted his finger from the trigger.

"I'm sorry I lied." He looked like he meant it. "About having the gun in my bag, I mean. I don't want to hurt you."

David's voice came out like a growl. "Your actions say differently."

McLaughlin sighed and then nodded his head. "You're right."

After a moment's hesitation, McLaughlin took a deep breath and stood up. Cassie felt her entire body tense, and David shifted more of his body to block hers. Her head grew light as the other man walked over to David's 9mm and picked it up.

When he turned back around, there was only a moment's hesitation before he moved again.

Then he walked straight up to David and handed him back his weapon.

37

"GOOD MANNERS WON'T KEEP YOU OUT OF JAIL, MCLAUGHLIN," DAVID said.

"Noah." McLaughlin looked tired. "And I know that. But I'm not here to hurt anyone. Was just saying some final goodbyes."

"You hurt Shapiro."

McLaughlin's smile held a tightness that betrayed his anger. "Shapiro deserved it. I think even you can see that."

"What you did was still against the law."

"I know."

"You don't seem worried about the consequences."

"I'm not."

"Regardless of your motivation and regardless of the type of person Robert Shapiro was, you're still going to jail."

"I'm aware."

Cassie wondered if David felt as frustrated as she did. She wasn't sure what kind of person she had built McLaughlin up to be, but it didn't match the man in front of her. She knew McLaughlin had killed a serial killer and not a random innocent person. But taking a life was still significant. Soldiers did it out of a sense of duty and morality, and yet many of them struggled with their decisions daily.

McLaughlin didn't look proud. He didn't look remorseful either, but he wasn't bragging or begging for his life. He looked weak and exhausted. His body, which must've once been muscular, now looked soft. His cheeks were gaunt. His eyes sunken.

"You're sick." The constant stench of cigarette smoke made so much more sense now to Cassie. "Lung cancer?"

"How did you know that?" McLaughlin looked confused.

Cassie shrugged. "Secret weapon, remember?"

"That's why you did it now." David nodded in realization. "You had nothing to lose."

"Only had a couple months left anyway. Maybe longer, if I was lucky. But no matter what I did, I wouldn't see a full sentence."

"Then why run?" Cassie asked.

"I guess I just wanted to live out my last days as a free man."

"You could've turned your evidence over to us." David's pleading tone surprised Cassie. "With the amount of overwhelming evidence you had, we would've nailed Shapiro to the wall."

"Shapiro killed twelve people in a brutal, horrific manner." McLaughlin's eyes once again flashed with anger, but the heat dulled quickly. Cassie noticed his grip on the gun loosen. "He didn't deserve to live out the rest of his days in a cell, with three meals a day. He deserved to feel the pain he had inflicted on others. And I made sure he did."

"You don't get to make that call, Noah," David said.

McLaughlin shifted and his gun clattered to the floor. He looked down at it but didn't bother retrieving it. "I'm not *supposed* to make that call, but I did anyway. And I don't regret it. Not in the least."

"They'll use that against you."

"It's already too late for me."

"Your cause was righteous if misguided, but—"

Cassie placed a hand on David's shoulder. "That's not what he meant."

It had taken her a moment to understand what she was seeing. His weakness, his frailty. The burst of energy that had left him exhausted. His apathetic resignation. He wasn't planning on making it out of this church, and considering his gun now lay on the floor, Cassie didn't think he was trying to go out like that.

McLaughlin must've seen her looking at it.

"I thought about doing it that way. Gun in the mouth, pull the trigger. It would've been fast. Painless. But violent. And I wanted to do it here, in a church. I'm not even that religious. But it felt right to come here, you know? I wanted to say goodbye to my sister. I don't think I'll be going where she's currently residing."

"Noah." David stood now but didn't approach McLaughlin. "What did you do?"

"Secobarbital." Noah's body slumped a little in the pew. He didn't right himself. "Did you know doctors used to prescribe it as a sleeping pill? Then they figured out they could use it in assisted suicide."

Cassie brought her hands to her mouth. "My God."

"How much did you take?" David had crossed the aisle and now had one hand under Noah's arm. He kicked the gun away. "When did you take it?"

"I took enough." His breathing was a little shallower now. "About twenty minutes ago."

"Why?" Cassie already knew the answer, but it was hard not to ask the question. She'd been around death more than she cared to admit, and yet she still had trouble comprehending it. Like looking at Shapiro's body in the morgue, it felt too wrong not to question whether this was real.

McLaughlin shrugged a shoulder. His eyes were heavy now. "It was either die today or die a couple months from now. Die painlessly or die when I coughed up half my lung. I decided I'd rather die here and now."

"For what it's worth," David whispered, "I would've done the same thing."

"Thank you." Through half-lidded eyes, he looked up at David. "What did you say your name was again?"

"David Klein."

The recognition was slow to build, but once it was there, McLaughlin smiled. "You worked the case back in the day, didn't you? I thought I recognized your name when you first said it, but I couldn't put a finger on it."

"Yeah, I did. I was a young man back then. Not a detective yet."

"Do you have any regrets?"

David's smile was sad. "More than most."

"Any regrets about this case?"

The ringing of church bells interrupted them. The pealing cacophony drowned out any other noise for a full minute. When it was over, Cassie's ears were still full of the sound. But she didn't miss David's next words.

"I wish I'd done more back then. I wish I'd tried harder. Spoken up more. Maybe I wouldn't have gotten anywhere. Maybe I would've been reassigned. But at least I could tell my kids and grandkids I didn't have any regrets."

"We all have regrets." Noah's slumped a little further. "It's what we learn from those regrets that's important."

"Is that why you killed Shapiro? Because you had your own regrets?"

"I wish I'd done more." His breathing was ragged. "More to help... my sister."

"You've helped a lot of people, Noah." David cradled the other man now. "And you brought justice to a murderer."

Noah looked up at David and moved his lips, but no sound came out. His eyes drooped until they were nearly closed. Cassie saw the subtle rise and fall of his chest slow, until she couldn't tell if he was breathing at all.

David looked up at her with pained eyes as he eased the man down.

There was nothing more either of them could do.

38

"And then the cops came. Then an ambulance. They pronounced him dead at the scene."

Cassie was sitting on one end of the couch in her living room, while her sister sat on the other. They were both snuggled under a thick, soft blanket. Apollo was curled up between them, his nose tucked under the tip of his tail. His soft purrs comforted Cassie in a way few other sounds could.

"I can't say I blame him," Laura said. "I'd want to go out on my own terms, too. But I don't know if I'd be brave enough to do it myself."

"Me neither. Still, it's strange."

"What is?"

Cassie furrowed her brow. She didn't have the right words for it. "He was a good person, at least as far I could tell. Usually, when victims come to me, something unspeakable has happened to them. Their killers are terrible, evil people. Like Baker and that doctor killing women and ripping out their hearts."

"Shapiro was a terrible person." Laura took a moment to compose the words that followed. "Technically, his victim came to you first."

"True." Cassie smiled. Laura was trying her best to accept her sister's abilities, as strange and foreign as they were, and Cassie appreciated the effort. "And I'm glad we got to solve that case."

"But?"

Cassie's smile faded. "But I feel strange about Noah's death. Like it was unjustified. Like he deserved better."

"The world isn't black and white, as much as that might make life easier. Good people can do terrible things, and terrible people can do wonderful things. Sometimes, an action is neither good nor bad. It just is."

"You know, David said something similar as we were leaving the church. Something about how legality and morality aren't always the same thing."

"He's got a point." Laura stroked the top of Apollo's head, and the cat purred louder. "Did you see anything when McLaughlin died? Like his spirit leaving his body?"

"No." Cassie laughed. "This isn't some cartoon."

"Hey, I don't know. It could be."

"I did feel him leave, though. The smell of cigarette smoke sort of faded into nothing, and then I could tell he wasn't there anymore."

"I'm sorry you had to witness that."

Cassie shrugged. "Wasn't the first time I've seen a dead body. Won't be the last."

Laura finally looked up from Apollo. Her voice was hesitant. "Are you okay? I mean, like, in general?"

Cassie didn't answer right away. She wasn't sure she had an answer to give her. "I think so."

"That's reassuring."

"All things considered, it kind of is." Cassie leaned her head back against the couch and stared at the ceiling. "I'm not perfect. I'm not ecstatic and jumping for joy. You should be concerned if I was."

"That's true."

"But I'm okay. I wish Noah didn't die, but I'm kind of glad he did it on his own terms. And I'm glad you're here." Cassie looked over at Laura. "Thank you, by the way."

Laura cocked her head to one side. "For what?"

"For asking me how I am. For caring about the answer." She swallowed back the emotion building in her voice. "For accepting me for who I am. For rolling with it, even though part of me still thinks you think I'm crazy."

"Crazy? No. Strange? Yes. But that has nothing to do with the fact that you see dead people."

Cassie clutched her imaginary pearls in mock offense. "Well, that's rude."

"It takes a special type of person to do what you do."

"Work in a museum?"

Laura pursed her lips. "Solve murders. Chase down bad guys. Bring justice to the victims who reach out for your help. I never got to say this before because of everything going on, but...I'm really proud of you. You're my hero, Cassie. I mean that."

Cassie felt tears prick the corner of her eyes, and before she allowed them to fall, she reached over and pulled her sister in closer. Apollo, now stuck between them, mewed in protest.

"Oops, sorry." Cassie let go and kissed him on the forehead instead of meeting her sister's eyes. "Squashed you."

Laura gasped. "I forgot to ask you the most important question."

Cassie waited as her sister paused dramatically, and then asked, "What?"

"What happened to the dog? Is David going to keep him?"

"For now. David's convinced that whenever Bear wanders around the house whining, he's looking for me. I don't buy it. I just think he doesn't want an upset ninety-pound dog around the fine china."

Laura's eyes got bright. "You have to take him. He's imprinted on you. How could you say no after that?"

Cassie pointed at the cat between them. "I don't know if Apollo would appreciate having a German Shepherd for a roommate. I'm not the only one who lives here, you know."

Laura scratched behind Apollo's ears. "I think Apollo would love having someone to hang out with while you're gone."

"Plus there's that. We're about to leave, remember? I can't adopt a dog and then run off to Charlotte."

"True. And there's something else we never talked about either."

"What?"

"What we're gonna say to Mom and Dad."

Cassie groaned and buried her face in a throw pillow. "I don't know. It's going to be so weird going home."

"You know they love you, even if things have been strained over the last couple years. It's still Mom and Dad. They'll be shocked to see us both on the doorstep, and then they'll feed us too much food and try to do our laundry and send us both home with knickknacks we haven't thought of in twenty-five years."

"Honestly, that's kind of what I'm afraid of. I don't really want things to be normal." Cassie smoothed out her hair as she tried to find the right words. "I want to talk to them about everything. About Novak. About what's been going on in my life over the last ten years. I want to know more about Mom's diagnosis."

"What about the ghost thing?"

Cassie scrunched her nose. "Do I have to?"

"No, but if you want to know more about Sarah Lennox, Mom and Dad are the best place to start."

"Do you think *they'll* think I'm crazy?"

"I don't know." Laura tapped her lip with her pointer finger. "Mom will try to reason it away. Dad will go find something to fix until he's thought about it long and hard and then he'll say, 'As long as you're happy.' And then they'll never talk about it again."

"You know, that's our problem as Quinns. We don't talk about anything. We keep it all inside until we burst or shove it down so deep, we can pretend we're over it."

"Hey." Now it was Laura's turn to clutch her pearls. "I thought I was the psychologist in the family."

"No, but really."

"I know. I know. It's just something we'll have to work on." She looked over at Cassie. "Together."

Cassie liked the sound of that. *Together.* It'd been a long time since she was together with her family. Seeing her sister and working out their issues was the first step, and now that they felt like a unit, Cassie felt a lot more comfortable talking to her parents about what had been going on inside her head over the last several years. She had to take responsibility for the role she played in forming distance between all of them. It would take a lot of time and patience to build their relationships back up to what they once were. But the best part?

She was more than ready to get started.

39

DAVID KNOCKED ON CHIEF OF POLICE SANDRA CLEMENTINE'S DOOR. The Chief, who had the phone cradled between her neck and shoulder, looked up and waved him inside. David shut the door behind him and sat down in a chair opposite her. The office smelled like oranges, and David's eyes automatically flicked to the garbage can, where he spotted a discarded peel.

The Chief was an imposing woman, even when she was sitting down. She was a tall, muscular black woman who could've played professional sports but had chosen the badge and done a damn good job of it.

"I don't need your excuses, Crawford, I just need you to do your job. Yes. *Yes.* Thank you." Clementine hung up the phone with a huff and gave David a tight smile. "Between you and me? Crawford is a goddamn pain in my ass."

"Mine, too, ma'am."

Clementine scribbled something down on a piece of paper and then folded her hands in front of her, giving David her full attention. "The Shapiro case was a tough one. You did the best you could. Don't hold onto the what-ifs."

David shifted in his seat. Sometimes he thought the Chief could read minds. She had this uncanny ability to just look at a person and read them like a book. David liked to think he was good about keeping his emotions in check, but Clementine had always gotten past any walls he put up. He liked her more for that. She was a good cop and an even better Chief.

"I know. I'll be okay. No need to worry about me."

"Do I look worried?" She flashed a smile. "I don't worry about you, anyway. I worry about dickheads like Crawford. Oh, did I say that out loud?"

"I didn't hear a thing." David's smile faded. "There's just a few more things I have to wrap up with the cold case, and then we can file it away."

"I don't think you came here to ask for a gold star."

"No, ma'am." David shifted in his seat again. He normally wasn't the bashful type, but he didn't like putting his nose where it didn't belong. "I know this was a bit before your time—"

"I'm three years younger than you, Klein."

He chuckled. "I meant before you joined our fine establishment in Savannah."

Clementine had transferred from Arizona. She was used to working the small towns, so there was an adjustment period when she came to Savannah, but thanks to her uncanny superpower, the Chief had no problem settling in. She demanded respect wherever she went, and if someone didn't give it to her, she sent them packing. She didn't suffer fools.

"Right. Carry on."

"I think the case with the original twelve victims was handled poorly. I don't think we did as much as we could have to solve it, and I think more people suffered as a result."

"Do you have proof of misconduct? Evidence of a coverup?"

"No, ma'am."

Clementine leveled him with a stare. "Then I can't help you."

"I know." He hung his head. "I don't even know why I'm here."

"You're here because you want someone to let you off the hook. I can do that, but I don't think my approval is going to ease your conscience. I've looked over the case, David. You weren't the lead. You were still green, had to do what your superiors told you to do. It's on the rest of them, and unless you have evidence, I can't bring any charges or file any complaints against them. What you really need to do is forgive yourself."

"That's not easy for me."

"It takes practice. Especially in this job. We make a lot of decisions that affect other people's lives. Learn to live with your choices, and if you can't, you need to learn how to fix them."

David sat with that for a minute. There had been moments when he'd done the wrong thing. Not out of malice, but maybe out of ignorance or haste. Hindsight and all that. McLaughlin had decided to do something about his regrets. And when he died, he did it, knowing he'd done the best he could.

"Now, I'd love to sit here and play therapist—God knows I'd make better money—but I'm a busy woman, and you have a lot of paperwork to fill out."

"Just one more thing—I'd like to take some vacation time sometime soon. I'm not sure when yet, but it might be a couple weeks. Think the precinct would be okay without me for a bit?"

"I think we can handle it. Harris has been looking to get some overtime, anyway."

"Does she ever stop?"

"I don't think so. She's a beast."

David stood up. "Thanks, Chief. I appreciate it."

"Just don't tell the others I've got a soft spot for you, Klein. They'll accuse me of playing favorites."

David left Clementine to her duties. As he passed through the main room, he noticed the mail had arrived. His stomach dropped. He hadn't had a letter in a little over a week now, and he couldn't help but wonder if his nightmare was over.

There was a pile of mail stacked on his desk, and he sat with some trepidation. His head was on a swivel to make sure no one else was paying attention to him. Harris was talking to Paulson at the front of the room, a coffee in hand. Two other officers were typing away at their computers. No one cared what he was doing.

David sifted through the mail quickly. Letters. Requests. Reports. He ignored them all.

Then, at the bottom of the pile, sat the one thing he was dreading. It looked inconspicuous. It was in a stark white envelope. A computer had printed his name on the front. No return address. Forever stamp in the shape of a liberty bell. Tightly sealed.

But instead of opening it then and there, he tucked it into the inside pocket of his jacket, where it burned against his chest. After the first one, he'd started a new routine—every time another letter showed up, he'd stash it, drive halfway home, pull over on the side of the road, and open it where no one else could lay eyes on the information inside.

It was his little secret. And he intended to keep it that way.

40

THE GHOST OF THE LITTLE BOY WAS WAITING BY THE CAR WHEN CASSIE
and Laura exited the house with their luggage. Cassie only hesitated
for a fraction of a second before popping the trunk and throwing her
suitcase in. Outside, she couldn't tell if the chill in the air was due to
the weather or her ethereal guest.

She felt like the mystery surrounding his spirit and the death of
Sarah Lennox was just within reach. She still didn't remember much
about that time in her life, but she was a mere four hours away from
discovering more. And maybe getting the answers to questions she'd
been asking herself for decades.

Speaking of driving.

"Hey, do you mind taking the wheel?" Cassie waited until Laura
had tossed her suitcase in the back before shutting the trunk. "I didn't
sleep well last night."

"Nerves?"

"Yeah, I just couldn't fall asleep. I think I only got an hour or two."

"No problem. Keys?"

Cassie tossed them to her and then slid into the passenger's seat.

As she shut the door, she glanced into the side mirror and saw the little boy's ghostly reflection. From this angle, it looked like he was watching Laura instead of her.

"All right, pedal to the metal time." Laura looked over and winked.

"You will go the speed limit. You will come to a complete stop. You will obey traffic lights."

"You will pass go and collect two hundred dollars."

"Hilarious."

"I will also choose the radio station."

"Acceptable. I'm going to get a quick nap in."

Laura turned the radio on but kept it low. Cassie pulled the handle on the side of her seat and laid as far back as she could. She wouldn't get the best sleep in the car, but she'd be able to get a couple hours, at least. Besides, it beat spending the next four hours to Charlotte worrying about what she'd say to her parents as soon as she saw them.

And even though it felt like they hit just about every pothole in Savannah, Cassie was asleep before they made it to the highway.

CASSIE GRIPPED *the steering wheel until her knuckles turned white and her hands ached. Her headlights dimly illuminated the road in front of her, and the rest was so dark she felt like she was driving through a void in space. She could sense, rather than see, the trees whipping by as she sped down an empty highway.*

She felt trapped in a time loop. Like she'd been here before, dozens of times. When she slammed her foot down on the brake pedal, she knew it would have no effect.

The inky blackness still held a grip on her. Fear bubbled in her stomach. She shook. Cassie felt the night closing in on her, pressing closer. When the car drifted, she let it happen. There would be no changing directions now.

A soft glow in the distance caught her attention. Forms took shape. She knew the light didn't come from another car, and when a figure material-ized, her only reaction was to grip the wheel a little harder. Then the second figure appeared. Then the third.

She already knew who they were. Her mother and father and sister. Either out of habit or instinct, Cassie tried once again to press down on the brakes.

This time it worked.

The car shuddered and slowed. Hope grew inside her, and for the first time since finding herself behind the wheel once again, she felt scared. She had resigned herself to the outcome, as horrific as it was. But now she had control. Now she could stop the accident from happening.

Her parents still had blank faces. The light still washed out their features, making them look pale and lifeless. They held hands with her father on the left and her mother next to him. Laura, only five or six years old, stood next to their mother, holding her teddy bear. She made direct eye contact with Cassie, but she wasn't crying this time. Instead, she had a slight frown on her face.

Cassie pumped the brakes and yanked the wheel to the side. The car squealed and slid, and she narrowly missed hitting her sister. The vehicle came to a complete stop about ten feet to the right of Laura.

Her family was alive.

Cassie pushed open her door and fell to the ground in her haste to get to them. When she picked herself back up again, she stumbled forward until she was right in front of Laura. When she knelt to meet her sister's eyes, she noticed Laura's frown had deepened.

"Don't you remember?" she asked, handing Cassie the teddy bear.

"Remember what?"

"That night. Don't you remember what happened that night?"

Cassie looked up at her parents, but they were still staring blankly ahead, like they were mere shells of their real selves. She turned back to Laura. "What night? What am I supposed to remember?"

Laura's voice was so frail it broke Cassie's heart. "It's your fault."

Cassie froze. "What?"

"It's your fault." Laura's voice was fading now. "You're the reason they took Sarah. You're the reason she died."

Cassie Quinn returns in Symphony of Bones! Order your copy now, or read on for a sneak peek:
https://www.amazon.com/dp/Bo8ViWMP6Z

Join the LT Ryan reader family & receive a free copy of the Cassie Quinn story, *Through the Veil*. Click the link below to get started:
https://ltryan.com/cassie-quinn-newsletter-signup-1

LOVE CASSIE? Hatch? Noble? Maddie? Get your very own L.T. Ryan merchandise today! Click the link below to find coffee mugs, t-shirts, and even signed copies of your favorite thrillers! https://ltryan. ink/EvG_

THE CASSIE QUINN SERIES

Path of Bones

Whisper of Bones

Symphony of Bones

Etched in Shadow

Concealed in Shadow

Betrayed in Shadow

Born from Ashes

Love Cassie? Hatch? Noble? Maddie? Get your very own Cassie Quinn merchandise today! Click the link below to find coffee mugs, t-shirts, and even signed copies of your favorite L.T. Ryan thrillers! https://ltryan. ink/EvG_

SYMPHONY OF BONES

A CASSIE QUINN MYSTERY (BOOK THREE)

by L.T. Ryan & K.M. Rought

SYMPHONY OF BONES: CHAPTER 1

Senator Lawrence Grayson stood inside his Charlotte office and peered out the window at the dark clouds above him. He didn't have a scenic view from this side of the building, but it couldn't be helped. Someday, he'd have a front-row seat at Jacqueline Kennedy's renowned garden, and that was enough to get him through days like this.

Grayson caught his reflection in the window and straightened his tie. He ran a hand over his hair and smiled. It was dark brown with streaks of gray, long enough to provide some style but short enough to give him a clean, groomed look. The window's reflection couldn't dim the bright blue of his eyes, which had won him favor from men and women alike. Even his beard, kept short and tidy, had turned more than a few heads.

But these days, Grayson noticed his hair was more silver than brown and his eyes had a few more bags underneath. Politics wasn't for the faint of heart, and if being in the state senate had aged him this much, he couldn't imagine what he'd look like by the end of his two terms as president.

Then again, that's why hair dye and Botox existed. He'd resisted until now, because so far, his looks had done him no disservice. It was only a matter of time before he wouldn't be able to rely on what God had given him. Once nature had run its course, he'd turn to today's spectacular technology.

Someone knocked sharply on the door, and Senator Grayson turned to find his publicist, Anastasia Bolton, entering the room with a tablet in one hand and a pile of paperwork in the other. She wore a black leather skirt and a maroon turtleneck sweater tucked into the waistband. Her nails were long and blood-red, perfectly matching her lipstick. She was an attractive woman, with high cheekbones and dark eyes framed by pin-straight black hair.

Grayson had once asked her if she was seeing anyone, and she'd gone on a five-minute tirade about how it was none of his business and that if he wanted her to continue to work for him, he would never ask her a single personal question again. He was so taken aback, he'd simply nodded his head, and they'd carried on like nothing had ever happened. That was over a year ago, and it had proven to be the best decision of his life. Anastasia had not only made him the talk of the town here in North Carolina, but she'd gotten him trending on Twitter on more than one occasion.

His future aspirations were within reach.

"Good morning, sir." Anastasia set the paperwork down on the desk just as Grayson sank into his chair. "You've got a full day ahead of you."

"Will there ever be a time when I don't have a full day?"

"When you're dead." She didn't even crack a smile. "First thing I need from you is a commitment to a charity."

"What will I have to do?"

Anastasia sat down opposite him and crossed her legs. She placed the tablet on her knee and began swiping and clicking with fervor. She was probably checking emails, answering Twitter questions, lining up interviews, buying him a new suit, and coordinating dinner with his colleagues. All the while, he'd only eaten half his breakfast this morning.

"You'll need to make at least three appearances. One will be volunteer work in either casual attire or without your jacket and your sleeves rolled up. Get a little messy. Real *of the people* vibes," she told him.

"Choices?" he asked.

"Children's hospital, vets, or animal shelter."

"You have a preference?"

Anastasia looked up, her finger paused an inch above the tablet's screen. "Animals are a crowd-pleaser, but it lacks depth. Unless your aspirations stop at President of the American Kennel Club."

"Right. So, children or vets."

She went back to swiping. "Children are always good, but they're unpredictable. You'll probably have to cry."

"I'm not good at crying."

"I know. I think we should go with the vets."

"You could've just said that from the start."

"It's better if it seems like your idea. Clients get defiant when they think their strings are being pulled, and that wouldn't be good for either of us."

Grayson resisted the urge to roll his eyes. She was still looking at her tablet, but she'd know. She always knew. "I'm well aware I sold my soul to the Devil. Getting *defiant* wouldn't service my purpose."

This time, she smiled. "You'd be surprised how many people know that and just can't help themselves."

Grayson liked to think he was different from all the others. More disciplined. But trying to convince Anastasia of that was pointless. "What will I have to do with the vets?"

She pointed a crimson-tipped finger at the paperwork in front of him. "There are a few different organizations in there. Read through their mission statements and volunteer opportunities. Let me know which one you like best. I'm thinking soup kitchens, meet-and-greets, maybe something with disabled vets."

"I have some friends in the tech industry. We can give a couple vets a new leg or something."

Anastasia bobbed her head up and down. "Perfect. I like that. Give me some company names by the end of the day. I'll see which one fits our image best."

He hated the way she talked about *his* image that way. Sure, she'd catapulted him from a nobody to a national sensation within a matter of a couple of years, but it was still his face on everything. His voice. His policies.

It made him feel a little better that Anastasia was just a cog in the machine, too. She didn't have any actual power. The power came from the company she worked for, Apex Publicity. They were the real puppet masters.

But in order to keep them happy, he had to keep Anastasia happy.

"No problem. Anything else?" he asked.

Anastasia didn't answer for a moment. She swiped her finger across the tablet's screen a few more times, then placed it on the seat beside her. Grayson sat up. She rarely let go of that thing.

"Your son."

Grayson deflated. If there was one thing he couldn't control, one thing he couldn't keep locked down and out of the public eye, it was his son. "What did he do now?"

"Nothing. Which makes me think we're due for another incident."

The last thing Grayson wanted to do was admit she was right, but when it came to Connor, he couldn't deny the truth. "What do you propose?"

"Are you still going to family counseling?"

"Yes, but I can't force him to go. And we've had to cancel the last two because of Mary's hospital visits."

"How is she doing?"

The question sounded robotic. It was like when someone asks how you are, and you're forced to return the inquiry even if they couldn't give two shits about the answer.

"She's doing better." Grayson leaned forward. "Look, I've done everything I can to handle Connor. I'm out of ideas."

"Ideas are our business." She tapped one of her crimson fingernails against her chin. "Let's see, he's nineteen. Good looking. Going to school for computer science. A little bit of a nerd, but has a rebellious streak. He's still doing drugs?"

"Yes." The word came out through gritted teeth. He hated that she knew his son as well as he did. Maybe even better.

She snapped her fingers. "A girlfriend."

"He has one of those."

She laughed. "We'll set something up. Get him to dump her. No, she'll dump him. Break his heart for a while. Then we'll introduce him to one of our girls. Someone that makes him feel like he's still rebelling, but someone who can keep him in line. A man in love is easier to control."

Grayson didn't know what to say. On the one hand, he knew there were relationships of convenience out there. In his line of business, compatibility and common goals were more important than romance. Sometimes it was easier to get to the top as a power couple. And if you didn't care about the sanctity of marriage, it was the perfect solution.

Senator Grayson loved his wife. From the moment he met her, he knew they'd get married. He'd always had political aspirations, and while she had been content as a kindergarten teacher, she'd given it up to become a politician's wife. Their marriage wasn't always perfect, but it was real.

Was he capable of manipulating his son like that? Was having a shot at the presidency worth allowing Apex to play his son like a fiddle?

Anastasia must've seen the gears turning in his mind. "It wasn't a request, Senator."

He swallowed the bile that had crept up his throat. "I'm aware, Ms. Bolton. I was momentarily considering the consequences should any of this come to light."

"It won't." She picked up her tablet again. "Apex is where we turn your dreams into reality. You want a son you can control? We'll make it happen."

Grayson's smile was tight. This wasn't what he had in mind when he had signed on with Apex, but he'd be lying to himself if he said he hadn't known who he was getting into bed with.

Another knock on the door interrupted his thoughts. "Come in."

A man in a black suit entered the room. His name was Alex Murphy, and he was the head of the senator's security team. He was an imposing man with short-cropped hair, a clean-shaven face, and eyes as piercing as Grayson's. He stood a head taller than the senator, and every day, Grayson was happy the man was on his team and not someone else's.

"What's wrong?" Grayson asked.

"It's your son, sir." Murphy didn't mince words. Another reason Grayson liked him. "We can't find him."

Grayson stood up behind his desk. "What do you mean you can't find him?"

Murphy gave Anastasia a quick glance, but he'd learned long ago that no topics were off limits when it came to discussing important matters in front of her. "After your argument last night, he crossed the border to South Carolina and spent the night in Rock Hill. On his way home, he gave my team the slip. We weren't too worried about it until he didn't show up to any of his classes today."

Anastasia finally turned in her chair. "How did a nineteen-year-old *boy* give your team the slip?"

Murphy's face was neutral, but Grayson saw his eyes narrow. "Unfortunately, it happens from time to time, ma'am. Tailing someone is not an exact science."

Grayson cursed under his breath. "Do you know what he was doing in Rock Hill?"

"Not yet, sir. I have someone retracing his steps. I just wanted to inform you of the situation. I'm sure it's nothing to worry about."

Everyone in the room knew that was a practiced lie.

Anastasia turned to face the senator again and raised one perfect eyebrow. "What did I tell you?"

Senator Grayson put his back to both of them. The clouds in the sky had darkened, threatening rain. He hoped his kid was safe, but at the same time, he wanted his son to learn a lesson he'd never forget. Connor's last scandal had nearly cost Grayson his seat in the senate. His opponent had brought up Connor's DUI, saying that if he couldn't handle what went on in his own household, how would he ever handle an entire state-worth of issues.

Grayson had skated through by the skin of his teeth, appealing to people's humanity and spinning a story about his family being just like everyone else's. Anyone who tried to present a picture of perfection was obviously lying, and he, Lawrence Grayson, was no liar. He was doing his best, just like his constituents, and he'd do better moving forward.

It had worked. Barely.

Grayson turned back to the room. "Keep me updated, Murphy. Every hour. Let me know what's going on."

Murphy nodded and left the room.

He turned back to his publicist. "Let's go through worst-case scenarios. I want to be prepared."

Anastasia was on the move. "I'm calling Apex. They need to know we might have a shitstorm ahead of us."

"Is that really nec—"

"Yes." She already had the phone to her ear. "You never win by keeping secrets from Apex."

When she left the room, Grayson loosened his tie and pulled out the bottle of whiskey he had stashed in the back of his desk drawer. It was for celebrations and emergencies only, and this felt like one more than the other.

Whatever Connor had done, Senator Lawrence Grayson knew deep in his bones it was about to change everything.

SYMPHONY OF BONES: CHAPTER 2

Cassie's eyes opened as soon as she felt the car shift into park. It took her a few seconds to remind herself where she was and what she was doing. Her neck ached and drool slid down the side of her cheek. She wiped it clean and brought the passenger seat back to an upright position.

Laura giggled to her left.

"What?" Cassie asked.

"You're a mess. Fix your hair. We're just around the corner."

Cassie's heart shuttered to a stop and then restarted. She pulled down the visor and checked herself in the mirror. Her sister hadn't been lying. She had some dried drool stuck to the corners of her mouth, her eyes were red, and her hair looked like she'd stuck her finger in an electrical socket.

Cassie attempted to tame her appearance. The last thing she remembered was pulling away from her house a couple hours ago. And then she had that awful dream where Laura had told her Sarah Lennox's murder was all her fault.

Cassie shook the memory from her mind. "Why'd you stop?"

"To make sure you were ready." Laura hesitated. "Are you ready?"

"You want the truth?"

"Always."

"No."

"Anything I can do to change that?"

Cassie flipped the visor back up and sighed. She took in her sister's perfect curls and bright eyes. "Not unless you want to turn the car around."

"Not really." Laura laid a gentle hand on her leg. "What's going through your mind?"

Cassie leaned her head back and stared at the roof of her car. Sometimes she hated that Laura was a psychologist, always trying to get her to talk about her feelings. And sometimes she was grateful someone pushed her out of her comfort zone.

"I'm nervous. Obviously. I know the plan was to surprise Mom and Dad, but I'm not sure how smart that was. What if they're upset we just dropped in like this?"

"They're our parents. They won't get upset. We have lifetime crashing credentials."

"You might. I'm not sure if I do."

"Look at me." Laura waited until Cassie met her eyes. "I talk to Mom and Dad all the time. They ask about you constantly. And it's not like you haven't spoken in the last ten years. It's just been a little more infrequent than usual. They don't hate you, Cassie. You know that, right?"

Cassie's eyes watered. She had to fight to keep her voice steady. "I just hate that I might've disappointed them. And I'm not looking forward to having *that* conversation with them."

"You did just fine with me, didn't you?"

"You're my sister. It's different."

Laura's laugh was light and clear. "It's going to be fine. They're going to be happy to see you, I promise."

Cassie nodded, but the pit in her stomach didn't loosen. She felt guilty for pushing her family away for the last decade, but part of her still felt vindicated in doing it. She hadn't known how to explain to her parents what she'd been going through—both after Novak's attack and while she was learning more about her abilities—and she didn't want to burden them with that knowledge.

And what if they didn't believe her? It hadn't taken Laura long to come around, but she'd also been involved in one of Cassie's investigations. She'd had a front-row seat to how Cassie's abilities worked.

But even beyond all of that, Cassie still harbored a kind of defiant independence. She loved her parents, but they could be suffocating. After the attack, all they had wanted to do was take care of her. It was nice in the beginning, but then it made her feel awful. She didn't want them to coddle her, and she didn't want to feel weak. It'd taken her a long time to come to terms with the idea that pain and fear weren't synonymous with weakness, but that realization had happened long after her relationship with her parents had fallen apart.

"Have you figured out what you want to say yet?"

Cassie scoffed. "About what? Why I'm showing up unexpectedly? Why I cut myself off from everybody? How I can see dead people?"

"All of the above?"

Cassie sank lower in her seat. "No."

Laura patted her leg and then put the car into drive. But she didn't pull forward yet. "You'll be fine. It'll be uncomfortable for a while, but I'll be there. They'll come around. We all want the same thing."

"I know."

"So, maybe 'are you ready' wasn't the right question. What about, 'Are you willing to do this even though it scares you?'"

Cassie wanted to say *yes* with resounding authority, but right now, she could only nod her head. Laura smiled at her and pulled away from the curb. She turned the corner and drove a quarter mile down Birch Street. Their parents' house was on the left.

The sisters had grown up in Savannah, but when Laura went to college in California, their parents wanted a change of scenery. The family had always enjoyed Charlotte, and it wouldn't be too far from Cassie, so it seemed like a practical move. Cassie had been to the house a few times, but it'd been a while. She'd forgotten how quaint it was.

The Quinns owned a nice little white Colonial home with blue shutters. It looked clean and tidy from the outside, and Cassie knew without stepping a foot across the threshold that it would be the same on the inside. The gardens out front had been trimmed up for winter, but she could see how well her mother had taken care of the flowers.

Time slowed down as Laura turned into the driveway. Her mother's red Camry was parked on one side, and her father's silver Buick on the other. It'd been a long time since they needed an SUV to haul their kids back and forth from sports practice, but Cassie still found it odd to see both of them driving sedans.

Cassie's palms began to sweat, and her breaths came in shallow. Spots erupted in front of her eyes. For a moment, she considered the practicality of finding her way to the airport on foot and flying back to Savannah.

Laura parked and placed another gentle hand on Cassie's leg. "It's gonna be fine. You'll see."

Cassie pushed open her door. Her legs wobbled, but she took two deep breaths to clear her mind. The crisp air alleviated some of her worry. Worst-case scenario, her parents didn't want to see her, and she'd have to drive straight back to Savannah. But at least she'd know where they stood.

The girls pulled their suitcases out of the car and made their way up to the front porch. Cassie looked around to see if she could spot the ghost of the little boy. He'd been right next to the car when they had left her house back in Savannah. Had he traveled with them? She'd spotted him around the city a few times, like at the airport and her therapist's office, but she wasn't sure if his presence extended to another state.

Seeing him now would've been an odd sort of comfort. But if he was around, he remained invisible.

Laura stopped in front of the front door and turned to Cassie. "How do you want to do this?"

"Just knock." Cassie was still breathless and her voice sounded miles away. "I'm just gonna wing it."

Laura rapped on the door. Cassie stood behind her, shifting her weight from foot to foot. Who would answer the door? What would she say? How would they react? A million different scenarios raced through her mind until she was dizzy again.

But when the knob turned, Cassie's mind cleared.

She stepped to the side just as the door opened, pulling her suitcase in close. Whoever it was, she wanted a few extra seconds to gather herself before she announced her visit. Laura shot her a look, but when she turned back to the door, a bright smile had replaced her confusion.

"Surprise!"

Their father's deep chuckle softened Cassie's heart. "What are you doing here?"

"We thought we'd surprise you guys. Hope you don't mind."

"No, of course not." He paused. "Did you say *we*?"

Cassie knew this was her cue, and before she could talk herself out of it, she stepped into view. Her father's gaze shifted from Laura to Cassie, and their eyes met with what seemed like an audible click.

Her father was a tall, thin man with silver hair and a mustache. His eyes were dark and gentle, and his face harbored countless years of laugh lines. He was the type of person who took refuge in the silences between conversations. He looked a few years older than Cassie remembered, but still every inch of the father she had idolized growing up.

"Cassie?" His voice caught in his throat. "Is that really you?"

"Hi, Dad." Cassie's eyes watered. "Surprise."

SYMPHONY OF BONES: CHAPTER 3

The entire world paused while Cassie's father absorbed his daughter's presence. When he stepped forward with open arms, Cassie caught sight of his watery eyes. She buried her face in his chest and breathed in his spicy cologne. His embrace was warm and firm and everything she'd been missing about him over the last ten years.

He was the first to pull away, and Cassie was quick to wipe away her tears. He held her at arm's length and drank in her appearance. "What are you doing here?"

It took a second for Cassie to find her voice again. "We thought we'd surprise you. I know it's been a while. I was hoping we could all talk and catch up."

His eyebrows knit together. "Is something wrong? Are you okay?"

"Yeah, yeah, I'm okay. I just thought it was time, you know?"

He took a minute to respond, but when he did, his words were heavy with meaning. "I know."

Their father led them through the front door and into the little entrance off the kitchen where they could kick off their shoes. He looked back and forth between them with an astonished smile on his face. "It's nice to see you both in the same place."

Laura shot Cassie a look that screamed *I told you so*, to which Cassie promptly rolled her eyes. She smiled back at her father. "Thanks. It's nice to be here."

Laura finished pulling off her shoes and stood up. "Where's Mom?"

"Upstairs." He leaned his head back and projected his voice. "Hey, Judy?"

A muffled voice answered from upstairs.

"We have guests."

There was rustling from upstairs, and the sound of her mother's footsteps made Cassie's palms sweat. Growing up, her father was the disciplinarian, but he was fair and just. He never yelled, and somehow that made everything worse. As an adult, Cassie could see how even-tempered he was. That made seeing him again after all these years much easier.

Her mom, on the other hand, had a bit of that Irish temper. She was a kind, giving woman, but she was also passionate and emotional. Cassie had seen her mom take more than one teacher down a peg or two in one breath and then invite them over for dinner in the next. She and Cassie had gotten into a few shouting matches when she was a teenager, but her mom could never stay mad for long. And neither could Cassie, especially when there was food on the table or ice cream in the freezer.

"Hey, Dad?" Laura whispered.

"Yeah?"

"I told Cassie."

Their father frowned. "Told her wha—" His eyes got wide. "I thought you weren't going to say anything."

"She has a right to know Mom's sick."

"I know that." He leaned forward. "But your mother is still going to kill me."

Cassie's mouth went dry. "Time to say your goodbyes, then."

Judy and Cassie's eyes met the moment her mom entered the room. A little gasp escaped Judy's mouth, and Cassie saw confusion, excitement, and apprehension cross her face in quick succession.

"Hi, Mom."

"Hi." She looked from Laura to her husband and back to Cassie, like she couldn't believe what she was seeing. "It's nice to see you."

"It's nice to see you, too." Cassie stepped forward and hugged her mom, breathing in the scent of cherry blossoms and hairspray. Judy Quinn looked exactly the same as she had ten years ago. She was a short, round woman, with bright red hair, deep green eyes, and a smattering of freckles across her nose. "Hope you don't mind us dropping in on you."

Judy hugged Laura and then turned to her husband. "Did you know about this?"

"Not at all. It seems like they conspired against us."

"Oh?" Judy turned to Laura. She couldn't quite look Cassie in the eye. "What's the occasion?"

"No occasion." Laura led the group into the kitchen and started rummaging through the refrigerator. "We just thought it was a good time to catch up."

Judy's face turned red, and she smacked her husband's arm. "You told them, didn't you?"

He had the wherewithal to look abashed. "Technically, I only told Laura. Then Laura told Cassie."

"Thanks for throwing me under the bus, Dad."

"Hey, if I'm going down, I'm taking you with me."

Judy threw her hands up and walked over to the cabinet with the wine glasses. She pulled two down as Laura retrieved a bottle from the fridge. As an afterthought, she grabbed one more for Cassie.

"I didn't want you to worry," she said.

"So, what was the plan?" For the first time, Laura sounded more hurt than exasperated. "Tell us after you had it removed?"

"In an ideal world, yes."

"And what if something had gone wrong?" Cassie's voice shook, and she hated the sound of it. "Then you would've taken away any chance of us being able to say goodbye."

The room fell dead silent. Cassie could feel the hypocrisy crawling across her skin. She'd pushed them away for ten years. She'd never given them room to work through what had happened right alongside her. And her last run-in with Novak? She'd waved it off like it was nothing, despite the fact that she'd almost died. Again.

"That was never my intention." Her mom's voice was quiet. Angry. Barely controlled. "I just didn't want you to worry, that's all."

Laura placed a hand on top of their mother's. "We know. And we're not staging an intervention here. We just wanted to visit. Catch up. Have a little family bonding time."

"Which I think is an excellent idea." When Judy shot him a look, Walter grabbed his keys from the hook. "I also think picking up some more wine is an excellent idea."

"And cheese. And orange juice. Eggs. We'll need two more steaks." Laura chimed in.

"I'll be back soon." Walter leaned over and kissed Cassie on the forehead. "I'm really glad you came."

Laura scoffed. "What am I, chopped liver?"

"No one deserves to be liver." Their father scratched his head. "More like moldy cheese. Or watery sour cream."

"Soggy pizza," Cassie offered.

Walter winked. "You could do worse than soggy pizza."

Judy tried not to laugh. "Go to the store, Walter."

"Yes, dear."

"Get me chocolate."

"Yes, dear."

The momentary easiness that came with their usual banter left the house as soon as Walter closed the door behind him. Cassie was too nervous to sip her wine, so she just left it on the countertop to gather beads of condensation.

"Well, you girls look tired. Let me get your room ready so you can take a nap before dinner."

"The drive wasn't bad—"

"I slept on the way here—"

Judy waved them off. "It has to be done sooner or later. Might as well do it now."

Cassie trudged up the stairs after them. The house was familiar enough, but the details were foreign. She remembered the bannister being an ugly pine color. Now it was a dark mahogany. The downstairs bathroom was pale green instead of an ugly mauve. She also could've sworn there hadn't been French doors leading out to the back porch.

They had done a lot of renovating over the past ten years.

Judy led them to one of the guest bedrooms and pushed open the door. She fluffed the pillows and slid back the closet door. "Laura, last time you were here, you left one of your sweatshirts. I washed it for you."

Laura pulled out a gray hoodie with the words *San Francisco* embroidered across the chest. "Sweet. I was looking for this."

Judy turned to Cassie. "Your room might take a little longer."

"That's okay." Cassie blushed. "I can help."

The second guest bedroom was piled with yarn and empty boxes and a portable wardrobe. "I turned it into my sewing room. I don't remember it being this messy."

"That's fine. I can...sleep on the couch?"

"You're not sleeping on the couch. I'll get the blowup mattress. You can sleep on the floor in Laura's room for tonight. Then we'll figure something else out." Judy stopped with the mattress bag halfway out of the closet. "How long will you be staying?"

"Oh, um—"

"We never actually discussed that." Laura chuckled. "At least a few days, if that's all right?"

"Of course." Her tone didn't betray her thoughts. "You can stay as long as you want. You both are always welcome."

The words sounded nice to Cassie's ears, but she couldn't help feeling like there was something going on underneath the surface.

Was she just overthinking the whole thing, or was her mom apprehensive about Cassie staying there?

Cassie didn't blame her. All four of them knew there was a tough conversation ahead of them, but for right now, it felt nice to pretend everything was normal.

It'd only be a matter of time before reality crashed in.

Order your copy now:

https://www.amazon.com/dp/B08V1WMP6Z

ALSO BY L.T. RYAN

Find All of L.T. Ryan's Books on Amazon Today!

The Jack Noble Series

Beyond Betrayal (Clarissa Abbot)

Noble Judgment

Never Cry Mercy

Deadline

End Game

Noble Ultimatum

Noble Legend

Noble Revenge

Never Look Back (Coming Soon)

Bear Logan Series

Ripple Effect

Blowback

Take Down

Deep State

Bear & Mandy Logan Series

Close to Home

Under the Surface

The Last Stop

Over the Edge

Between the Lies (Coming Soon)

Rachel Hatch Series

Drift

Downburst

Fever Burn

Smoke Signal

Firewalk

Whitewater

Aftershock

Whirlwind

Tsunami

Fastrope

Sidewinder (Coming Soon)

Mitch Tanner Series

The Depth of Darkness

Into The Darkness

Deliver Us From Darkness

Cassie Quinn Series

Path of Bones

Whisper of Bones

Symphony of Bones

Etched in Shadow

Concealed in Shadow

Betrayed in Shadow

Born from Ashes

Blake Brier Series

Unmasked

Unleashed

Uncharted

Drawpoint

Contrail

Detachment

Clear

Quarry (Coming Soon)

Dalton Savage Series

Savage Grounds

Scorched Earth

Cold Sky

The Frost Killer (Coming Soon)

Maddie Castle Series

The Handler

Tracking Justice

Hunting Grounds

Vanished Trails (Coming Soon)

Affliction Z Series

Affliction Z: Patient Zero

Affliction Z: Abandoned Hope

Affliction Z: Descended in Blood

Affliction Z : Fractured Part 1

Affliction Z: Fractured Part 2 (Fall 2021)

Love Cassie? Hatch? Noble? Maddie? Get your very own L.T. Ryan merchandise today! Click the link below to find coffee mugs, t-shirts, and even signed copies of your favorite thrillers! https://ltryan.ink/EvG_

Receive a free copy of The Recruit. Visit:

https://ltryan.com/jack-noble-newsletter-signup-1

ABOUT THE AUTHOR

L.T. Ryan is a *USA Today* and international bestselling author. The new age of publishing offered L.T. the opportunity to blend his passions for creating, marketing, and technology to reach audiences with his popular Jack Noble series.

Living in central Virginia with his wife, the youngest of his three daughters, and their three dogs, L.T. enjoys staring out his window at the trees and mountains while he should be writing, as well as reading, hiking, running, and playing with gadgets. See what he's up to at http://ltryan.com.

Social Medial Links:

- Facebook (L.T. Ryan): https://www.facebook.com/LTRyanAuthor

- Facebook (Jack Noble Page): https://www.facebook.com/JackNobleBooks/

- Twitter: https://twitter.com/LTRyanWrites

- Goodreads: http://www.goodreads.com/author/show/6151659.L_T_Ryan

Made in the USA
Middletown, DE
12 April 2024